CROSSING LINES
COLBY MILLSAPS

Printed in the United States of America

First Printing, 2017

ISBN-13 978-1978460492
ISBN-10 197846049X

For all the ones who said I wouldn't.
But mostly, for all the ones who believed I
could.

Noah

I clenched my jaw tight and flicked my eyes to the clock on my computer when Grant strode into the room. 5:37. It was way too early to be dealing with this again. Especially after sitting awake all night wondering what the hell I had done. I was sure the dark circles under my eyes would alert him to the fact that I hadn't slept a wink, yet he had the audacity to walk in here looking as if nothing had changed. Looking as if my entire world hadn't blown up yesterday…or had been on the brink of blowing up. All because of him. Not that it was his fault. It was my own damn fault. But I was angry and hurt and it was easier to blame him.

"Look Grant, I don't want to hear it honestly. It's over. I kept my end of the deal, I need you to keep yours."

"Noah…"

"I don't need another lecture, okay?" I snapped. "If you're here about what I think you're here for, save it. I took care of it like I said I would. Just let it go, please. I'm begging you. You don't understand the circumstances."

"Noah, I didn't come to-"

The door swung open again and I inwardly groaned. If Carter walked in right now, Grant wouldn't believe a word I was saying. Everything I went through yesterday would have been pointless. I braced myself and turned to look at the door, but it wasn't Carter who stood there.

"Samantha," I said, surprise clear in my voice. She was one of Carter's friends. "Is there something I can help you with?" Anything that would end this conversation with Grant.

He wouldn't be deterred though. "Noah, I just need to talk to you for a minute," he hissed. "Miss Greene, could you please give me a moment with Mr. Sweeney?"

"Actually, it's kind of an emergency, Mr. Olsen." Her voice shook as she tore her eyes from me and glanced at Grant. Something was off about her. Her hair wasn't perfectly straight like it had been every other day this year. And she looked like she was wearing the same shirt from the day before. Her eyes looked smaller without their normal layer of makeup, and they were red and swollen.

"Mr. Olsen, I'm sorry but we'll have to discuss whatever it is you need at a later time. It was nice to see you," I lied. He gave me a pointed look, begging me to reconsider, but I didn't change my mind. After a tense silence passed between us, he finally backed out of the room without another word.

I turned to Samantha earnestly. "Samantha, what's wrong?"

She swallowed hard and glanced around as if to make sure no one else was here and my panic rose. "Sam…"

"Someone needed to tell you," she finally croaked out, her voice shaky. "You should know."

"No…" I was already shaking my head because there was only one reason for her being here, for her being a mess, and it wasn't good.

"It happened yesterday. She was on her way home."

"No." My stomach turned. On her way home. Her way home from talking to me. *No.* I screamed in my head, refusing to believe this was possible.

"They say it wasn't her fault. He was texting and swerved into her lane. There was nothing she could have done except maybe be driving slower. But

6

you know, I guess that doesn't matter now. The car was a mess. They had to cut it open to get her out. They showed me the pictures and-" Her words started running together but I had tuned her out. I was just imagining the last time I had been in the car when Carter was driving.

"You drive too fast." I had finally told her as I eyed the speedometer inching towards twenty-five miles per hour over the limit. I had always wondered why there were so many handles in a car. Then, as I clutched one for dear life, I finally understood.

"But," she said earnestly, "I *want* to go faster."

"What does that have to do with anything?" I gasped as we whipped around another sharp corner.

"It's all relative. So I'm practicing some restraint in not going any faster."

"Oh good. That's great. That will help us so much when we get pulled over. Or die." I had added only half sarcastically. She looked over then and smiled at me and although I had the urge to yell at her to keep her eyes on the road, I knew it was okay. That it was alright so long as she was around.

Samantha was still talking when I finally focused back on her. Tears had started to fall down her face and I knew I needed to ask but I was having trouble forming words. I also wasn't sure I wanted to know the answer.

I forced my legs to bring me to stand directly in front of her and made her focus on me. "Is she... Samantha...did she..." I took a deep breath. "Is Carter dead?"

"No."

"No?" I repeated, not willing to get my hopes up. Sure I had misheard. "She isn't dead?"

"No. They flew her to Mass General."

7

"So she's still there? She's still alive?" Sam nodded. "I've got to go. I have to get there." Suddenly I was throwing random papers and folders back in my bag, rummaging for my keys.

"Wait, you can't go." I heard Samantha saying but I ignored her as I rushed towards the door. "Mr. Sweeney, stop."

"Look Sam, you can stay in this room or you can go, but I'm leaving."

She hurried after me as I practically sprinted down the hall and then took the stairs two at a time. "Mr. Sweeney! You have classes to teach!"

"Someone else can teach them."

"What are you going to tell the office? You can't just say you're going to see her. What are they going to think?"

"I don't give a damn what they think." I knew I was being harsh and that Samantha didn't deserve it. I knew I was supposed to be the rational one but all I could think about was Carter and how she looked when she was sad or scared. How she looked yesterday after everything that had happened between us. All I knew was that I needed to get to wherever she was.

I reached the front doors of the building and stopped before turning to face Samantha. "I need you to do something for me, okay? I need you to go to the office and say an emergency came up for me and I won't be able to teach today. Say I can explain it all later. Can you do that for me?"

Samantha nodded and swiped a stray tear away. "Mr. Sweeney," she called softly once I had turned to push open the doors. I paused with my hands on the door but didn't turn back to face her. "She loves you, you know."

The pounding of my heart echoed in my ears.

"Mass General you said?"

"Mass General," she confirmed.

AUGUST – NINE MONTHS EARLIER
Carter

"Business or pleasure?" A guy's voice asked from above me. It wasn't some deep baritone or a voice that would cause me to melt in a puddle, but there was something different about it. Despite being low, there was an authoritative edge that made me look up. I slowly lowered my book, folding the corner of the page to hold my place, and took in the man behind the voice. It wasn't fair for guys to look like that. His hair was dark and fell in waves upon his forehead, almost too long but not quite. His eyes were deep set, impossible to decipher what color they were, and it bothered me that I wanted to know their color at all. He was older than me, that was for sure, but not by too much. And there was something about him, a certain air that he didn't belong on a beach full of sunbathing girls and boisterous teenagers. Somehow he just seemed more refined than any boy I knew.

I scrambled to remember his question and replied in a voice so calm I even surprised myself, "Pleasure."

"Huh," he muttered to himself as if he hadn't been expecting my response and was taken aback. "Ambitious."

"Yeah well, it's one of my life goals so…" I trailed off.

His head cocked to one side at that admission. "Your life goal is to read *The Complete Works of William Shakespeare*?" he asked, quoting the title of my volume. Instead of sounding turned off or confused as I assumed a guy like him would be, he sounded fascinated. Intrigued even.

"One of," I clarified. "I have a lot of life goals. But yes, it is."

"Huh," he repeated while running a hand through his hair. It was a simple enough gesture but it had me wanting things I had never wanted before. "There's a lot of tragedy," he noted.

"There's plenty of comedy," I countered. A smile lit his face and right then I knew if that was the only smile I saw for the rest of my life, I would be perfectly content.

Before he could respond again, a hand came down on my shoulder. I flinched at the contact and hoped he wouldn't notice. "Come on, C. It's the last day of summer. Stop reading and come swim with us." My friend Nate grabbed my hand and tugged me to my feet, causing my book to go tumbling to the sand. I bit my lip and shrugged my shoulders at the mystery man.

"Wait, aren't you going to tell me your name?" he asked as Nate relentlessly pulled me towards the water.

"I really don't see any point," I replied coyly over my shoulder.

A smile spread across his face and he chuckled at me. Then I saw him slowly bend down and carefully place my book back on the blanket right side up, his fingers gently skimming over the gold lettering. He looked back at me and shook his head, that perfect smile still on his lips. "Don't give us a story like Romeo and Juliet where I don't know your name until it's too late!" he called after me, but I only laughed and turned back to face the water. "My name's Noah! Just so you know. Noah Sweeney!"

I laughed at his effort but didn't look back again, only picked up my pace until I was running into the waves in an attempt to catch up with Nate. When I finally turned back to face the beach, my hair dripping salt water now, I expected him to still be there. I expected him to be standing there, still looking perfectly out of place on the hot sand watching me. But he wasn't. I frowned for a minute, disappointed.

"Noah Sweeney…" I whispered to myself. Then I smiled slowly. What I didn't know was that he was wrong. Knowing his name wouldn't change anything for us.

Noah

"Hey, where'd you go this afternoon? I must have fallen asleep for a bit but when I woke up you weren't there."

I thumbed through another folder, making sure I had the class list and a copy of the syllabus for this class. "Oh, I went for a walk down the beach. You know I don't like just sitting there." I replied distractedly while I placed the folder back in my bag and grabbed a second one. I began flipping through the pages of this one until Whitney suddenly snapped my bag closed on my hand as I reached for another folder.

"Noah!" she snapped, clearly exasperated with me.

"What are you doing?"

"What are *you* doing?" she fired back. "Relax. You're going to be fine. You're always fine."

"This isn't just going to a new class, Whitney. This is important."

"I know that," she huffed. "but Jesus, Noah. I haven't seen you smile or laugh in a week. Well, it's been even more than just a week. It's been months. I thought going to the beach would give you a break."

The beach was something she liked, not me. She hadn't thought it would help me. She had thought of herself, just like she always did. I only sighed and the girl with the book came to mind. I almost smiled just thinking about her. When I blinked, Whitney's defeated face came back into focus. She couldn't be more different from that girl; I could tell that from the few short moments I spent with Juliet. But I reminded myself that I loved Whitney, because I did. Right? I did love her. I had to after dating her for so long. She had dealt with my bullshit for so long. So I took a deep breath before replying, "It did. It was nice. But I need

13

you to understand this is a big deal for me, Whit. This internship could be the difference between me actually getting a job to support us or not. A job that will allow me to get him back. I need this. *We* need this."

"What *we* are you even talking about, Noah?" she said angrily, her eyebrows raising in a challenge. "Because it seems to me that the only *we* you'll ever care about does not include me. It just includes him." I bit my lip in regret. I didn't want another fight. Since Keaton had left us I thought she would have been happier; that it would have relieved some part of the strain from her and put it squarely on my shoulders. Clearly, that wasn't the case. All it had done was make me miserable and her even more dissatisfied with me.

"I didn't mean it like that. I meant us...you and me. You know that."

"No, actually, I don't know that," she snapped.

"Whitney, come on. Can we not do this right now?" I pleaded. She rolled her eyes and swiveled away from me, quickly stalking out of the room. Her dark hair had only just disappeared around the doorway when the phone rang. Seconds later, she was back in front of me, thrusting the phone at my chest.

"It's for you," she hissed before turning on her heel. I rolled my eyes at her back and lifted the receiver to my ear.

"Hello?"

"Noah Sweeney?" A deep voice boomed back at me.

"Uhm, yes?" I stammered.

"This is Principal Goldsworth."

"Oh, right, of course. Hello, Sir." I squeezed my eyes shut and inwardly groaned at my lack of finesse.

"Yes, good evening. Well you see Mr. Sweeney, the reason I'm calling is because there has been an accident. With Mrs. Granger."

My breath caught. "What do you mean an accident?"

"She passed away last night. An unexpected heart failure."

"Oh my God," I gasped, "That's terrible."

"Yes. As you can assume, it has put us in a bit of a predicament. School opens tomorrow and it seems like our staff is one English teacher short. I, of course, could find a substitute in the interim. But then I realized we have you at our disposal."

"What do you mean exactly, Mr. Goldsworth?"

"If you want it, the position is yours for the year."

I sat down at the counter in shock. "I...I'm not sure what to say."

"Yes would be acceptable."

"Yes. Yes, of course I want the job, Sir."

"Wonderful," he said brusquely. "We'll go over the details tomorrow morning. Please arrive early to meet in my office. It is my understanding that you are prepared to begin tomorrow? Mrs. Granger had everything ready at school. Other than that, you should be prepared from the last week."

"Yes, Sir."

"Very well. I'll see you bright and early tomorrow, Mr. Sweeney." And with that, the line went dead.

*****

I picked up the remaining syllabi and counted them out, making sure I had twenty-four to match this class roster. I was tired and more than a little overwhelmed. Most of all, I was sick of the sidelong glances and hurried whispers I got whenever I walked through the halls. For the last half of the day, I had stayed hidden in my room to avoid the throngs of high school girls. I kept reminding myself this was what I wanted, but more than that, this was what I *needed*. If this year went well, I could get Keaton back even sooner than I had anticipated.

There was a soft knock on my door and it was pushed open to reveal another teacher who looked only a few years older than me. "Hey, I'm Grant," he extended his hand and I shook it.

"Noah."

"Yeah, I heard." His smile was a more reserved one but one that exuded a sense of calm nonetheless. For some reason, he gave off a feeling of positivity. "It gets better you know."

"What?"

"This. All of it," he extended his arms to encompass the classroom around us. Then he smiled at me again. "It's overwhelming at first, trust me I remember it well. But it's great, you'll see. If you ever want to grab a beer some time, let me know. You'll probably need one after this week."

I gave him a small smile. "Thanks. I'll keep that in mind." I wondered what it would be like to go get a beer and take time to hang out with friends just for fun. It struck me just how much I had missed out on in the past years. Did I even know what a friend was at this point?

"Great! Well, it was nice meeting you, Noah. I'm sure I'll see you around."

16

"Yeah, yeah...Nice meeting you, too." He gave me one last reassuring smile before the door clicked shut behind him. Only seconds later, the bell rang and I took a deep breath in. *Almost over.* I repeated in my head for what had to be the tenth time this afternoon. The door swung open again and students began filing in. A pair of girls walked in and instantly blushed when I happened to glance their way. Their whispered giggles soon followed, and I inwardly groaned. *One more class.*

I uncapped my marker and turned my back to the classroom, meticulously spelling out my name on the board as the remaining kids found their seats. When the last bell rang, I turned to face my final class of the day. "As you can see, if you can read, my name is Mr. Sweeney. And I sure hope you can read seeing as this is senior English. Now, I know your schedules may say Mrs. Granger for this class, but she is no longer with us. So it'll just be me this year. And if you couldn't already tell by my lack of finesse, this is my first year teaching but I'm going to do the best I can."

I made my way around the desk and took a seat on the edge of it to survey this group of kids, half of which had their heads down. "I could lie and tell you that if I had known I was going to be your teacher today, I would have planned some fun activity. But even if I had time to plan, it probably still would have been less than exciting. So instead, I'll be cliché and we're just going to get to know each other today. I'll go around to everyone and you have to tell me your name and one thing about you. Then you can ask me any question you want and I have to answer honestly. Sound fair?"

There were a few groans, as I had been expecting, but for the most part the students nodded along. After teaching five different classes, I was pretty sick of this game myself but I didn't really have any other plan. Maybe this class would surprise me. I reached behind me for the class list to follow along with the new names and readied myself.

"Okay, so I guess we'll start here." I nodded my head to a girl with a pierced lip sitting in the first desk to my right. A lock of pitch black hair fell over one eye, a single purple streak capping off the look of teenage angst. "What's your name?"

She didn't even look up at me when she muttered, "Jade."

A pair of girls snickered from the back corner and I shot them a glare. "Okay, Jade. And something about you?"

She finally looked up from chipping off her own nail polish long enough to level me with the most bored expression I had ever seen. Her words came slow when she spoke. "I'm only here because I need this class to graduate. And no, I'm not asking you a question. Frankly, I don't give a damn about you."

I bit my lip to keep from laughing and attempted to regain my composure by checking her name off on my attendance list. I probably should be scolding her for her use of language or lack of participation. A real teacher probably wouldn't be on the verge of laughter from her response, but I couldn't help it. "Right then," I finally managed to get out. "Moving on." I focused on the girl to Jade's right. She couldn't be more opposite from the previous student. She sat with her back straight, hands folded before her. Her golden hair fell in perfect ringlets despite the heat of the late summer afternoon and it was neatly tucked into a ribbon tied with a bow.

"My name is Abigail. Something about me is that I've gone on three mission trips with my church to Ecuador, Haiti, and Guatemala." She proudly told me and beamed her blindingly white smile. I subconsciously blinked and flinched away from it in response and fought to give her a closed lip smile as a part of me struggled to picture this pastel-covered, prim and proper girl in a third world country.

"That's amazing Abigail." I replied politely, checking her name off and looking up again.

"So Mr. Sweeney, what do you do in your free time?"

I had answered this question in each one of my classes now but I continued to smile and paused as if to think of my answer. It wasn't a complete lie…it just wasn't the complete truth, either. That was the nice thing about being a teacher, though. No students would pry into your personal life. I could reveal as much or as little about myself as I wanted to. "I read a lot. Or I go for a run. I also play pick-up soccer if I have the time. So who's next?" I focused on the boy next to her. Max who raced motocross. I continued on, answering my favorite book, my favorite food, what music I liked, where I went to college. All the mundane questions.

I came to a girl in the back last who had an empty seat beside her even though she gave off the aura of popularity. Her dark hair was pin-straight and framed her face perfectly and her makeup gave her an intimidating, yet almost porcelain look. "I'm Samantha. Don't think of making it cute and calling me Sammie. It's just Samantha. I'm the class president. How old are you, Mr. Sweeney?" She said all this without pause, just calmly stared back at me, her eyes holding my own long after I had chuckled awkwardly at her forward question. Not one student had been so bold as to directly ask my age yet. Age seemed a taboo topic, but not to Samantha apparently. A few other girls began giggling yet again.

"Yeah Mr. Sweeney, how old are you?" One called out. Mariah I believed her name was.

I licked my lips and pushed off my perch on the desk to make my way behind it again. I stole a glance at the clock on the back wall while I fought back my initial response of *Too old for you*. Only three more minutes of class. I looked back to Samantha and she only folded her arms across her chest and raised one brow.

"Twenty-three." For the most part, the class remained silent, though I could hear some whispers rustling through the room, people calculating how many years older I was. Samantha for one, kept a perfect poker face as she gazed back at me until the door burst open and her eyes swiveled to see whoever had just walked in. I worried it would be Principal Goldsworth, already coming to check in. I straightened up in an effort to look more professional and turned to face him, but upon seeing the late arrival, my breath caught. Then, an uncontrollable smile spread across my face before I even had time to process.

"Juliet," I breathed.

Carter

My feet immediately came to a halt, my pre-rehearsed excuse lost in my throat. That smile, the one I thought I'd never see again. There was no way. I had to be wrong. But there he was. My eyes quickly scanned him over from head to toe, taking in his new attire. The same wavy, dark hair and strong jaw, but now there was a dress shirt covering his torso, the sleeves of which were rolled to his elbows. A navy tie dangled from his neck and I could see his hands were loosely fisted in the pockets of his slacks. He was breathtaking. And now he was my teacher.

"Noah Sweeney," I whispered so quietly he didn't even catch it.

"Carter, over here," I finally heard my friend Samantha snap impatiently. No doubt I was embarrassing her yet again by just standing at the front of the classroom like a gaping idiot. I tore my eyes from Noah to find her in the very last seat in the back, an open chair between her and Nate pulled out waiting for me. Mariah and Jenny glared at me as I passed, immediately putting their heads together, surely gossiping over why I could possibly be late. If they only knew. I stopped a foot from them and turned back.

"If you two have any intelligent thoughts to contribute to the world, I'm sure we're all dying to hear them. But seeing as I have yet to hear a single scintillating observation from either of you in my life, we really would all be better off if you could just keep your mouths shut. Thanks." I smiled at their shocked faces sweetly, tossed my bag on the ground beside Samantha, and took my seat sulkily. She offered me her most winning smile that I studiously ignored.

"His eyes haven't left you," she whispered. "He thinks you're amusing."

21

"Wonderful," I spat. I was no longer interested in her comments that had anything to do with the so-called "hot new English teacher." I no longer wanted to hear anything to do with English teachers at all.

"Hey, McMillan," Nate drawled from my other side. I didn't want to deal with him, either. Luckily for me, the bell rang just then because I had no idea how I planned to sit through a class right now.

"Come on," I muttered to Sam, pushing my way to the door. I almost made it, too.

"Juliet," his voice caused my feet to stall involuntarily. "A moment. Please."

Samantha gave me a questioning look, but I only shook my head at her. "Text me," she answered swiftly as she sashayed into the hall.

I hung back until everyone had exited the classroom. I didn't even turn to face him until the last footsteps had long since faded on the stairs. He stood behind his desk, both hands placed palm-down on it, almost bracing himself as his head hung down between his shoulders. I didn't speak, just waited until he finally lifted his head to look at me. He was no longer smiling, just staring at me with a curious intensity. Then he pointed to the board and the neat, blue lettering.

"I'm Mr. Sweeney, your new English teacher. It's nice to meet you," he extended his hand to me and I burst out laughing while I crossed my hands over my chest.

"Oh come on, Juliet. Work with me."

"First off, my name isn't Juliet," I snapped. "It's Carter."

"It's not my fault you didn't tell me your name before," he replied, matching my stance by folding his arms. I kept my mouth shut and eyed him. "Look, I don't know what you want me to say. Just forget we've ever met before I guess."

"We haven't met before. I don't recall ever introducing myself to you." I surprised myself when my anger dissolved and a teasing smile spread across my face. Something about him made me feel free. Free to feel anything, to say anything. I didn't remember the last time I had felt that way.

He opened his mouth, clearly exasperated with me, but then he saw my face. His eyelids fluttered closed and I vaguely marveled at how long and dark his lashes were. But then he shook his head and reopened his eyes. When he stared back at me, this time with a soft expression, I was able to pick out the dark blue in his stare. So dark as to be the color of wet denim. His mouth quirked up on one side in a smirk and I knew I had no reason to be angry. I never had been terribly angry, just caught off-guard. And he had to have been even more surprised than me. Suddenly, the whole situation seemed comical and I found myself laughing. I dropped my bag on a nearby desk and walked over to him, then hopped up so I was sitting perched on the desk directly in front of him. He gave me an odd look, one that said I was the most amusing thing he had ever laid eyes on. I was unsure if I should take offense to it or revel in it. For now, I just went with it because I liked this feeling of freedom being near him gave me.

"So Sweeney, how'd we get here?"

He sat down slowly in his chair across from me and continued to give me that look, one I had a feeling I was going to get a lot of. "What do you mean?"

"You. I've never seen you around before. What's your deal?"

23

He leaned back in his chair, his hands coming back to cradle his head. I saw him tense, though he hid it well, and I wondered how one question seemed to put him on guard. But then the tension melted from him as he took me in and a moment later he had morphed back into the guy I met on the beach, no longer the uptight teacher.

"It's my first year."

"You don't say," I replied dryly. He gave me an annoyed look but for some reason I already could read him. I knew he wasn't actually angry.

"You weren't even here. You can't attest to my teaching skills."

I quirked an eyebrow at him. "I was busy. Besides, you should know by now you're the talk of the school."

He rolled his eyes at my last comment, choosing to ignore it. "So I'm expected to let you get away with skipping class? What kind of precedent would this be setting Miss…" he trailed off, expecting me to fill in my last name, but a part of me liked making him work for it.

"I told you my name's Carter."

"You do realize it won't be hard for me to figure it out, right? I am your teacher," he raised his eyebrows at me but I only shrugged so he continued. "No nicknames?"

"Not unless you intend to call me Cart, which I would highly suggest you don't do for your own good."

He smirked at me. "Then I'll just have to come up with something else, won't I?" I only narrowed my eyes at him. He chuckled softly. "You missed today's lesson regardless. Tell me about yourself."

"That was your lesson? Get to know each other?"

"Don't scoff at me."

"Be a little more redundant, why don't you?" I laughed at him. "Last class of the day with a bunch of seniors? We've gone through that routine for years now on the first day of school. You must have gained a lot of fans that way." My voice dripped with sarcasm.

"Well actually, I did. Seems to me that I'm the 'talk of the school.' I think the two who sat over there particularly enjoyed the class." He nodded towards Mariah and Jenny's seats. I immediately swiveled back to glare at him. I was met with questioning eyes. "Touchy subject?"

"They only liked you because they think you're attractive," I spat.

A grin took over his entire face, crinkling his eyes, before he asked, "And why do you like me?"

"Who ever said I like you at all?"

He nodded his approval at my response and fell silent, but the smile I was already falling in love with stayed in place. His eyes continued to bore into mine until I hastily looked away. His stare was unnerving, as if with one look he could see through me and the entire wall of sarcasm I hid behind. So instead of meeting his eyes, even though I knew I was becoming easily mesmerized by them, I took time to glance around his room. I took in the thick volumes lining the bookcases and the posters of inspirational quotes adorning the whitewashed walls.

"'Swim in your own direction?'" I questioned disdainfully as I eyed one featuring a brightly colored fish amongst a sea of dull grey ones. Despite the quote, it looked to me like all the fish were going the same way. I met his bemused gaze.

"I didn't decorate," he replied dully. He answered my questioning look before I could speak,

"Mrs. Granger was listed on your schedule I presume?" I nodded. "She died."

I gasped and he gave me a sad nod. "Did you know her?" he asked.

"No," I paused. "So you're just a substitute?"

"Yes and no. I was supposed to be an intern. They asked me to take over for the year and then depending on how I do, they could offer me a job."

"So your future relies on this one job?"

"In a way," he conceded, but there was something hidden in his eyes that showed me there was more than what he was saying.

"And you'll probably be monitored pretty heavily?"

His wry smile answered me. "I'm not a prisoner, Carter," he took a deep breath and cocked his head to one side and I looked away again, afraid of what I was getting myself into. "I suppose they'll check in on me a bit, yes."

Just then, the door swung open and I quickly hopped off the desk, instantly on guard. But why? It wasn't as if a teacher couldn't talk to their students. Yet for some reason I felt guilty.

"Miss McMillan!" A voice called out from the door and I immediately beamed facing Mr. Olsen.

"So McMillan's your last name," I heard Noah mutter from behind me with a smile in his voice and I stepped into Mr. Olsen's outstretched arms.

"How have you been, kid?"

"Good, you?" I stepped back from him, taking in his calming smile, the same one I had known since freshman year.

"Can't complain. I see you've met our new arrival," he nodded his head towards Noah who was giving me a questioning smirk, but in a way his uptight air had returned.

"I have yet to determine what I think of him," I replied dryly. Mr. Olsen's smile widened.

"Best of luck to you, Mr. Sweeney. She's a handful." I gasped in mock disgust while Noah chuckled.

"Trust me, I have no doubt. But I have a feeling I can handle it." He gave me a conspiratorial look and my insides squirmed.

"McMillan," Mr. Olsen nodded at me, signaling my dismissal, and I took it. "Don't be a stranger."

I grabbed my bag from the desk as I passed and took one last glance as the door swung shut behind me. Noah's eyes caught mine, dark and mysterious, and he ran a hand absentmindedly over his jaw.

*****

"Talk," Samantha's voice cut through the static on my phone as I pulled my keys from my bag.

"About?" I tossed the bag in and climbed into the drivers' seat.

"Don't be coy with me. It's unbecoming of you."

"Touché. What do you want me to say?"

"Well, let's see... You leave me alone in a class full of half-wits until the very last minutes. Then low and behold, you cause a scene upon your entrance. Not only did the new teacher that everyone's been going crazy over look like he *knew* you, you also managed to snap at Mariah and Jenny. Much appreciated by the way. I'm proud of you for finally standing up to her. But, my favorite part of all; 'Juliet' was asked to stay after class. Pray tell Juliet, what is going on in that secretive head of yours?"

I sighed as I pulled out of the lot. There was no use arguing with her. She was relentless and only the truth would do. "I met him the other day."

"Where?" she immediately demanded.

"The beach."

I heard her make a grumbling noise on the other end of the line and then it was silent for a while. "So what now?" she finally asked.

"What do you mean?"

"What did he have to say today?"

"Nothing really," I replied, thinking back on our conversation. It wasn't a lie, nothing about our talk had been exciting by any means. Yet at the same time, it had given me something I hadn't felt in a long time. Peace, happiness even. Because in those few minutes with him, nothing else had seemed to matter. I hadn't been stuck within my shell, powerless and scared. I had been able to be myself, a person I wasn't even sure I recognized anymore. I realized now, this was not going to be a good thing. I could not have these feelings from my teacher.

I had learned long ago to rely on no one but myself and yet in just two days of knowing him, I could tell Noah Sweeney was going to be something different. The happiness that only he had been able to give me would become something I depended on. The thought terrified me, but not enough to stop.

SEPTEMBER
Carter

"Why'd you choose here? This town. This school," I asked as I took my seat in front of his desk. The other students had all filed out, their raised voices dying down as they poured into the fall sunshine to head home. But I stayed behind. It was clear it was becoming a routine for me, although I wasn't sure how pleased Mr. Sweeney was with the arrangement. It was in the afternoons that I was able to catch glimpses of the man I had first met that day on the beach. It was a slow process though. There was just something about Noah Sweeney that made me want to crawl into his head and live in it, even though I already knew he would never allow anyone that close. It was also stupid. He was a teacher. I shouldn't want to know what was in my teacher's head.

"What do you mean?" he asked now.

"Well, you choose where you work, right? Why here?"

He scratched the back of his head with one hand while the other swiped over the words he had written about *Macbeth* on the board today. "It's near my college, so I applied here just because that's what everyone did who was in my teaching program." He chuckled as he set down the eraser and glanced at me. "I applied to all the high schools around the state. This one just happened to have an opening. Does that count as choosing?"

"No other school gave you a job offer?"

"Yeah, they did. I liked it here, though. At least, I thought I did."

"So you're reconsidering now?" I questioned.

He gave me a teasing grin. "I don't know. Some students are...eh," he trailed off, raising his shoulders in a shrug.

29

I laughed. "Liar. I'm a great student."

He laughed with me but had to agree. "Are you going to major in English?" he asked as he packed his bag.

"No."

"No?"

I shook my head but didn't elaborate further. I wasn't used to people actually being interested in me. Instead, I asked him another question. "Why English for you?"

He chuckled at my topic change but took it in stride, pulling his bag over one shoulder as I followed him out of the room. "Because I was good at it?" It came out as more of a question than an answer to one. I pegged him with a look and waited for more. He took his time locking the door behind us, readjusted his bag on his shoulder, and then turned back to answer me. "I guess I like to write. And read. So I figured why not make others like to write and read."

It was a simple answer, but I liked it a lot. It fit him. Because even though it was so simple, it seemed to mean so much. "I'll see you tomorrow, Carter." He said softly as we parted ways, him heading to the teachers' lounge and me heading to the student lot.

"Bye, Noah Sweeney." He rolled his eyes but didn't chastise me and I was rewarded with one more of his half smirks before he turned away again.

Nate was leaning against my car as I pulled my keys from my bag and I gave him a quizzical look. "Hey, C. What's up?"

"Uhm, nothing," I hedged, the guard I put up for most of the world immediately back in place. "Did you need something?"

"Some of us are heading to Baker's field tonight. You know, just a small thing. Samantha's got

it all organized. I'm sure she's told you all about it."
She hadn't, but I smiled at him like I knew what he
was talking about. Samantha didn't tell me all that
much about social gatherings. She knew I had my
limits. She understood I didn't really like half of her
so-called friends. It had taken me a long time before I
would even talk to other people. "Anyways, I was just
hoping that'd you'd be there. I know, parties aren't
really your thing but…I just wanted you to come. So
if you wanted to come…that would be cool."

He was stammering and losing his finesse
with each sentence he spit out that I didn't reply to. I
couldn't imagine Noah ever stuttering around a girl.
He had a calm that nothing could penetrate. But why
was I comparing Nate to Noah at all? I shouldn't have
even been thinking of Noah. I should have been happy
to have one of the most popular guys in school asking
me out. If that's even what he was doing.

"Sure. Yeah. I'll be there." I gave him a small
smile and he beamed back at me, the relief rolling off
him in waves.

"Awesome. I'll see you there." I watched as
he loped off, tossing me one more large grin over his
shoulder before climbing into his truck.

*****

"I didn't think you'd want to come."
Samantha hissed at me as she reapplied lipstick in the
mirror of my passenger seat. "You never come. I gave
up trying two years ago."

"I know. I just figured, why not?" I glanced at
her as I whipped around another corner and she
clutched the handle on the door but didn't comment.
She was accustomed to my driving by now. "You do
realize it's going to be dark. No one's going to care
what shade your lips are. No guy even notices that
crap in the daylight."

31

"Not the point, Carter. We don't dress to impress boys. We dress to impress ourselves. You got that? You don't change for a boy. You don't do things for boys. You do things for yourself. Girl power, baby."

I rolled my eyes in the darkness as I pulled up next to the other trucks and cars lining the edge of the field. I wasn't sure if she was trying to convince me or herself, but I let her either way. I felt like I missed out on all the fun girly friend things I was expected to do. I wasn't a conventional friend.

"Stop tugging on your shirt," she snapped at me as we made our way to the bonfire in the middle of the field. "You look fine. It's supposed to be tight."

"I'm not trying to pick up a guy," I hissed back.

"I'm confused." She stopped and grabbed my arm to pull me back before we reached the group. "You came because Nate invited you, but you're not looking to hook up with him?"

"Not everything is about boys, didn't you just tell me that? Girl power?"

She studied me hard, her eyes already a little glassy from the shots she had taken before we left her house. "Something's different about you," she declared after a moment. "You laugh more."

"I always laugh a lot." I retorted. She opened her mouth, and I already knew what she was going to bring up so I held up a hand to stop her before she could start. "Not now. Now, we have fun. Okay? Because I haven't done this before. Too many walls, right?"

"No more walls," she told me adamantly. It was a saying I heard from her all too often. "Let's go."

Just then, Nate came strutting over with two red cups in his hands. "Ladies, come join us." He held out the cups as an offering and Samantha eagerly grabbed hers and gave me a pointed look before leaving me behind with Nate.

I gave him a small smile and politely declined the drink. "So you're the responsible one," he said.

"Between me and Samantha? Of course," I laughed. He reached out without asking and took my hand. My first reaction was to pull away, as it always was. Even if I had very slowly gotten used to his overly friendly ways, I didn't want his skin on mine. But I knew that would look rude and Nate really was a friend. I also knew Samantha would yell at me for it later because I could still feel her eyes on me, making sure I was taking down my walls for the night. So for now, I let Nate's meaty hand dwarf my own and pull me towards the fire.

I knew almost everyone who sat on the logs and overturned buckets around the flames. It was a big high school, but the people who sat here tonight were the ones everyone knew. They were Samantha's friends, not mine. But I was Samantha's friend, too. So instead of looking down on me, they were polite to me. Sometimes *too* kind. I wasn't sure if I liked it or not. As the night went on, they each got steadily more drunk until Nate was blatantly hitting on me. I had done my best to ward off his subtle attempts since this summer but he was having trouble catching a hint. He found me again late in the night as I was sitting by myself on the far edge of the fire. Samantha had long ago snuck off with the lacrosse captain. I was pretty sure his name was Ryan. Or maybe Brian. It wasn't hard to imagine what they had gone to do. So instead, I sat by myself, tearing at the grass beneath me, wondering if this was what kids did every Friday night.

"McMillan!" Nate called as he stumbled over and sat next to me heavily.

I struggled to think of his last name and I felt a little bad when I couldn't remember it. He even sat next to me in physics and English and I didn't know it. "What's up, Nate? Think you've had enough to drink?"

"Enough to drink? No. I don't think so. You see, I still know you aren't into me. So if I know that, then no. I haven't had enough to drink." His words slurred together, but he gave me a winning smile nonetheless and I had to chuckle.

"I'm sorry," I said, unsure how one even responded to something like that.

"Why is that, McMillan?"

"Hm?"

"Why aren't you into me? Plenty of other girls are. Those two over there?" He squinted and pointed across the fire at two blondes giggling with each other. Macie and Candace I think their names were. They were on the gymnastics team with Samantha. "They won't leave me alone."

"Kind of like you won't leave me alone?" I countered with a laugh so he knew I was kidding.

He clutched at his heart and beer sloshed out of his cup and onto my shoes. "Ouch. Your words hurt." I laughed but didn't respond. I didn't talk about myself. I didn't talk about my real feelings. The closest I had gotten to opening up in years had been to Noah and I had no idea why. I had no idea why he kept coming to mind now, when I was with arguably the most attractive boy in our school. When I was supposed to be acting like a typical high school senior. "Last year, I thought you were the hottest girl in school."

His words shocked me. I wasn't anything special. I was just average. Add that to the fact that I stayed away from everyone except for Samantha, I was surprised he even knew my name when we had a class last year. But as the year went on, he had slowly become a friend to me. If you could consider it that. Then this summer, it became clear he wanted more than a friendship. I could never give him that, but I also didn't want to lose what little connection I had gained with someone.

He kept going when I didn't speak. "You were also so mysterious. You didn't talk to anyone except Sam. I wanted you to talk to me. I liked your eyes the most. They scared me at first."

"My eyes scared you?" I gasped. I wasn't sure what flirting was exactly, but I had a feeling he wasn't doing a very good job right now.

"Yeah. They're so big and sad and painful."

"Nate, that's not a very good thing to hear." His words hurt because I knew they were true. I didn't want them to be true, I tried to deny they were true for a long time. But I couldn't.

"I wanted to know why. If they were always like that. Were they always like that, Carter?" He focused on me fully now and I saw just how drunk he was. He wouldn't remember this conversation in the morning.

With that thought, I felt comfortable in saying the truth. "No."

"Did you know this year they aren't as sad? This year they don't look so hurt. Do you know that?" I shook my head and he smiled at me. "Want to know what I used to think?"

"What did you think?" I whispered.

35

"I liked to think it was because of me. Because we became friends this past year. Right? We're friends, C?"

"Yeah. We're friends."

"Yeah. So I told myself your eyes were happier because of me. Isn't that silly?"

"It's not silly…"

"I realized tonight it's not me. Because you don't want me, do you?" I opened my mouth to reply, then shut it again. I was at a loss for words. I didn't want to hurt him. He was good to me. "It's okay. I get it. I do. But there's someone isn't there?"

"Uhm…" Was there? Was Noah really mending me more than I even realized? Was he the reason my eyes were happier, why I laughed more as Samantha pointed out? "I don't know."

"I like him." Nate proclaimed. "Whoever he is. Or maybe it's a she. It's not a she, is it?" he asked me suddenly, as if this was the only logical explanation for why I hadn't been interested in him.

I chuckled awkwardly. "No, it's not a she."

"Okay. Then yeah, I like him. You don't need to tell me who. Until he hurts you. You tell me if he hurts you, okay? Because we're friends. Yeah?"

"Yeah, Nate…we're friends." I looked at him hard, maybe for the first time in the past two years of knowing him. He was handsome with olive skin and dark hair that matched his dark eyes. He wasn't Noah though. No one was Noah to me.

"Thanks, Carter. Thanks for coming tonight." He threw an arm over my shoulder heavily and pulled me into his side before kissing the top of my head and I didn't even flinch. I actually enjoyed it. Letting someone else hold me, knowing they were my friend. I wondered if this was one of the high school experiences everyone claimed were so great. Maybe I had missed out on things after all.

*****

That Sunday, I threw open the door to our small-town restaurant without thought, almost as if I owned the place. Not that I did of course, but my uncle did so I had basically grown up in this little hole in the wall populated by only locals. That person who I barely recognized? The girl who was always completely herself? This used to be the only place I found her. It was a little piece of the person I used to be, filled with memories of my brother and I with our two cousins and nothing could touch it. No grief or guilt could come into this place.

However, when I came barreling in this time, I barely had time to catch myself from tripping into the guy standing just inside the door. Clearly, he didn't belong here. His hands were tucked into the pockets of his cargo shorts and he was wearing a faded grey t-shirt but was rocking back on his heels as if he didn't know what to do with himself. Yeah, there was no way he belonged here. I kind of felt bad for him because it was clear he was waiting to be seated, something we did not do here.

I reached up and tapped him on the shoulder. "It's seat yourself-" My breath caught. Yet again I was running into Noah Sweeney outside of school hours.

"Carter," he gasped and the shock was evident on his face.

I grinned up at him. There was something about being with him that made me let go of every single reservation I had. Maybe it was because he didn't know how I had been the past four years. He didn't know who I was then. But for the first time, I wanted someone to really know who I was *now*.

"You're wearing a t-shirt," I remarked as I took him in again. It was a stupid thing to say, I was painfully aware of that. But I wasn't used to seeing him in just a t-shirt. It drew my eyes to his tanned biceps which I hadn't seen since that day at the beach. I focused on trying not to stare and pulled my eyes back up to his face. His cheeks were flushed from my perusal, but that was all he would give away.

"Is there something wrong with my t-shirt?"

It gave me a chance to study him again, this time with permission. It wasn't fair for someone to look so good in just an old, grey t-shirt. I hid my approval and squinted my eyes back at him. "I guess it's acceptable. It is a Sunday after all. I suppose you can't always live in dress shirts."

He chuckled. "You're right. It is indeed Sunday."

"And you're at Sonny's Chicken Coop."

"The name of this place is seriously 'Sonny's Chicken Coop?'" He craned his neck as if to see it written on a sign somewhere.

Okay, so my uncle wasn't exactly the best at choosing names. But I was extremely defensive of the diner; my little home away from home. "Don't knock it 'til you try it."

And with that, I walked past him to hop up on a stool at the bar. I couldn't just stand there and talk to him, even if I wanted to do that all day. He made me feel alive; normal. He made me feel things I had never felt before. Him in that t-shirt made me remember what else he was hiding under his dress shirt and tie every day. He was also my teacher. That was not okay. I shook my head and attempted to get my mind out of the gutter.

Before I had even settled into my seat, I felt him slide onto the stool next to me. Not leaving an empty stool between. Not sitting a few seats down the almost empty bar. No, out of the five other empty seats, he chose the one immediately to my left. I half turned to raise one eyebrow at him. "What are you doing?"

"Some girl told me it was seat yourself here at Sonny's Chicken Coop," he said in the most chipper voice I had ever heard. And that smile. God, when he smiled like that I couldn't think straight.

I narrowed my eyes at him even though it took everything I had not to laugh. "I hate you." I knew as soon as I said it, I shouldn't have. That's not how you talk to teachers. There was just something about him when I was with him that made me lose all sense.

He threw his head back and laughed and I wanted to memorize the sound so I could play it over and over again later. I definitely wasn't regretting saying it now; not if it would make him laugh like that. Man, I was seriously messed up. He was my *teacher. Teacher.* But here now? This wasn't my teacher, Mr. Sweeney. No, this was just the Noah Sweeney I had met on the beach.

"What you feel for me is so the opposite of hate," he joked. I scoffed and shook my head. If only he knew just how right he truly was. *So* the opposite of hate.

"Carter!" My cousin Tally came barreling out of the kitchen just then but immediately stopped short when her eyes landed on Noah Sweeney. He had a tendency to cause that reaction. She made an effort to appear a bit more professional as she sauntered the last few steps to the bar but it was a fruitless attempt. I could still feel Mr. Sweeney's half amused gaze locked on me.

She batted her eyelashes as she handed a menu towards him. "Welcome to Sonny's!" Mr. Sweeney

39

barely looked at her as he took the menu and placed it down in front of him. "Can I start you with anything to drink?"

"Just coffee would be great, thanks." He replied smoothly and just like that his teaching voice snapped back into place. The wall of professionalism came down on Tally hard.

She reluctantly turned back to me when she realized Sweeney wasn't going to reciprocate her interest. I leveled her with a bored expression, telling her I was unamused by her attempts, but she just waved me off. "Usual?" she asked.

"Yeah, just-"

"Make sure it isn't crunchy. Yeah, we all know." She finished for me before turning and sashaying her way back into the kitchen. I smirked when I saw from my peripheral vision that Sweeney didn't even look at her retreating backside, despite it being clear that's what she had wanted. I was just about to look down at my phone to busy myself when his voice interrupted me.

"Crunchy?"

I swiveled on the stool to face him and eyed him curiously. I was confused at what he was doing. I was confused at this whole thing. Whatever it was. "My waffle."

"Your usual is a waffle?" he asked. He seemed genuinely intrigued by this, like he may actually need this knowledge at some point in his life.

"Yes..."

He took in my words for a moment longer and I thought that would be it. I was a little bit sad because I liked the sound of his unprofessional voice. I liked everything about his unprofessional self. "You do realize the whole point of a waffle is to be crunchy, right?"

"No."

"If you didn't want a crunchy waffle you should have just ordered a pancake."

"That's completely different."

"It's made out of the same batter!" He argued, clearly not understanding anything.

"If I ordered a pancake, it wouldn't waffle."

He stared at me in utter dismay. "Did you just use waffle as a verb?"

I had to think back on what I had just said. "You know what I mean."

"I have absolutely no clue what you mean."

"You know, the waffle holes. The waffle pattern. Pancakes don't waffle. Only waffles waffle. And without the waffle, where would your butter and chocolate go?"

His mouth quirked up on one side in the most adorable smirk. "You are the single most amusing person I know."

I bit my lip and tilted my head to one side. "I'm not sure if I should be offended or flattered." His smile only grew as he shrugged his shoulders. "I really don't like you," I reiterated. It caused him to laugh and internally, I did a little happy dance because I had caused him to make that beautiful sound yet again. He was still laughing when Tally came back to take his order and place his coffee in front of him. She gave me a curious look, as if she didn't believe I was capable of making a guy like him laugh but there was no one else at the bar to blame it on.

"So have you decided what you'd like today?" she asked him. He hadn't even opened the menu yet, so unless he was here for something specific I doubt he knew what he wanted. Instead of answering her, he turned to me.

"What do you recommend?"

41

I never even got a chance to reply before Tally's laughter cut me off. "She's not the person you should be asking."

That got his attention. "What's that supposed to mean?" There was a bite to his voice but Tally didn't pick up on it.

"She's so particular about her breakfast foods. You won't end up eating anything if you ask her for a suggestion."

Noah turned to me to gauge if what she was saying was true or not. I only bit my lip and shrugged my shoulders in response which caused him to chuckle. He turned to Tally. "Well, I really wouldn't like a soggy waffle," his eyes darted to me playfully. "So I'll just take the pancakes. With a side of bacon. Thank you."

Once Tally had left us again I tossed a glare his way. "There is nothing similar about pancakes and waffles." He shook his head at me. "Also, bacon doesn't go with pancakes."

"You're impossible." He smiled at me but there was something else there in the back of those dark blue eyes. Something I couldn't decipher.

OCTOBER
Carter

His eyes caught mine as they had so many times over the past weeks. I watched them as the critical, professional look melted from the blue and they grew lighter, playful. I smirked to myself while I took my time packing my bag after the bell rang. It had been a couple weeks since our run-in at the diner and since then we had established even more of a routine. Samantha narrowed her eyes at me, but didn't say anything. She only followed the trail of other students out the door. She had become steadily more suspicious about my after school ritual.

When the final footsteps disappeared, I made my way to his desk and sat before it yet again, my feet dangling. "Hey," I said softly.

The rest of his uptight façade faded as he loosened his tie and pushed his sleeves up higher. "Hey," he crooned back. My eyes shifted over him and I felt the familiar calm settle in as my smile grew.

He waited for me to speak, but I wasn't ready to just yet. Sitting in silence with him was enough for me. His hand ran over his jaw again and I traced it with my eyes. Everything about him was sharp, almost intimidating. His eyes were hard, always impenetrable whether they were their steely grey or the dark blue from when I first met him. Even so, everything about him fit and I found myself silently cataloguing every detail I could while he was preoccupied with thinking about something else. I longed to know every thought that flitted through his head but I knew I never would. He wouldn't let me.

He was so private, nothing about him came easy. He could sit silent for minutes on end and yet still appear completely at ease. Other than the very first day, he hadn't told the class a single thing about

43

himself. Yet I knew I had gotten somewhere with him. He had told me his backstory, his interests, more mundane facts that were slowly piecing him together for me. However, it was the things he didn't say that mattered even more to me. The way he appeared totally at ease when I was around and yet restless if others were nearby. It was as if he trusted me, but only me, and that was something I could not take lightly. I smiled to myself but as soon as his eyes turned back to me, I looked away. I knew my time to stare was up because if anyone could win a staring contest, it would be him and I had no intention of giving him free access to read every thought that crossed my brain.

He gave me a small smile and pushed off from his chair to start packing up his things for the day, throwing them into his bag and straightening papers on the desk. I watched his hands as they deftly sorted and flicked through different things then lifted my eyes to his face where he wore a content smile.

"What's your favorite place to go?" If he were at all caught off-guard by my question, he didn't show it. I was sick of only seeing him in a classroom; I wanted to know where else he could be. I had loved the him I got to see at the diner, the one who had let all his reservations go as well.

"Want to see it?" he asked as he slung the bag over his shoulder. My breath caught on his words and his jaw clenched for a moment, a flash of some unknown emotion crossing his face before he could safely stow it away.

"Yes," I breathed, scared if I spoke too loud he would take back his offer.

"Well, let's go then," he held the door and I ducked under his arm into the deserted hallway, then fell into step beside him. I kept glancing up at him, waiting for him to tell me this was a bad idea. That this couldn't happen. Instead, his jaw continued to clench and unclench as my little legs struggled to keep up with his long strides.

He didn't speak as he opened up his passenger door and tossed the CDs that were littering the seat into the back. He didn't speak as he hastily shut the door behind me and slid in behind the wheel. He didn't speak even after we had been driving for ten minutes, the whole time my eyes had been fighting to steal glances at him. Finally, his jaw loosened, his fingers unclenched from around the steering wheel, and his eyes flicked to me.

"Why do you keep looking at me like that?"

He dared to ask me a question right now? After punishing me with this excruciating silence? I deflected, asking him a question in return. "Are you regretting this?"

His eyes fluttered shut and his knuckles turned white on the steering wheel again. "No."

"No?"

"I don't regret my time with you, Carter." He stopped but I didn't speak. I let him have time to continue because it was clear a but was coming. "But there's still a part of me that knows the difference between right and wrong. And you know it, too."

He turned the car off the main road and onto an overgrown dirt path. "Yes...I know right and wrong..."

He didn't fill in my blank for a while but I wasn't about to continue. "We both know we shouldn't be doing this."

"This isn't wrong," I countered.

"I'm your teacher, Carter." He sighed. The trees that had been blurring slowly by my window began to thin and a lake came into view. My breath

45

caught, our conversation forgotten for the moment. He threw the car in park and I was immediately fumbling for the handle and stepping out into the crisp fall air.

The sun was just beginning to dip below the horizon on the opposite shore and it was casting tendrils of golden light high into the slowly darkening sky and onto the still waters below. The leaves on the trees hanging over the banks were bursting with color. Reds and oranges and yellows fought to cling to branches while their brothers who had already fallen bobbed atop the ripples of the reflected sunset. It was absolutely breathtaking.

I turned back to find Noah standing behind me, bathed in golden light, softening all his sharp features, and it took everything in me not to gasp again at the mere sight of him. He had been watching me, his face expressionless, but as soon as I turned he focused his eyes on the horizon above my head and shoved his hands deep into the pockets of his slacks.

"This is my favorite place," he whispered into the growing darkness. "It's perfect. Every single time, it's perfect. Every time it's something different and I think that's amazing. I like different; I like being surprised. Some days, like today, the sun will set perfectly over it and you get to see the bloody reflection in the water and the leaves float like little boats on top of it." My eyes traced the path of one dull yellow leaf as it drifted across the orb of light mirroring the sun dipping below the trees as he talked. "In summer, there actually are boats. Hundreds of them, all white sailboats bobbing in the breeze, each holding their own little story. Each with their own little worlds. Other days it looks angry or freezing, the steely grey waves seem to attack the shore. Then the next day it will be so calm it looks like a sheet of glass that I could walk on. But every time, it's beautiful."

His eyes finally drifted down from the horizon to meet mine. They were lighter than I had ever seen them, the color almost completely leached out of them so they were a white-grey now. They reminded me of his description of the water. Calm and serene at one moment, and stormy grey in the next. He breathed out heavily as he stared at me and for once I didn't look away. There were no words to describe him. He was gorgeous, but his mind…I was slowly starting to fall in love with his mind. That was a very dangerous thing.

His eyes were everywhere on me, heating every inch of my body they landed on, and I was completely at his mercy waiting for his next move. "Yes," he muttered out of nowhere, so quiet I might have missed it if everything in me hadn't been straining towards him.

"Yes?" I asked.

"Yes, I'm regretting this." The air seeped out of my lungs and suddenly the darkening twilight didn't seem so beautiful anymore. He walked past me before I could respond and sat atop one of the large rocks above the lightly lapping waves. I turned and trailed behind him.

"Noah, don't." But I didn't even know what I didn't want him to say. I just knew it wasn't going to be good.

Hearing his first name out of my mouth caused him to flinch. He dropped his head into his hands as I sank down onto a rock below him. "What was I thinking?" He looked down at me as if he actually wanted an answer. "You were in my *car*. You're here alone with me." He stood up suddenly, distancing himself from me, acting as if I may attack him. "Oh my God…If anyone saw you leave with me…" He turned away from me and I heard him mutter something else, but I couldn't make it out.

Each new word that fell from his lips caused a new wave of pain and shame. "Stop. Stop it," I pleaded.

"That's exactly what needs to happen. This needs to stop." He said, clinging to my words as he paced back to me. His finger waved between the two of us as I slowly stood up. "Mr. Sweeney. Carter McMillan. Not Noah. Noah doesn't exist to you."

His words hurt but I couldn't let him know that. I couldn't let him know how attached I had gotten in such a short amount of time. But I also couldn't let him panic over nothing. "Listen, this isn't wrong, okay? We're not doing anything! We've *never* done anything. Just calm down." The words I was speaking were completely true. We hadn't done anything. Running into each other in the diner had just been a coincidence. Since then, all we had done was talk. I couldn't even consider us friends. Because although I had quickly come to rely on him in these past weeks, he kept himself locked up. I had no way of knowing what I meant to him. I had no definite knowledge if he even enjoyed my company until today. Today was the first time he had ever shown what could be considered overt interest in me. And he was already taking it back.

"Carter," he sighed, completely fed up with me. "I don't think administration would be too concerned with the opinion of a student and a fill-in student-teacher. It just takes one person seeing something and thinking it's more than what it really is. This is so much more than just us."

I shook my head but had no rebuttal for him. He was right. Part of me had been choosing to ignore that fact. I wanted to ignore it because I was reveling in the idea that he actually wanted to spend time with me. Outside the confines of a classroom. I had used this trip to determine that I wasn't just another student to him. But he was right. This wasn't okay. And I wasn't sure how I had allowed myself to believe it was okay. He was my teacher. Yet for some reason, I had become drawn to him like I had never been drawn to anyone else before.

"What do you mean this is more than just us?" My brain had finally caught up to the last thing he had said.

He quickly paused his pacing and glanced at me. It was clear I had hit a nerve and my stomach clenched before he could even say anything. "Wh-what?" he stuttered. Noah didn't stutter. I swallowed hard.

"There's someone else isn't there..."

His eyes were wide. "Carter, I..."

"You have a girlfriend?"

He seemed to breathe a sigh of relief at my question, which I found odd, but his hand was still clutching the back of his neck in agitation. "Yes."

One word. All he said was one word, but it was enough to make my knees weak and I sank back down to the cold rock. I couldn't think of a single thing to say to him right now. Any ideas my brain had been entertaining for us over the past weeks, right or wrong, were completely dashed. How could I have been so stupid? How could I have even had those ideas in the first place?

His back was still to me and I could see every muscle pulled taut. The silence seemed to stretch forever before he finally turned back around to face me, his arms falling limp by his sides. He didn't speak; just stared at me in an attempt to gauge my reaction. It was a look I knew well, paired with a barely there smile. But there was no smile now and I purposely kept my face devoid of any emotion. I wasn't in awe of his ability to stay silent anymore.

"How long?" I finally asked.

"How long for what?"

"Have you been dating. How long have you been dating your girlfriend?" I was fighting hard to keep my anger in check. He didn't need to see how much this affected me. I wasn't necessarily mad he had a girlfriend. I was mad he hadn't told me about her. Clearly, I was not a very important person in his life if he had failed to mention a girlfriend. Just because I wanted him, didn't mean he wanted me.

"Two years."

I laughed without humor and stood again, striding past him and pulling open the passenger door. He followed without a word, sliding into the drivers' seat and glancing at me cautiously. I folded my arms over my chest in an attempt to keep him away and to keep myself together.

"Please talk," his voice sounded loud in the silence of the car. He hadn't even turned the key yet so the engine could drown out some of his words. I didn't acknowledge him, just gazed out the window. The breathtaking scene didn't seem so gorgeous to me anymore. "Carter. Tell me *something*,"

"Can you drive please? People are probably wondering where I am." That was a lie. I was staying with Samantha tonight and I already texted her I would be late.

He sighed like he wasn't happy with my response but started the car nonetheless. After a few tense moments of nothing but the radio faintly playing, his voice cut through me again. "I'm an ass." I smiled at his words without thinking and before I could wipe it away he saw. It gave him enough hope to continue talking. "Please, Carter."

I rolled my eyes. "I don't know what you want me to say. Clearly I'm not your friend, *Mr. Sweeney.*"

The stress I put on his title and the fact that I was throwing his own words back at him caused him to flinch. He ground his teeth and waited a moment before speaking again. "I panicked, okay? I didn't mean to make you upset."

"Why?" My question stopped him and I watched as one hand reached up to rake through his hair. I had already learned it was a nervous habit of his, something he did when he was uncomfortable. He didn't justify me with a response though, and I knew by his face he wasn't going to. "I just want to be your friend," I said quietly, even though in my heart I couldn't say if that was the truth or not. All I knew was that in a few short weeks, he had begun to mend parts of me I didn't know had been broken. For the first time, I had learned what it felt like to need someone and not be afraid.

"I know. I know." His eyes found mine in the growing twilight. They looked black now, and despite their darkness they still gave me the feeling that he could see everything in me. Luckily, they refocused on the road after only a couple seconds. I blew out a breath I didn't realize I had been holding and turned away from him completely. He didn't know, though. He didn't know how much I had begun to need him. Even I didn't know I needed something until he came into my life.

He didn't say anything else for the rest of the drive. He didn't even fidget, leading me to believe his mind was completely blank. Our confrontation had meant nothing to him where it meant everything to me and my mind was a whirlwind of thoughts I couldn't

51

even string into sentences. He never said we could still be friends. He never said if we even were friends or not.

He pulled into the student lot and I directed him to my car. Silently, I snatched my bag from the floorboard and pushed open the door, feeling the night cut into me. Just before I slammed it shut, I paused and looked back in at him. He was staring at me with so much intensity my stomach immediately filled with knots, but I still managed to find my voice.

"Why didn't you mention her?"

His face barely changed at all and when the only answer he gave me was a slight shrug, I shoved the door closed and practically threw myself into my own car, not bothering to look back.

Noah

The sound of my door slamming shut felt as if she had physically slapped me. I watched as she pulled her own door closed and revved the engine. My fist flashed into the steering wheel as I watched her taillights fade away before I dropped my head into my hands. I had only known her for a few weeks and she was already completely altering my life.

She asked why I had panicked and I couldn't give her an answer. She asked why I hadn't told her about Whitney and I just shrugged. What the hell was wrong with me? She had every right to ask those questions. We had become friends in these weeks. Friends told each other things. They asked each other things. And they answered honestly. But I couldn't do that. The right answer for why I couldn't do that would be because she was my student and teachers are not supposed to be friends with their students. They tell you that in school. They teach you all about ethics and the lines you can't cross. There are a lot of lines. I knew them all. I was a good student. I wanted to be a good teacher. I *had* to be a good teacher. So why was it that I couldn't stop thinking about all those lines in the past weeks? Because every time I watched Carter's mouth twitch up in a smile while she talked to me, I became mesmerized by it. Every time she told me a story and got so excited her hands started waving around, I wanted to hold them in my own. Each time she laughed and her whole face lit up and she tried to cover it with her hands, I wanted to grab them and pull them away from her face so I could see her happiness. She was becoming more and more happy.

That first day, those first weeks, there was a sadness in her. A deep regret in those eyes that I wanted to remove. It was something I knew well, a feeling I had myself. I wanted to know what had happened to put it there. After that day at the diner, I knew I needed to have more of that exasperating girl in my life. So I let her stay. Every day after school, I let her stay. I let her talk and I let her probe into my own life, if only a little. For the first time in years, I found myself happy to talk. Happy to have someone to share my laughs with and my past with. Not all of it. But happy parts. She became my friend. I couldn't tell her that, of course. Those lines again. The bigger problem was that in my head, I knew I wanted more. But I kept it all in check. I was good at keeping everything in check. Until tonight. I groaned and tapped my head against the steering wheel once more before I pulled out and turned towards my apartment with my mind completely tangled.

I couldn't answer her questions tonight because I didn't have all the answers. Sure, I could give her the rudimentary answer of why I had panicked. If anyone had seen her get in my car, I would be fired on the spot. Line number one: students are not allowed in teachers' vehicles. Up until that point, we hadn't done anything wrong. But I had crossed that line tonight. More than anything, that was why I had panicked. Because I had always been the smart one; the responsible one. Yet in one month with Carter, I seemed to lose all sense. I didn't think straight with her. I was good at being guarded, completely closed off to the world, because that's how I stayed safe. And yet she had gotten under my skin. For some unknown reason, I wasn't afraid to answer her incessant questions. I wanted to talk to her for hours; I *wanted* her to know me. I hadn't felt that way in over four years. I panicked because I was terrified I was getting myself into something I wouldn't be able to get out of. And it would ruin everything.

I hadn't told her about Whitney because in all the time I had spent with Carter, Whitney had never once been on my mind. She wasn't my priority. I was the worst person in the world. My girlfriend of over two years should have always been in my mind. Carter, a student in my class, should not have had any influence on that. I punched the steering wheel again as I drove. I was mad at myself. Mad at Carter, even though she wasn't to blame. No one was to blame. Whoever was pulling the strings of life didn't seem to care that I didn't want her in my life right now. I didn't want all these feelings she was stirring up in me. I didn't ask for these.

I pushed open my apartment door and flicked on the lights while reaching for my cell phone. My fingers deftly punched in the number from memory and she answered on the third ring, slightly out of breath. "You know it's not a good time."

A smile spread across my face at her controlling tone, the same one that had bossed me around for years. "Nice to hear from you too, Sis."

"Yeah, yeah. So nice, except you only call when you want to talk to Keaton, and you know he's already sleeping. Plus, this is a bad time for me." To attest to this, I heard a sudden burst of noise from the other end and traffic rushing by. I could picture her in her scrubs with the phone pressed to one ear attempting to hail a cab. After a moment, she came back to me. "So what it is, Noah?"

"Well..." Before I could even begin to formulate what I was about to say, she was cutting me off again.

"Oh, wait I've actually been meaning to call you about Keaton. You need to take him next week."

"Keaton? What?" My mood lifted and fell all at the simple mention of his name.

"I have a conference I can't miss and I know technically this isn't allowed but I know you would never let me just leave him with Sean. And you wouldn't want him to be with Mom and Dad, either. So I figured, it's just a weekend. You're not working. What's the worst that could happen, right?"

"Oh. Wow. Yeah, that would be amazing. Thank you so much, Sarah." Just the idea of Keaton being back here, in this apartment, with me, made me almost forget why I had called her in the first place.

"Great. So anyways, why are you calling when you know it's a bad time?" she rushed on.

I took a deep breath, my mess crashing back down on me. I wasn't sure what I wanted to say. Not sure how I wanted her to respond. "Hello? Noah? I don't have a ton of time, I'm on my way in now."

"I just left a student," I finally let out in a rush.

"It's a little late for that don't you think?"

"That's the point," I replied blandly.

"I'm sorry...tell me this was some weird teacher-student conference thing."

"It wasn't."

She laughed without humor. "And Mom and Dad always thought you were the responsible child."

"Sarah!" I snapped.

"Is she at least of age?"

"It isn't like that."

"Alright, then I'm confused," she muttered. "Listen, just tell me the truth. Are you sleeping with her or not?"

"No."

"No?" she questioned. "Okay... so this is not ideal, but at least it's okay still. What's the big issue?"

"It's different." I sighed and paced around my kitchen, grabbing random things only to put them back down in a different spot. My feet finally stalled and I hung my head. "It's more than that."

"More? What do you mean-" She stopped herself as what I was saying made sense to her. "You have feelings for her." I nodded even though I knew she couldn't see me. "That's worse, isn't it?"

"I don't know what to do. All I can do is hurt her. Because this can't happen. I can't mess up, you know that."

"Yeah," she replied sarcastically. "I'm well aware of that. And Whitney," she added, her words falling like another punch to my gut and adding to my guilt. "How is Whitney?"

"Fine," I muttered. "Not here."

"What do you mean she's not there? Again?"

"She got a job as an assistant to some fashion guru this time. She hasn't been to the apartment in three weeks. She won't be back for another month or so."

"Do you love her?"

"Who?" I asked.

"Wrong answer, Noah." I could see her look of disapproval as if she was standing right in front of me. "Look, I just got to the hospital. I wish I could help you more, but my shift starts in five. I'll see you Friday with Keaton and we can talk then, okay? Just…don't do anything to screw this up for yourself. You've worked too hard. You're a good guy. I love you. Talk soon."

"Bye, Sis." I sighed as the line went dead and my head fell to my arms on the counter.

My chair rolled into the wall as my bag fell onto it and I turned to look around the empty room the next morning. Something about the school before students arrived always left me with an eerie, empty feeling. I'd been teaching for over a month and yet nothing in this room reflected that. The walls remained plastered with ridiculous posters and even the board still bore a quote about new beginnings in Mrs. Granger's flowery handwriting. I was just beginning to erase it when my door creaked open and quickly fell shut.

I turned, not ready to face Carter after last night, but it was only Grant. "Good morning, Noah."

"Hey, what's up?" I asked casually as I relaxed again and turned back to the board.

"I'm not sure. You tell me."

The eraser flashed over the last of the blue letters and I faced him with a questioning look. He gazed back at me hard with his hands on his hips and for the first time I realized he could be an intimidating man when he wanted to be. Maybe I should have taken him up on that offer for beers all that time ago, maybe I should have made better friends with him. "What are you talking about?"

"I saw her get into your car last night."

My eyes widened at his words. There was no use in lying about it, so I gave my head a slight nod. Grant pinched the bridge of his nose and closed his eyes as if my confirmation pained him. "It's not what you're thinking." He only stared at me for further explanation. "We're just friends. Nothing more. She's a good kid."

"That's the thing, Noah. She's not a kid. I know that. I've known that since I met her freshmen year. I'm scared you've realized that as well and have easily forgotten she's still in high school. I can understand that. It's just, she's an incredible person and I would hate to see anything screw that up."

"I'm not screwing it up. I'm not some terrible person to come in and ruin her life." I hated that he thought so little of me. But then again, hadn't I doubted my own character last night? Maybe I was the person he thought I was.

"I know that. I like you, Noah. I think you could be a good teacher and I'd like to see you stay. I just had to ask. There's a line you don't cross. I'm worried that you're close to crossing it."

"I know the line," I said through gritted teeth. He didn't respond, only cocked his head to one side as if to say *do you, though?* A small part of my brain echoed his sentiment and I wondered if I really had forgotten those lines so soon, because those lines were more important than even he could understand.

Grant backed a few steps towards the door and I figured our conversation was over for now, but then he spoke again. "I'm not saying this because I think you're a bad guy, Sweeney. I'm asking because I think the opposite of you. You've become my friend, and I'd like to think I've become yours. I'm only trying to help you. You have to help yourself, too."

"I appreciate it," I muttered. "I just slipped."

He nodded, appeased for now by my response.

*****

Carter and I danced around each other for the remainder of the week. I could feel her eyes follow me through every lesson of the past four days, but she never once spoke or made to approach me after class. I avoided looking in her direction altogether, although that didn't stop my mind from wandering to her every other free second. That sadness and regret in her eyes? It was creeping back in. It hurt even more to see now because I knew I was the reason behind it this time.

Today was the first day of the week I wasn't rushing from the room directly after her class. There was a staff meeting in a half hour that I needed to be at even though I had quickly learned to dread them.

When the final bell rang, I pulled out a stack of papers to grade and sat back in my chair.

I hadn't even glanced at the first one when I heard her soft footsteps padding towards me. I didn't have to look up to know it would be her, but instead of taking a seat in one of the first desks, she kept walking until she was by the wall beside me and slid down to sit on the floor. She did this all so casually, like sitting on the floor in a classroom was the most natural thing in the world.

I looked down at her and almost burst out laughing. "What are you doing?"

"Sitting," she replied simply.

"On the floor?"

"Yes."

My chair swiveled so I was facing her straight-on now. Her eyes stared back at me, taunting me with their swirl of green and blue and the highly amused smile I always fought so hard to hide from her emerged. She stretched out a hand towards me. "Sit on the floor with me."

I laughed aloud, our stalemate from the week completely forgotten in this moment. "No."

"Come on, Sweeney," she flexed her fingers at me. "Just sit with me."

She was completely ridiculous and though I was shaking my head at her, for some reason I found myself taking a seat beside her with my back pressed against the wall. I could tell myself it was because I wanted to help erase whatever hurt she always felt, to erase the hurt I had caused her, but I knew it was really for more selfish reasons.

A maze of chair and desk legs were spread out before me, looking so much more cluttered from this perspective than they did from when I was standing. Carter's hand dropped down to what little space there was between our thighs and I stared at it for a long while before tracing back up her arm, along her collarbone, and back to her face.

"Why are we sitting on the floor?"

"Sometimes, you need a new point of view." Her eyes left mine to survey the room again. I scrunched my nose at her philosophical line of thinking but decided to humor her.

"Okay...And what does this new perspective tell you?"

"Well, it tells me life seems more confusing from a different view." She quirked her head to one side, intensely studying the clutter in front of us. "We live in a world of extremes. It's all blacks and whites. Because it's easier to handle that way. But the truth is, there's so much grey in between. And it's the grey stuff that matters."

Her attention turned to me and she met my eyes fearlessly, never once looking away as she continued. "I'm sorry. I'm sorry for not thinking more. I'm sorry for getting in your car. I'm sorry for not seeing your side of things. But I am *not* sorry for this. I'm not sorry for us. We're in the grey, Noah, so stop trying to label it as black or white. We just have to figure out how to work this grey area."

I wondered for the millionth time where she came from and how she had gotten into my life because everything about her was so unprecedented. I would agree with her. I'd tell her what she needed to hear. But we weren't grey to me. She could never be a color so dull as grey.

I nodded at her words and her body seemed to relax a little, as if she had been scared of my reaction. She leaned her head back against the wall, facing forward yet again. After several seconds of silence, she spoke in a whisper. "I wish you weren't a teacher."

I pulled my hands from my pockets and rested them against my knees. Her words hurt even though I knew she didn't intend them to. "You wouldn't know me if I weren't," I reasoned.

"Sure I would."

I smirked at her certainty. "You wouldn't even tell me your name that first day. We never would have seen each other again if I wasn't your teacher...and maybe that would have been for the best." I said the last part so quietly, even with her sitting inches away I couldn't be sure if she caught it or not.

The next second, the intercom crackled to life and my spine immediately straightened. "Mr. Sweeney?"

"Yes?"

"There's a visitor here in the office for you. May I send her up?"

"Yes, of course. Thank you," I stood hastily and brushed off any dust that might have been on my pants. Carter took her time standing beside me and grabbing her bag from the floor.

"Visitor?" she asked. Before I could even tell her I didn't know who it was, the door to my room burst open and a little boy with unruly brown hair came bounding in. I was laughing as he careened into my knees and I scooped him up. "Hey, little man!" I pulled back to take a closer look at him and feigned confusion. "Wait a minute; I thought you were someone I knew. But Keaton's way smaller than you. And he has short hair. Who are you?"

"I am Keaton! I am!"

"I don't know..." I looked around him to where Sarah was standing at the back of the room.

"Have you seen Keaton? I could have sworn he was supposed to be with you."

"Noah! It's me! I am Keaton!" He slapped at my chest and I faked dropping him a few inches to make him giggle.

"Huh, I guess you are Keaton! You've gotten so big, buddy."

"I eat all my veggies so I can be just like you." He gave me a gap-toothed smile and I chuckled as I put him down to embrace my sister.

She felt like home and a familiarity I had been lacking for too long. "I've missed you," I mumbled into her hair. She didn't get a chance to reply as Keaton's voice called for our attention again.

"Who are you?" he was pointing to Carter, who had squatted down to his level and was giving him a look of adoration.

"My name's Carter. You must be Keaton?"

"Carter isn't a girl's name."

"Keaton! That's not very nice," Sarah scolded, but Carter was already laughing.

"It's okay," she said quickly. "I get that all the time."

The intercom interrupted again, this time a school-wide announcement for the staff meetings of the afternoon that I had almost completely forgotten about. I hastily grabbed my bag. "I have to go. I'll meet you at the apartment in about an hour and a half, okay?" I asked Sarah as I ushered everyone out of the room. Her apologetic look wasn't the answer I wanted.

"My flight got changed. I have to be at the airport in an hour."

My feet stalled halfway down the stairs. Keaton continued on ahead, keeping a running conversation with Carter who cast a questioning look at me over her shoulder, but stayed with the little boy as Sarah and I lagged behind. "Sarah, what the hell. I can't take him right now. I can't just walk into a staff meeting with a three-year-old."

"What do you want me to do? Miss my flight?" she snapped.

"You could have at least warned me! I could have figured something out!"

"Can Carter take him?"

"What?" I asked in shock.

"He seems to like her." She pointed to the two of them already at the doors, him giggling over something Carter was saying.

"You don't even know her!"

"But you do,"

I laughed without humor and shook my head. "This is why I had custody of him even though I was only in college."

"What's that supposed to mean?"

"You're okay with just handing him over to someone you haven't even met! I don't know why I ever thought it was a good idea to send him to New York with you."

She dropped her voice and chose to ignore my last comment. We both knew it wasn't my idea. It was just the best option I was given. "That's the girl you were with the other night, isn't it?"

"What does that have to do with anything?" I hissed.

"If you're willing to jeopardize *everything* for her, I'm willing to trust her with Keaton for two hours."

I made to reply, but she was already striding away from me. "Carter, are you doing anything right now?" I heard her asking as I hurried to catch up.

"No. Why?"

"Well, I need to catch a flight and Noah has his meeting. So if it was at all possible, could you maybe watch Keaton for a bit? It wouldn't be long."

"No. It's fine. Don't worry about it; he can just-"

Carter cut me off, "I'd love to."

Sarah beamed at me in a triumphant way before turning back to face Carter. "Thank you *so* much," she gushed. "You could just bring him to Noah's apartment, if that's okay. He won't be long. We can go grab all Keaton's stuff from my car now."

I winced at her words and glanced around hastily. "No, Sarah. No way," I hissed as Carter stared at me with wide eyes. I noticed Keaton had been clutching her hand this whole time.

"Please, Noah, please," he said now. "I want Carter to play." I looked down at his hopeful little face and inwardly cursed. My hand scrubbed over my jaw and my eyes caught a clock by the entrance. I had no more time to argue. I needed to go now if I wanted to make that meeting on time, and there was no way I could be late for it.

"Sure. Fine. I've got to go. Just text me what's going on." I pulled my bag higher up on my shoulder, gave Sarah a one-armed hug, and tossed Carter what I hoped to be a neutral look. In reality, my mind hadn't even begun to catch up to this situation.

I barely made it to my meeting on time, much to my department head's displeasure. I then proceeded to fidget throughout the entire thing, not even hearing the words being said. My phone vibrated in my pocket just minutes after the meeting began and my hands had been itching to pull it out for the excruciating hour that followed. And of course, someone had to bring up a new topic with only two

65

minutes left, ensuring I was stuck for another fifteen minutes. When the discussion was finally called to an end, my bag was already over my shoulder and I was the first one standing. Just as I reached the door, I heard my name called from behind me. I spat out a curse under my breath and turned to face whoever it was with my best attempt at a smile.

The speaker was my department head, a balding man who could have easily been my grandfather. "Just a moment, please."

I paced back to him as calmly as I could. "Almost thought you were going to be late today."

"Sorry about that, Sir. I got held up."

"Not a problem. I figured it was about time I check in with you, seeing as the first term is coming to a close. Did you have any problems or questions you want to run by me?"

I put my hands in my pockets and fought to keep my foot from tapping impatiently. "Not right now, no." I replied. "I'll probably take you up on that offer later when it comes time to finalize grades."

"Of course," he chuckled. "Any trouble with students?"

My mind reeled to Carter. Trouble. Trouble could be defined in many ways. "No, Sir. My classes have all been very good for the most part."

"Wonderful. Well, I'm sure you have places to be on a Friday night, a young man such as yourself." Another grandfatherly chuckle and I smiled despite how wrong he was about me. "You're doing well, Sweeney. Keep up the good work." His meaty hand came down on my shoulder and I forced a smile while my inner guilt resurfaced. Was I really doing all that well? If he only knew.

I practically sprinted out of there, one hand fumbled for my keys while my other hastily pulled my phone from my pocket on the way to my car. I had two missed texts from Sarah.

I brought her to your apartment. Stop panicking. She's great. Keaton loves her. Just relax.

I fought down my anger and scanned the second one, which alerted me that she was boarding her plane and would have to turn her phone off. Just my luck. My only option was to call my own apartment and hope Carter would pick up. That she was still there like Sarah had claimed.

The call went all the way to my voicemail as my distress for this whole situation rose. When the answering machine finally clicked on, I called out. "Carter, if you're there, please pick-"

She cut me off before I could even finish. "Noah?" I noticed the hesitation in her voice, as if she wasn't sure what she could call me. I breathed a sigh of relief.

"Oh, thank God. You're there with Keaton?"

"Yeah. He's fine. He was hungry so I made him a sandwich earlier. I hope that's okay. He seemed to know where everything was."

There was a question there that she didn't fully come out to ask. Why he was so comfortable there. Why he looked so much like me. What the whole story was. I took a deep breath. "I'll be there in a half hour."

It was weird; knocking on my own apartment door before pushing it open. I didn't want to startle her though. She looked up at me as I came through the door from her spot on my floor where she was sitting cross-legged with a half-assembled Lego set in front of her.

"Look, Noah! Carter built part of my castle!" Keaton pointed to the two fully-formed walls proudly. I tossed my bag onto a chair and ruffled his hair, but

67

my eyes stayed locked on Carter. Something about seeing her here made it as if there wasn't enough air in the room.

"That's awesome, buddy. Why don't you keep building while I talk to Carter in the kitchen, okay?"

"Okay," he mumbled, his little fingers already fumbling to fit pieces together again.

Carter pushed herself to her feet and trailed behind me to the kitchen, divided from the living room by only an island with a couple bar stools so I could still keep an eye on Keaton. I pulled out a stool for her and made my way to the other side, needing to put space between us. "You want something to drink?" I asked. I didn't even wait for her response, just pulled out two glasses from a cabinet and filled them with water. I slid one across to her and looked over her head to check on Keaton. It made me so happy to see him back here, I had to keep checking he was real. But he was, and another castle wall had been assembled. I gulped down half my water in one go before yanking off my tie and refocusing on Carter. Her eyes immediately fell to her glass, which she absentmindedly swiveled in her hands, but an amused smile remained on her lips.

"What are you smiling about?"

She looked back up at me, and though I could see her fighting to hide it, her smile grew. "You," she finally said. "You're so flustered. It's funny to see you so different from the professional role you play at every day."

I sighed. "It's not a role, Carter. It's my job. And this isn't funny. If anyone ever found out you were here-"

"Oh, give it a rest, Sweeney. No one's going to find out, okay? Please, just let it go."

I swiveled away from her and grabbed a bowl, placing it on the counter none too gently. "Let it go?" I scoffed. I pulled out an egg from the refrigerator and cracked it into the bowl. I could feel Carter's eyes following my hands as they mixed the egg and bread crumbs together. It helped ease my stress, but didn't change the situation. I wanted to just let it go, she had no idea how much I wanted to let it all go, but it couldn't be that simple. "We can't *do* this."

"Why not? Look, can we please just stop fighting about all the logistics. It's tiring and it gets us nowhere. We both know the rules, but do you really want me to leave right now? Tell me you hate me here, and I'm gone." I opened my mouth and closed it and before I could spit out the words to hurt her, she continued, "I'm already here so just let it go. At least for tonight."

I took my eyes off her to focus on the chicken I deftly cut into strips and tossed into the bowl. I was weak. Weak enough to concede to Carter on this point, against my better judgment. "Fine."

"What are you doing?" She finally asked as I rolled the strips in my breading. I lifted my eyes to meet hers again and allowed myself to let go as she suggested. To stop worrying about my career and this mess we were in…at least for tonight.

"Keaton's favorite meal is chicken tenders."

"You make your own chicken tenders?" The surprise in her voice wasn't hidden at all.

I rolled my eyes. "What, I don't strike you as the chef type?"

She laughed and I couldn't help but quirk a smile. "No, actually. Chef was not on the list of skills I envisioned you having."

"So there's a list, huh?" I teased as I turned to put the tenders in a pan with oil. I heard her groan from behind me and I laughed again as Keaton's little footfalls came into the kitchen.

"French fries?" he asked from my knee.

I scooped him up with one arm and balanced him on my hip. "I don't know, little man. Do you think you and Carter can manage to make them?" I swiveled to face Carter and smirked at her.

She gave me a questioning look. "You make your own French fries, too?"

Keaton giggled and squirmed down from my arms before dashing to the freezer. "No, silly," he pulled a bag of frozen French fries out and ran them back to Carter. "Fries!" I watched as she smiled down at him and then followed him around the counter to join me by the stove.

"I believe we need a cookie sheet, Master Chef." Her eyes flashed at me, always with that hint of challenge I so wanted to accept. For now, I only reached into a cabinet and pulled out a tray for her while preheating the oven.

Carter and I didn't really get a chance to talk much after that, as Keaton was constantly asking her questions or telling her about life in New York with Sarah. I noticed her probing eyes every time he referred to her as his aunt, but I didn't explain. Explaining could come later. For now, I ate my meal silently and watched as they interacted. How easily Carter slipped into it all, when Whitney had been here for years and still never made it comfortable. So when it came time for Keaton to take a bath and go to bed, she asked if she should leave. And for some reason I found myself shaking my head; telling her it wouldn't take us too long and directing her to the couch.

When I finally did come back out after ensuring Keaton was asleep, she was curled on the couch under one of my blankets. The sight caused me to pause and swallow hard before stepping forward. She startled and sat up straighter. "Hey. I hope you don't mind, I put away the dishes and Keaton's Legos."

I smiled and sat down beside her, careful to lean into the opposite arm of the couch. Her smile drooped a little and part of me felt bad for hurting her feelings. If she only knew I put this much distance between us for her own good. She didn't need my mess in her life.

She didn't press me for information. Didn't even ask a single question. After a moment though, I found myself speaking softly. "I was only nineteen when he was born. Almost finished with my freshman year. That was lucky, that he was born in April. It meant I had a whole summer to learn how to deal with a newborn before school the next fall. He's been with me ever since. Well, up until this year. He moved in with Sarah towards the end of the summer…" I didn't continue. I didn't like this next part. Yet there was something about Carter that made me feel safe. Safe enough to tell her anything, not worried that she would judge me. Although, this was just the beginning. "He didn't just move in with Sarah. He was taken from me. Somehow, the courts decided I was no longer a fit guardian for him this past summer, even though he had been with me for years at that point. I was the only parent he knew. I still don't know what changed their minds, why they came and deemed me unfit. I couldn't let him just go into the system though, she would never forgive me. So I pleaded for them to appoint Sarah as his other legal guardian."

Carter stayed silent for a while, her eyes slowly playing over my features. There wasn't even a hint of judgement in her eyes. "I'm so sorry," she

71

whispered. "From what he's told me, and what I've seen, I can't imagine anyone ever thinking it was a good idea to take him away from you."

I smiled at her, or I at least attempted to, but I had a feeling it came out more as a grimace. "That's why I panicked the other day. That's why you can't be here. If I can prove to the courts that I have a steady job, that I'm stable and can support Keaton again, I can get him back. I *need* to get him back."

Now there was a pain in her eyes. A sadness, not just for me, but for herself. "I mess that up for you, don't I?"

I took a deep breath. "I don't want you to."

She looked away from me for a long time and I wanted so badly to know what she was thinking. Her eyes were so easy for me to read, but I was lost when she wouldn't look at me. I was bracing myself for what she may say next, but I had no way of knowing what it may be. "So his mom…"

I wasn't anticipating that question. I guess it was more solid ground than our current situation. "My other sister Kelly." I could tell that hadn't been the answer she was expecting. It opened up a whole different story. One I had never once told in its entirety. Yet here I was, telling it for the first time. I had to make her understand. She needed to see that this mess, this mess was my life and she should run the other direction as fast as she could. It would be better for both of us. "She's five years older than me. It goes her, then Sarah, then me. She and Sarah always fought growing up, but I was the baby and they both loved me. I was always closer to Kelly, though. I idolized her. She was constantly doing things, things I never even knew anything about. Especially when she got to high school. She had it all. Then she got a modeling contract and moved to New York instead of going to college. We were all happy for her. I think I was the most upset to see her go, though. I missed her the most. Missed her stories. I didn't think New York was for her. But who was I to say? I was just a kid.

"She called a lot those first few years, back when everything was just beginning. She said she missed me, told me about all the crazy things she was doing, told me I needed to get out more. Sarah moved out there once she graduated and they shared an apartment. Kelly would call to complain about her a lot. Said Sarah was always yelling at her to get her life together. They only lived together for two years. Sarah told our parents she was done babysitting her older sister. None of us really knew what she meant by that. Those next three years, I never really heard from either of them. I was graduating and going to college, Sarah was swamped with med school stuff, and judging from all the magazine covers and billboards, we all assumed Kelly was doing fine."

I looked at Carter now. She was still staring at me with rapt attention, the light from a nearby lamp reflecting off her eyes. For the first time, I let all the guilt I had held inside for over three years come out. "I should have *known*, Carter. That's on me. It's all on me. I was supposed to be her best friend. I was her brother, and she didn't feel like she could come to me. I can never forgive myself for that."

"Did she...you know..." Her implication of suicide was clear enough and I shook my head.

"No, she's still...well, she's alive at least. But when she had Keaton, she snapped. The type of snap you hear about in movies. Where no one can find a definite reason and the person ends up in a psych ward. It didn't happen immediately. Like I said, he was born in April. I didn't get a call until early June. It was her agent. He asked me if I had heard from

Kelly; said he knew she called me a lot. He also told me that her maternity leave ended a week ago and she still hadn't shown up for any shoots. I laughed when he said it, thinking this was all an elaborate joke she had planned. But it wasn't. I hopped on the next train to the city and was at her place the same day.

"She was there, but she wasn't. I can't even describe it to you, Carter. Have you ever looked into someone's eyes and not seen them? Like the person you love isn't even there anymore, even though they're standing right in front of you?"

"Yes..." Carter whispered so softly I barely caught it. But I did and I knew there was another story there. For another time.

"So she's still here, but she's not. I got her checked into a psychiatric ward. My parents moved her into a better facility later on. She signed over parental rights to me, though. It was the only time we ever saw her act like her old self at all. She refused to sign Keaton over to anyone but me. It broke my parents' hearts. They didn't want me to take him, tried to fight us both on it. They said by doing that, she was ruining my life just as much as she had ruined her own. But I wanted it. I wanted him. To me, it was the only way I could make it up to her. I would never abandon him. I would never make that mistake again."

"Noah, it wasn't your fault..."

I gave her a weak smile. I had heard those words plenty of times, but they never changed anything. "To this day, she hasn't changed since when I found her and Keaton in her apartment. The doctors still can't pinpoint what happened or how to treat it. It was like post-partum depression, but a thousand times worse and no treatments were fixing it. We don't know who Keaton's father is. He wasn't at the hospital when Keaton was born and Kelly never mentioned him. I found out later from some of her friends that before she got pregnant, she had been doing pretty bad. Parties, drugs, God only knows what. Some said if she hadn't gotten pregnant when she did, she would have probably been found dead in a matter of months. In a way, having Keaton saved her life. She quit everything cold turkey when she found out she was pregnant. At least, that's what I've been told. No one knows how or where she found the strength to do it. Sometimes I wonder if quitting like that had anything to do with how she snapped. I guess we'll never find out."

When I had started this story, I had meant it as a way to push us apart, scare her away. Yet here I was, letting my fingers trail over to Carter's blanketed feet where I traced patterns absentmindedly. I heard her breathing hitch as my hands skimmed so close to her, only a layer of fabric separating our skin. Something about her gave me strength; enough strength to speak the words I had tried for years to banish from my brain.

"If she was so strong to quit all those drugs, why wasn't she strong enough to stay with Keaton? Why isn't she strong enough to come back from wherever it is her mind has gone?" My eyes lifted from following my own fingers to Carter's face. In the semi-darkness she looked years older and her dark eyes looked like they could hold all the answers.

"You can only be strong for so long."

I let her words sink in. Then, without looking away, I spoke again. "Sometimes I wonder what would have been better."

"What do you mean?"

"Maybe she should have just overdosed four years ago. Maybe she was done then. But now she's stuck here. Alive, but not really. And I wonder if she blames Keaton for that. That's why I never let him see her. I don't know what she'd do if she ever saw him. Maybe she even blames me. And now I've let her down."

Carter didn't gasp. She didn't pull away from me further as if I was a horrible person for even thinking my own sister would be better off dead. She didn't look at me differently at all. Instead, she tentatively scooted closer to me, her eyes full of question. I didn't move or give her an okay, but for once I didn't stop her either and she gently curled into my side, wrapping one arm around my stomach as if she could possibly hold me together. I didn't realize I had been holding my breath until I let it all out in a long exhale. She didn't offer me any kind words. Didn't tell me I shouldn't feel that way. She just held on to me. And somehow, that was the best thing she could have ever done for me.

Carter

I woke up to something tugging at my shirt. Not something, but someone. Keaton held one little finger to his mouth in an effort to keep me quiet. I blinked slowly and made to sit up, but something was holding me in place. Noah's arm had come down to hold me to him at some point during the night, an act I was sure if he knew about he wouldn't be proud of. At least now I knew why.

I carefully slid out from his grasp and stood up stiffly. Noah shifted on the couch, spreading out more but not waking up. He looked so peaceful now, so different from the torn man he let me see last night. I stood and stared for a moment, knowing I probably would never see him like this again. All too soon, Keaton was tugging on my hand before dragging me to the kitchen and attempting to crawl up on one of the bar stools. I lifted him up so his little feet swung back and forth happily, his dark hair a tangled mess from sleep.

"Noah never sleeps," he whispered conspiratorially.

"What do you mean?"

"He's always awake before me and after I go to bed. That's why we have to be quiet. He needs sleep. Auntie Sarah says if you don't sleep, you can't grow. Maybe that's why Noah never gets any bigger. But I do. Because I sleep."

I chuckled at his logic, all so straightforward at age three, but a part of me was sad for Noah. "So you grew up with him?" Keaton nodded. "But now you're living in New York?"

"Yeah. There's more kids there. Noah's fun, but there's never little people around. When I go to school with Auntie Sarah, I have lots of friends. And I like Auntie's friend, Sean. He takes care of me when she works. He's fun too. I never liked Noah's friend, Whitney. She was mean. But I like you. You're funny." He beamed at me, the same boyish smile I loved to see on Noah, despite how rare it was. But his reference to Whitney was a reality check, one that had me remembering just how many lines we were crossing. No matter how much I wanted to deny it, I knew Noah was right. This wasn't okay. Because for me, I wanted so much more from him. He couldn't give me that. Not only because of the simple answer, that he was my teacher, but because of the little boy sitting in front of me.

"Can you make Mickey Mouse pancakes? Noah always makes me Mickey Mouse pancakes."

He directed me to all the ingredients I needed, all the while chattering away while I struggled to decipher his little kid dialect. "Are you going to stay around like Whitney used to?"

I bit my lip and glanced over the counter to where Noah was still sleeping on the couch. I felt terrible. I had spent the night. In his apartment. While he was my teacher. And he had a girlfriend. This was bad. "I don't think so, buddy."

"But why? You're better. You're nice to me. And you're nice to Noah. Whitney wasn't nice to Noah when she was here. She wasn't here a lot, though."

I somehow managed to remember to flip Keaton's pancake while I processed his words. "What do you mean, she wasn't nice to Noah?"

"I liked it when she went away a lot. Because when she was here, she yelled lots. When she didn't think I could hear. It was about me mostly. I felt bad. I made Noah's life messy." His shoulders drooped and I immediately came around the counter to squat down in front of him.

"Don't you ever say that, Keaton. Don't even think it. It's not true, you hear me? Noah wants you in his life so much. He loves you more than you know, okay?" He nodded slowly, but I could tell I hadn't completely convinced him. I had never met Whitney. I didn't want to. But for her to say such terrible things made me hate her.

"Hey, what's going on out here?" Noah's voice was scratchy from sleep and I immediately stood up straight and turned to face him. He smiled at me slowly and then tried to hide it. "Morning."

I ducked my eyes and made my way back to the cooking pancakes. "Good morning."

"Noah, can we go to the park today?"

"Of course we can."

"And Carter can come?"

I paused in flipping the pancakes onto plates and caught Noah's eye. He cocked his head to one side while he studied me, one hand protectively on Keaton's shoulder. "I'm not sure. She might be busy today…"

"Carter, will you come?"

I held Noah's gaze for a beat longer, trying to find any warning in it, any hint of how I should answer. But all I saw was curiosity, as if he was waiting to see what *I* wanted for once. I turned to smile at Keaton. "If you want me to come, I would love to come."

And so an hour later, I found myself shivering on a park bench beside Noah while he absentmindedly sipped on his coffee, as if we did this every weekend. He smiled as Keaton slid down the slide in front of us and then leaned forward so his elbows were resting on his knees. After a few more moments of silence, he spoke.

"I'm sorry, too."

"What?"

"What you said yesterday? In my room? I'm sorry I haven't been thinking of your side of things, either. But you're right, I'm not sorry about us."

His words caught me off guard. I wasn't expecting him to admit to an "us" at all. Instead of making me pleased as it should have, it just made me feel worse. "It doesn't matter." He turned his head to look at me and waited for me to continue. "Whatever this is…was… it's never going to happen again, is it?"

He took a slow sip of his coffee and then looked back at the ground between his sneakers and the dry, browning grass there. He didn't need to speak any words for me to know he agreed. I nodded and pulled the sleeves of my sweater over my hands. "You love her?"

His head dropped lower and I saw him bite his lip. "We've been together for over two years." It wasn't answering the question I asked and so he continued on. "She's going to start expecting things."

It took a moment for the meaning behind his words to sink in. "You can't honestly be thinking about marrying her?" I scoffed.

He shrugged his shoulders, as if I had merely asked him what he planned to make for dinner that night. "She's hinted at it before. It's something that should be thought about."

"You've got to be kidding me…"

"I don't really think you're one to have much say in this."

"And yet you brought it up to me. Come on, Noah! Look at yourself. Look at her. Oh, wait. You can't! Because she's never here!"

"She has a job, Carter." He finally put down his coffee and sat up straight to look at me fully. "How would you even know if she's around or not?"

"Keaton. Why don't you stop and think about Keaton. He doesn't like her, Noah. And from what he's said, she's no good for you, either."

"Oh my God," he muttered mostly to himself as both hands raked through his hair and tugged. He stood and spun away from me, laughing without humor. "I can't believe I'm having this conversation right now. You're going off information from a three-year-old!" He swiveled back to face me. "You think me and Whitney aren't in the same place?"

"You aren't." How I could say that, I wasn't sure. I had been resigning myself to the fact that nothing between Noah and I could ever work a moment ago. Yet now, the thought of him marrying Whitney, someone I didn't even know, made me sick.

"Look at us, Carter!" He gestured between us rapidly and then spread his arms to encompass the whole park, full of laughing children and tired mothers drinking tea on a cool Saturday morning. "You think we're in the same place? Because if you do, you're out of your mind. See this? This is my life. I take care of a child. I go to work all week. I don't go party on the weekends or hang out with friends every day. I haven't done that in years. Do you understand that? We could never work out."

"This isn't about us!" But wasn't it? Wasn't that why I was so upset over this? Over him with someone else? Everything in me knew we could never work. I *knew* that. And yet I couldn't fathom the thought of him with someone else. Life was cruel that way.

"Then what the hell is this about? Please. Enlighten me. Because I thought we were getting

81

somewhere. Finding a balance. But I can't have you freaking out on me for this."

"I don't know," I said quietly, so out of place in our shouting match. "I don't know. All I know is that I'm here."

His eyes fluttered shut as if my words pained him. "And in a year, Carter? Where are you going to be in a year?" I didn't have an answer for him. I didn't want to answer him. "You need to go." His calm, composed voice hurt more than any shouting he could have done. I stood and for once offered no argument. Instead, I turned and walked away without looking back.

I drove straight to Samantha's, as that was where I had told my mom I had been all night into today. She was waiting on the front steps of her house when I pulled up.

"Alright, I'm done," she said before I had even shut the car door.

"So am I. What's up with you?" I responded as I followed her through the enormous entryway and into her kitchen.

She spun on me and pierced me with her patented glare that could make almost anyone else in our school shake. I only pulled an apple from the fruit basket on the counter and raised an eyebrow at her. "You are. I can't keep covering for you if you're not going to give me anything in return. I thought I didn't have to worry about you. You were the one who always covered for *me*. Now, I'm covering for you and I don't even know what's actually going on."

I knew she didn't want any favors from me. She just wanted to know information. "I was with Noah."

"Noah who?" she questioned.

"Noah Sweeney."

"As in, our English teacher, who most other high school students refer to as Mr. Sweeney?"

My apple crunched satisfyingly and I nodded. "The very same."

"You're sleeping with him," she proclaimed. She wasn't appalled like many people would be. In a way, she gave off a sense of pride. Probably because it was something she would do. Sleep with a teacher. I'm not sure how that made me feel. The idea was wrong. I knew that. With me and Noah though, it felt different. Not that we were sleeping together. Just that being with him never felt wrong. It felt right, even with everything he had told me last night.

"Nope."

"You're sleeping at his house...and not sleeping with him?" I shrugged my shoulders and half nodded. "You're missing an opportunity."

"Samantha!"

"We all know what he looks like. I'm just stating a fact." She said with one raised eyebrow as she popped open a can of Coke and took a seat across from me. She took a sip and then concern flashed across her face. "Wait a minute. Are you okay? Is he pressuring you? Is he trying to take advantage of you? Carter, you can tell the police. He'll get fired and you'll be okay."

"Woah, Sam, calm down. It's not like that. We aren't like that. Besides, he's apparently thinking of proposing to someone."

She narrowed her eyes at me, attempting to decipher if I was telling the truth. Apparently I passed her test for now because she jumped to the next thing I mentioned. "I didn't even know he was dating anyone."

"Do you know much about him at all?" I countered. *Did anyone?* I thought to myself.

"No," she took another sip of her drink. "Carter, all jokes aside, be honest…do you think this is a good idea?"

"Is what a good idea?"

"You and him. You know he could lose his job. Even if it isn't because he's pursuing you. If it's a mutual thing. It's still not, you know, legal. And it wouldn't exactly look good for you, either. I know you think you fly under the radar, but you don't. And people are mean."

"You do realize you're friends with a lot of those mean people," I pointed out. How I ever became best friends with the leader of the social ladder is beyond me, but here I was. She only rolled her eyes at me and pegged me with a determined look. I wasn't going to avoid her questioning any longer. "I know. We know. But I keep telling myself that we're just friends. We aren't doing anything wrong if we're just friends."

"Are you?" she paused. "Just friends?"

"Yeah…"

She pursed her lips. She had heard something else in my one word answer and I was scared of what she was going to ask. "You think you love him?" She studied me intently, waiting for an answer to appear on my face just as much as she was waiting to hear the words from my mouth. As it turns out, I never even had to speak. "Oh, Carter. It's only been a couple months. I know you've never really been serious with anyone before. How would you even know?"

"I'm not saying I do!" I quickly defended. "I don't know. I think I could. And yes, you don't need to tell me that that's probably against the rules. I know that. I know just how complicated this is."

She took a deep breath. "Do you ever think you're in love with him, or just the idea of having him?" When I opened my mouth to immediately shut her down, she held up a hand. "Just hear me out. There's no way this could go right, Carter. I know you don't want to hear that, but I also don't want to see you more hurt than you need to be. So if you're idealizing this relationship in your head, I just want you to take a step back for a minute. Is it really him, or do you just want to find someone to fix you?"

"I don't need to be fixed, Samantha!"

She winced. "I didn't mean it like that. It's just..." she sighed as if debating what she wanted to say next. "I won't lie, I've seen you happier than maybe I've ever known you in the past couple months. And a part of me wants to be happy for you, that he's able to do that. I know you don't think you need to be fixed...but Carter, do you remember when we became friends?"

I didn't want to hear half of her words, but I went along with her anyways. "Yes..."

"I wanted to fix you. I know it was a while ago, and I know you will never ever say that you need anyone to fix you. You aren't exactly broken. It wouldn't hurt to have someone help fit you back together, though. Can you at least see where I'm coming from?"

I knew exactly where she was coming from. I knew it because I had never been the same after what happened all those years ago. Samantha was the one who made it better. The girl I never would have dreamed to be my best friend. In a way, maybe she had fixed me. At least, as much as she could. Yet, I still felt like I had been missing something.

"He can't fix you, Carter. He can't be the one to do it. So just stop and think if you love him or if you just want to love someone.

NOVEMBER
Noah

I kept my gaze fixated on Carter's empty seat as the bell went off. It had been two weeks since our argument in the park. Now that Keaton had gone back to New York with Sarah, I had nothing else on my mind but Carter. And the fact that she had shown up to my class for all of two days in the past ten. I had tried my best to avoid even looking in her direction then, but now I wished I had. Without even realizing it, I had grown accustomed to her always being here; seeing her every single day. Now suddenly she wasn't around, and I wasn't handling it well. I was worried. I didn't worry about anyone other than my family, it was a rule I had made after everything had happened with Kelly. I figured if they were the only people I worried about, I would never again let them down. Especially after this summer, nothing would get in my way of getting Keaton back. Yet here I was, worrying about Carter. If she was okay. If she was hurting. I was in too deep. Way too deep because she was doing exactly what I should want, what I had even told her needed to happen. She was staying away from me and I should be thanking her for that. Instead, I was hurting.

Against my better judgment, I had caved and asked Grant if he had seen her. He had. He also gave me another warning look that I chose to ignore. She was around. She was just choosing to not be around me. Now, I gritted my teeth and made a split second decision as the last students of the day filed out.

"Samantha. Can I have a word?" I caught her as she was halfway out the door. She sighed but didn't look surprised by my request as she made her way back to my desk. Never one to make the first move, she just stood before me with both hands on her hips.

"I hate to ask this, but it's getting out of hand. Carter hasn't been to class in almost two weeks," she opened her mouth as if to give a rehearsed reply, but I held up a hand to stop her. "And I know she's been here. She just won't come to this class. She's in danger of failing, Samantha."

In addition to her hands-on-her-hips-no-nonsense look, her foot began to tap and she rolled her eyes at me. "She could never fail English. You know it and I know it. We also both know that you would never fail her."

My eyes widened at her implication but she only smirked, causing me to wonder just what she knew. Before I could think on it further, she became serious again and glanced around us as if to make sure we were alone. I braced myself for what she was about to say. She licked her lips and looked disdained. When she spoke next, it sounded as if she knew that Carter wouldn't like what she was telling me. "I would check the special education building if I were you." Then she checked the jeweled watch adorning her wrist. "She'll probably still be there if you hurry. Best of luck, Mr. Sweeney." She put extra emphasis on my name before swiftly exiting my room.

I ran a hand through my hair and exhaled a breath I didn't realize I had been holding. Then I packed my bag and slung it over my shoulder before locking the door behind me. I didn't need her in my life, I knew that. All she did was make it more complicated. I should just let her go right now, let her keep thinking I would someday marry Whitney. She would have to come back to class eventually and then the only way I would worry about her would be as my student. In a few short months, she'd graduate. Case closed. So why had I flown out to meet Whitney last weekend and instead of being happy to finally see her after two months, I broke up with her? The same reason I found myself passing my car in favor of the special education building across campus. Carter had a hold on me that I didn't know what to do with.

When I pushed open the door, I was met with a bustle of activity. Some kids were laughing, others were wailing, some were running, some just stared at me staring at them. There were also helpers everywhere, so I knew that amongst the chaos there must actually be order.

"Can I help you?" An older lady asked as she gave me a dazzling smile that made it seem like just being in this circus of activity made her the happiest person on earth. Before I could answer her, I spotted Carter's long blonde hair in a far corner.

"I just have to see someone," I pointed to the corner. "Thank you though." She nodded and continued to beam at me. I weaved my way around her and towards Carter, then paused to watch her for a moment before she knew I was behind her.

She sat crouched in front of a boy in a wheelchair with spikey blonde hair, although it looked more silver than blonde. He didn't move at all as I watched. In fact, his face never really changed. He seemed to stare straight ahead at her, unseeing, yet I knew she was talking to him. She stood and grabbed a coat off a nearby hook, all the while keeping a running conversation. Then she carefully lifted each of his arms and slid them into the sleeves and adjusted it behind his back. At one point, she even threw her head back in laughter and I knew I was smiling at her like an idiot but I couldn't help it. When she stood back up from adjusting it, her eyes met mine and she froze instantly. I rubbed the back of my neck nervously, then stuffed my hand back into my pocket and rocked back on my heels.

"Hey…" The boy in the wheelchair appeared more mobile than her at the moment because his eyes swiveled to me and he raised one arm to point.

This seemed to snap her out of her trance. "What… What are you doing here?" she sputtered.

I took a few more steps so I was closer to her, standing directly in front of the boy who still hadn't put his arm down. "I came to find you." She still didn't move so instead I decided to try my luck with the boy. I squatted in front of him and extended my hand to shake. "Hey, I'm Noah. What's your name?" He didn't move and his face still didn't change, his eyes remaining dead. That was the hardest part. Looking into his eyes and not seeing who was really in there. It reminded me too much of my sister and I flashed a glance at Carter for guidance. Luckily, she had regained some composure.

"He won't shake your hand. I'm surprised he even lifted his arm to point. That's almost unheard of." Gently, she touched his outstretched hand and lowered it. "He also won't answer you."

"Alright then." I sat back on my heels and she came around to squat beside me as she had been doing when I first arrived. I didn't say another word, feeling like she would fill anything else in if she wanted to. She had heard my story the other week and let me tell as much or as little as I wanted to. I would give her that same right.

"He doesn't speak at all," she continued after a minute. "Do you, Johnny?"

Johnny looked at her, but didn't really look at her, and she smiled in response. "This is my fr-" She halted and closed her eyes as if in pain. "My teacher," she spat. "This is my teacher, Mr. Sweeney. He came to say hi to you, Johnny. Isn't that nice?" She smiled at him, to no response, and then swiveled to face me and sat cross-legged on the floor before me. "So why are you really here?"

I mirrored her and crossed my legs and had a sudden feeling that we were young again. As if we had both been in kindergarten together, though I knew that was impossible. "You haven't been in class all week."

"You came here to fail me, Noah?"

Just hearing her say my first name gave me a rush and I smiled involuntarily. "No," I paused. In all honesty, I wasn't sure why I had come. I looked around us again at the chaos. "This is where you come instead of my class?" At least she had the sense to look a bit guilty. "Who is he, Carter?"

"Johnny." she answered automatically. I only stared at her, not asking for more, just letting her know I wanted more. "Johnny Talcoma."

I let the unusual last name register. "You mean, as in Mariah Talcoma?" She nodded. "But, I would have thought...I'm not sure. She would have mentioned...?"

"No," she snapped quickly, then looked away. Her fingers were tugging at her long sleeves even more so than normal. She was anxious. "I'm not proud of who I was, Noah. Don't get me wrong, I'm starting to like who I'm becoming. But I'm not proud of who I was then." I stayed silent as she took a deep breath and continued.

"They're twins," she started and I fought down my shock. "When we were younger, we were all friends. Family, really. I basically lived with them. But Mariah never wanted to tolerate Johnny. She tormented him mercilessly. And I never did anything. I should have done something to stop her, told someone how bad it was so they'd know. He wasn't okay, she made sure of that. But I was only thirteen and I just didn't think. I didn't help. I should have helped, Noah. Sound familiar?" Only she had an excuse for not helping. She had been too young. She didn't know. Tears were threatening to fall off her lashes now and everything in me was screaming to hold her just as she had done for me. Yet even though I knew exactly what feelings of guilt she was consumed with, I couldn't even touch her hand to comfort her. I knew that no words I offered would change how she felt. Sometimes, that's just how life was. You had to deal with it on your own. But if you were lucky, you found someone to stand by while you dealt with it. I realized now, I wanted to be that person for her.

"One day, we were all walking home from the bus stop. I don't even remember what he said, but she got mad. She pushed him. Into the road. As a car was coming." The tears finally overflowed as I gasped, appalled at the story. The regret and sadness that used to be so prevalent in her eyes? I had wanted to know where it came from all those weeks ago. This was the reason why. She blamed herself for this. "He's paralyzed. From the waist down. But to be honest, he doesn't move much of anything. As far as doctors can tell, no damage was done to his vocal chords, but he doesn't speak, either. Brain scans have shown that all parts of his brain should be fully functioning, but it's as if he doesn't hear anything. I have a feeling that he does, though."

The whole time she had been studying her hands intently, but now she looked up, completely skipping over my face in favor of his. "I know you hear me, Johnny. You're probably sick of hearing about all my daily drama by now, right? You'll miss it next year when I'm at college, though."

92

It was the first time she had acknowledged college around me. I wondered where she had applied. Where her top choice was. What she was going to major in. The information suddenly seemed crucial to me. I wanted to know everything about her. But for now, she started talking again and the only thing I could focus on was her face and the way her eyes always let me read every emotion she had.

"That was five years ago this past spring. For a whole year, I didn't talk to anyone. My mom and dad wanted to take me to a shrink, but I refused. There wasn't anything wrong with me. I had witnessed a person who I thought was my best friend become a monster. I watched her almost inadvertently become a murderer. I didn't trust anyone. I didn't trust myself. How could I? When the person I had trusted most of all had turned out to be someone I didn't even recognize. I had lost all faith in people. I blamed myself. I should have told someone she was awful to him. I should have realized she was turning into a monster. I should have broken up their argument before it started. Maybe if I had reached out quicker, I could have pulled him back onto the sidewalk in time. I'll never be able to erase any of that guilt and doubt.

"Then a year later I came here, and for the first time since it happened I was able to forget myself. That's one of the perks of going to a large school; no one knows when you're there but not really there. And Johnny was here. When being surrounded by people became too much, I came here, to him. The one person I hadn't lost faith in. It's where I met Samantha the winter of that awful freshman year.

"Almost two years since it happened, and I was still a walking zombie with fortified walls around me. She has a brother with Down syndrome. He was

93

a great kid and I knew him well from spending so much time in here. Anyways, she came in one day because he must have told her about me. The thing was, I didn't know about her. I probably should have. You know her; she's the most popular girl in school without even trying. She always has been. But I didn't know that. Maybe that's why she liked me so much. Because I didn't like her. She came in with a sledgehammer and dismantled every wall I put up to block her."

Carter stopped here and smiled softly at the memory. Then, despite the fact that we were on school property, she reached out and took my hand. My first reaction was to give an answering squeeze of reassurance, but the next response to recoil came only seconds after that. She held on tight though, wrapping her fingers in mine, her small hand disappearing in my long fingers as if she was a part of me.

"Carter…" I warned. She just shook her head and while I was glancing around to see if anyone had seen, she bent low to kiss our joined hands. Before I could react, she was already standing, pulling on my hand as if we had joined them simply to assist each other in standing. Then she winked at me and laughed at my shocked expression. Actually laughed, when just minutes ago she had tears running down her cheeks. This girl was going to destroy me.

"Your mom's here, Johnny." And just like that, she was rolling Johnny towards the door I had just come in, although that felt like a lifetime ago now. Except then, I had no idea what I was doing. Then, I had thought I would just convince her to come back to class; tell her we would figure out a new balance. I had no idea that new balance would include me beginning to slip in love with her. Yet when she gave me a look over her shoulder as if to say 'are you coming?' I answered with a reassuring smile, my feet already following after what my heart wanted. Even as my brain screamed no.

It was still screaming no as I watched her lean against her car in the student lot, long ago vacated in teenagers' rush to begin their Friday nights. "Are you busy tonight?" I found myself asking without preamble. Clearly, my brain was losing today. She shook her head and then smiled.

"My parents are gone until next week. I've seen where you live. I want you to see where I live." My face retained the permanent smile it always had around her. It was all so innocent with her. A simple sentiment that was anything but when it came to us.

"I'll follow you."

She beamed and I had to take a step back because I could have sworn she would have thrown her arms around my neck if I hadn't. I laughed and backed away further, watching her eyes follow me until finally I turned around fully to head back to my car. Even then, it was a long while before I heard her door open and shut with a thud in the distance.

I parked my car behind hers in front of a modest house surrounded by trees on all sides. To the left passed a clearing, the land rose up in a hill. It was small, more of a bump in the landscape than a hill, but it was this I saw her focusing on as I got out of the car and joined her on the front walk. I studied her studying it for a moment and when she didn't turn to acknowledge me at all, I turned my attention to the bump as well, wondering what secret it could possibly hold for her. It didn't seem like she planned on telling me, so instead I reached down silently and folded her hand back into mine. It was weird; ever since she had taken my hand in that room it was as if my skin craved hers. It was a feeling I had never experienced before. Ever.

I was a twenty-three-year-old guy. I should have felt this so many times. I had been attracted to plenty of girls, slept with some of them, but it was nothing like this. I didn't want Carter for that. I wanted her for so much more. That's why I kept convincing myself this was okay; that I wasn't jeopardizing everything.

Her fingers laced in mine and she cocked her head to one side so it was leaning on my shoulder. "When I was younger, that was my mountain. I always wanted to be up there, high enough to see everything. Or at least, I thought I could. I would make little teepees, pretend I was an Indian. Or an explorer. Or a hunter. That tree at the very top?" She pointed with her free hand. I shook myself from picturing her blonde head tracing through the woods and followed her gaze to a pine tree which looked more than a little sad and half dead.

"It was the biggest, greenest tree. Always; all year long. One time, my friend climbed all the way to the top. I was always too afraid. Too scared of falling. I'm not so scared of falling anymore."

Her voice grew quiet by the end and she turned to face me full-on, her eyes telling me there was more to her words. I heard them loud and clear. Then, when she was sure I understood, she turned back to face the hill, not allowing me to read any more from her.

"It's so small now. The tree isn't scary anymore. It's no longer a mountain. Everything changes, you know? For better, for worse, everything changes. Or maybe you just look at things differently than you first did."

I hadn't even begun to start comprehending her words, but she was already pulling me towards her house, a happy, carefree smile in place. Yet again I found myself laughing simply because she never failed to surprise me.

As soon as we walked in and she had shut the door behind us, I heard footsteps charging towards us. A grey cat came tearing into the entryway and immediately wrapped himself around Carter's ankles. He was tiny, but clearly not a kitten, and dark grey stripes covered him from tip to tail, as if he were a grey tiger. I had never seen anything like him before.

She bent down to rub his chest once he had successfully flopped himself down in a half roll on her feet. "Hey, Monte," she crooned affectionately.

"Monte?" I repeated, making sure I got it right.

"Mmhm," she kept petting him. "Short for Montague."

I straightened and looked at her with one raised eyebrow. She laughed and stood up, casually tossing her coat on a chair in the entryway and holding a hand out for mine. I shrugged it off, noting her carefully following my movements, and handed it over. "I'm sorry... Montague? As in, *Romeo and Juliet*?"

"Are there Montagues in anything else?" She quipped as I trailed behind her into an open, welcoming living room.

"Sorry I'm confused," I replied snidely. "But if I do recall, you've expressed your extreme dislike of *Romeo and Juliet* to me plenty, despite it arguably being his most famous work. Why in the world would you name your cat after Romeo? Of every single character in that play, he's the one you despise most of all."

She laughed and shrugged all at once. "True," she conceded. "And as I've also told you before, I don't care if it's Shakespeare's most famous play. Fame has no bearing on quality. As for Monte, I'm not exactly sure to be honest. I guess because I believe that even from things you hate, there can be stuff you love. Maybe I just wanted to believe that at the time. I got him after the accident, during my so-called depression. In any case, I love him more than anything. So I suppose I achieved my goal. I found something I love from something I hated."

I took a seat on the couch beside her, far enough away so I could have a clear view of her. "Do you have any idea how unprecedented you are?" She laughed at my words, but I just stared back at her hard. "You make this impossible, Carter." I said quietly after we hadn't moved an inch in over a minute. I could tell she was struggling internally, her breathing increasing under my stare, but she didn't look away from me at all. It was another challenge and I groaned at the sight of it. She called me on it.

"What?"

"That look," I found myself saying. "You've got to stop giving me that look. Like you're challenging me. Because I am so close to taking that challenge. And I can't do that. I can't tell you the things in my mind. I can't tell you what that look makes me want."

Her answering gasp was enough for me to know she understood exactly what I was saying. Any ghost of a smile that had been left over from our playful conversation about Shakespeare was gone now and I wasn't sure what look I liked on her better. Her challenging attitude, while at times exasperating, was my favorite thing about her. She challenged me every single day I had known her. To laugh more. To look at things in a different way. To let go and be myself, when I hadn't been able to do that in years. I had been afraid for anyone to truly see me. Me and my situation.

Instead, I had just accepted that Whitney was all I had. She knew my situation and, at first at least, had seemed fine with it. It became increasingly obvious she disliked Keaton playing as my son as time went on. She didn't want a kid. She just wanted to be with me and only me. She was all for appearances. Hers always had to be perfect, and it took hours for her to even get ready to go out. Mine apparently had been deemed acceptable and at times I wondered if the only thing she ever cared for were my looks. But my looks with Keaton? That wasn't an appearance she was pleased with. Somehow, I kept overlooking every red flag with her. Up until a few weeks ago, I hadn't really stopped to think that I had other options. Even though she had all those red flags, I never thought she would have stooped to the level she admitted to me after I broke up with her.

Carter still hadn't responded and suddenly I felt like she needed to know. "I broke up with Whitney last week." What little composure she had gained back after my last confession was shattered at this revelation.

"What…Why?"

"You made me think. We don't match up, you were right on that. It just took me a little while to realize that. You made it pretty apparent. I had been avoiding signs for a while, so I flew out to break it off with her. When I did, she was angry. She told me what she had done…this past spring." Carter didn't speak, her face was a mask of confusion. I swallowed back the hatred burning my throat that I had tried to keep in this past week. I never shared things with people, I was used to holding it all in. But I wanted to share with Carter.

"I would have never imagined she could be so cruel. She told me she was the one who went to child services. She filed a complaint, saying I was an unfit guardian. That a college student with no steady job could not be supporting a toddler. When they reviewed the facts from the complaint, it wasn't inaccurate. I was currently unemployed, I hadn't picked which school to intern with yet. Even when I did, I would still have to wait a year before being able to teach on my own and support myself and Keaton. So they took him, allowing that if in a year I had secured a job, the case could be revisited." My hands scrubbed over my face, attempting to wipe away the shame of this whole thing.

"Oh my God, Noah..." I felt Carter shift closer to me on the couch but kept my head in my hands. "How could she have done that to you? After being with you for all that time? That's horrible. I wish I could fix it for you."

I turned my head in my hands to face her, and her face was so close to mine it made me catch my breath. "Thanks. But you can't fix it. You can only make it worse." She flinched away from me, the pain my words caused her was so clear to see written all over her face. I groaned. "Carter, I'm sorry. I didn't mean that maliciously. It's just the truth. If anyone were to find out anything about us, going to the lake, my apartment, *here*." My hand scrubbed over my jaw and I shook my head. "I don't even know what I'm doing." I said this last part more to myself, but I knew exactly what I was doing. I was following every stupid thing my heart was saying and it was going to cost me sooner or later. I just hoped that it was later, because every single time I looked at Carter I needed to be closer. It wasn't just a want at this point; it was a need.

She didn't answer for a long time. Instead, she chose to look out a picture window above my head and I watched as her chest rose and fell while she took steadying breaths. "Sometimes Samantha still has to remind me not to put up walls to keep everyone out," she said finally. I didn't know where she was going with this, so I preceded cautiously.

"You don't strike me as a shy, cold person."

Her eyes flitted down to meet mine for half a second before returning to observe the outside world and the few birds left pecking for food on the dead grass before the first snow of the year. "I don't have many friends. I keep to myself a lot. I refuse to open up to basically anyone. Samantha also has to remind me to be myself a lot. To just have confidence in myself and say what I feel. Do you think I'm a confident person?"

Still, I was wondering how this tied to our conversation about how wrong this was, but I nodded my head immediately at her question. I had trouble thinking of one person I knew that was more comfortable in their own skin. The returning smile she gave me never reached her eyes. "Because I'm not. It's something about *you*, Noah. Around you, I'm okay. I can be myself and it's okay. I don't have any wall up for you. For some reason, I'm not even afraid. Maybe I should be."

"Carter…"

"It's fine," she said quickly. "You don't need to say anything. I just want you to know I'm sorry if I'm screwing everything up for you. I don't mean to. I wish more than anything that I wasn't. That this could be simple, one of those easy things you see in books or movies. But it's not. And I can't help it. I can't stop."

I didn't know how to respond, because I felt it, too. I felt that pull to her as if she was a magnet and no matter how wrong I knew this was or how much I tried to fight it, I still got pulled back in. I stood up and paced away from her, knowing I needed to put some space between us now. My heart had swelled at her words, that I had made her feel like that. It made me feel amazing, because I wanted more than anything to make her happy. The logical part of me was screaming yet again how horrible this was. I needed something to distract myself.

I found a row of photos in the hall that I chose to scrutinize. There was her as an infant, building a sand castle with another little boy, more pictures with who I assumed were her parents. She had her mother's eyes and her dad's smile. Somehow they fit perfectly together on her. I hoped if I asked a question she would go with it and we could leave that excruciating conversation behind, at least for now.

"Who's that?" I asked of the boy who adorned as many frames as she did.

"My brother." Her voice was right beside me even though I hadn't heard her walk up. "He lives out west now. He's six years older than me." I glanced at her studying the pictures with me, wondering what she saw in them. A million different memories that I only got one snapshot of.

"What are you doing next year?"

"Hm?" She turned from the wall of pictures with a surprised look on her face.

"Next year. Where are you going to school? Or where do you want to go?"

Her face fell. I hated that her face fell. This was something she should be excited about. A new chapter in her life.

"I've looked into a few schools. I'm not entirely sure. I want to be a photographer. I suppose it doesn't really matter where I go to school. It's more a matter of experience."

Her words caught me completely off guard. "A photographer?" I tried to picture her in a studio, taking countless pictures of models or graduating seniors or babies in little pink dresses. It didn't seem to fit. She didn't fit the image I had in my head of short-tempered men in skinny jeans ordering around models at any of Kelly's shoots I had to sit in on.

"Yeah. Of wildlife. Just of this earth. I want to travel the world, see all the places I've only seen in pictures. My parents travel all the time, they work for a travel magazine, and I always want more than the articles they write or the few pictures they bring home for me. There's got to be more. I want to see the places you never knew existed and the animals in those places. My parents write about the places, but I want to be the one to take those pictures that make other people want to travel the world."

I had never stopped to think like that. That there were people out there taking those pictures for the magazines and posters of the Great Wall of China or of the tiger stalking through the forest. I was always in awe of them, but I never wondered about the people behind the camera. She would be great for that. I knew it the moment she started talking. She already had such a different view of the world around us, I knew she would bring something amazing to any picture she took.

"What? You're smiling. What are you smiling about?" she laughed.

I shook my head. "Nothing. You're going to be great." My eyes found a huge print framed at the end of the hall with the sun setting behind a lone horse in the desert. The entire thing had a red glow to it, from the sand, to the sky, to the blazing sun peeking out behind the dark outline of the horse. "You took that?" I asked, nodding towards it.

"Yeah. We went on a family trip to the Grand Canyon. I took it while we were there. In a way, I've found an escape in photography. It could take me far, far away from here and for a long time, that's all I wanted." I noticed how she didn't say it was what she wanted now and I wondered what that meant.

"So you're going to travel a lot." It wasn't really a question.

"Well, there are many things I have to check off my list that involve travel..."

"List?"

"I have a lot of life goals, Mr. Sweeney." She drawled playfully before slipping by me down the hall and turning in an open door on the right.

I trailed after her, letting the same words she had said to me so many weeks ago on the beach sink in. "So I've heard," I said as I came to stand in the doorway. From what I could see, her room was a pale blue. However, you could barely see any of the paint. Instead, the walls were covered in pictures. Quite a few featured Samantha, others showed family, different scenes from nature had me wondering how I could have possibly missed how beautiful this part of the world was. She had a sheet of paper in her hand and she patted the blanket beside her.

Her room was so small, it only took me two steps before I was at her bed and again I had that feeling that there wasn't enough air in the room. I hesitated before sitting beside her, as if I was a nervous teenager again and couldn't be alone in a girl's room. The effect she had on me was ridiculous. I looked over her shoulder at the paper in her hands and saw it was covered in her careful lettering, each line with a tiny little box beside it.

"'Ride on a motorcycle at midnight?'" I quoted as I picked one out from the middle of the list. She laughed.

"I don't know why. Something about freedom I guess. You wouldn't happen to have a motorcycle would you?" She turned to face me fully, one knee swinging into my lap, and I stiffened. The expression of pure joy on her face was enough to make me gloss over the fact that a part of her was in my lap and I had to laugh.

"Do I look like a guy who would own a motorcycle?"

She took a deep breath and then blew it out with a pout. This look was almost as adorable as her excitement had been. She bit her lip in frustration and looked back down at the box beside that line, still blank with no intention of being checked off. "No. You don't."

"I might know a guy though…"

"Are you serious?" The excitement was back in an instant and my answering grin took over my face.

"We'll see." I left it at that as my eyes scanned further down the list. There were some common bucket list ideas here: climb the Eiffel Tower, see the Coliseum, sit atop a Mayan ruin. I had no doubt she had plans to make each one of them extraordinary, though. But then there were others, ones I would have never dreamed of. Swim with a full grown tiger, kayak with Orca whales, go underwater spelunking.

"I don't even know what spelunking is."

"Exploring caves. But underwater." In the next second she was pulling out her phone to show me pictures of scuba divers as a small light going through endless caves of dark water. To me, it looked terrifying. To her, it probably looked amazing.

"What happens if you run out of air?"

She looked at me as if I had four heads despite it being what I thought to be a logical question. "You don't," she replied plainly. I snorted a laugh and reached around her shoulder to let my finger skim down the list, stopping briefly over the line that stated: read every significant play by Shakespeare.

"You're an odd child, you know that?"

"'Let me be that I am and seek not to alter me.'"

I bit my lip as I fought to remember which play she was quoting. She studied me with an amused look on her face. "*Much Ado About Nothing?*" I asked after a moment.

"*Much Ado About Nothing,*" she confirmed. Her voice had dropped to a whisper and it had me watching her lips more than I should have been.

My tone matched hers, "I should go..." My eyelids fluttered closed when she turned into me more and I could feel the heat from her so close to me.

"Don't," she whispered back. My eyes remained shut as I shook my head and swallowed hard. Then I leaned back and separated myself from her before this went too far. She didn't look hurt or upset, just disappointed. I felt it too, as much as I should have been feeling relief.

I backed out of her room and made my way back to the front door where I hastily pulled on my jacket. In the time it took me to get it on, she had planted herself between me and the door. I hadn't stepped back at all and we were chest to chest with her smell blurring my thoughts yet again. "Carter, what are you doing?"

"I don't want you to go." She was so close her words fell like waves upon my lips. If I leaned forward an inch, my forehead would rest against hers. I gave into the urge and her breathing quickened against me. Another inch and our lips would be touching. I clenched my teeth because everything in me wanted to lean into that inch and if she didn't move now I was going to lose any and all willpower I had somehow managed to hang on to.

"I have to go," I said. But I wasn't sure if I was telling her that or telling myself. I closed my eyes and took a steadying breath in, having every intention to extract myself, but then her smell completely overpowered me. It was like cinnamon and apples and I just wanted to taste her; to see if she could possibly taste as good as she smelled.

I pulled my mouth away from hers and buried my face in her neck, but that did nothing to lessen my desire for her. If anything, the cinnamon and apple scent was stronger here and suddenly I felt my hand curve around her neck, brushing aside her hair so my lips could have better access. If my head had been screaming "no" while I was in her bedroom, it was wailing at me now.

She easily complied with my gesture, tilting her head into my hand and exposing more of her throat. "Tell me to stop," I groaned, my lips mere centimeters from her skin. "Tell me I can't do this."

Her breaths came quick, her pulse rapid beneath my palm which still cradled her neck. "Please, Noah," she pleaded and I broke. My lips connected with her neck and I could feel her gasp against me. The taste of cinnamon and apples flooded my mouth as her body became pliant. I had to hold her up as her hands fisted in my jacket. "Noah…" she whimpered. "I need you to kiss me."

I forced myself to pull my lips from her skin and what I was sure had just become my favorite flavor. I knew what she wanted. An actual kiss. But I couldn't give her that. This was a moment of weakness, one I shouldn't have let happen. I wished I could pretend I was unaffected, that I was okay, but it took everything in me to just steady my breathing again. "No."

"Noah." Her voice was weak. Her knees were weak, but I released my hold on her nonetheless. When I looked down at her, her eyes were still shut tight, but it was no longer in pleasure. Now I was sure it was to hide the tears forming behind her eyelids. "I need you. I just need you to kiss me. Please."

I hated that I did this to her, that I was so selfish. She was literally begging me for something I wanted to give her. And yet I wouldn't. I was the worst person. But a part of me still thought I would be worse if I gave in. I hated the world for putting us in this position.

"I'll see you Monday." I almost didn't recognize the voice that came out of my throat. It was cold, as detached as I wished I truly was. I watched as she recoiled like the words had actually struck her and slid away from the door. Then I quickly pulled it open before I could do any more damage and strode out.

Carter

We didn't talk about what happened, or what almost happened, at my house. It was wrong. So wrong. Ask anyone and they would agree. Yet for some reason I couldn't help but wish it would happen again. It didn't feel wrong. I felt his eyes follow me every time I came in and out of his class and that was enough for me to know I wasn't alone in this. He could push me away all he wanted, but I knew there was something on his end, no matter if it was right or wrong.

For now though, his eyes skipped over me as he scanned the class. "Don't forget, I need that analysis next Monday. I know none of you want to do it over break, but you've known about it for a week so no excuses. Have a good Thanksgiving, everyone." Some students mumbled a reply as they filed out after the bell, but I hung back for the first time since that night.

"Carter," he said it like he was surprised. I guess in a way, I was surprised I had hung back also.

"Hey..." I wasn't exactly sure where I wanted to go from here. I was just sick of only seeing him as his professional persona lately. I wanted the real him back.

"What's up?"

I swallowed hard. "Is it wrong to say I miss you?"

He tilted his head to one side and gave me a smirk but I could have sworn there was a pain in his eyes. A longing. "Probably."

"I don't think I like the concept of right and wrong anymore." I matched his half smile.

"I don't think we have much say in the matter."

"But we're a 'we' again?" I picked up on his word choice.

He took a seat in his chair in front of me and kicked his feet up on the desk. Then he bit his lip and looked down at his hands for a long while before speaking. "Pretty sure we always were a 'we'. Even if it can't happen." His eyes met mine and they were a hard, steely grey. I knew from one look that was all he would say on the matter, but it was enough for now. It was enough to know there was something worth fighting for. So for now, I just chose a different topic.

"Any plans for Thanksgiving?"

"I'm supposed to go to New York to have it with Sarah and Keaton. But we'll see. The weather doesn't look too good."

"Oh right, snow."

He nodded. "What about you?"

"My parents fly out to Utah tomorrow to have Thanksgiving with my brother."

"You're not going?"

"No," I shook my head. "They're staying for a week and I didn't want to miss school. I'm going out to stay with him this summer anyways."

"So you're home alone for Thanksgiving?"

"Samantha invited me over for dinner. I'll probably go there. Which reminds me, I'm supposed to be meeting her. Have a good Thanksgiving. Tell Keaton and Sarah I say hi."

He smiled at that. "I will. Have a good Thanksgiving, Cub."

I paused halfway out the door. "Cub?"

"I told you I would think of a nickname."

"And you settled on Cub?"

"I felt like it fit you." I didn't know where it came from or how he had thought of it, but I liked it. I liked that he had a name for me that no one else did.

Samantha was waiting for me impatiently in her car. "You're going to get caught," she chastised after we had rode in silence for a while.

I rolled my eyes and glanced out at the dead trees blurring by. "Can't get caught if we aren't doing anything wrong." She just gave me a bored expression before turning her eyes back to the road. "I haven't talked to him in weeks. I don't think wishing him a happy Thanksgiving is breaking any rules."

"Carter, if you were just telling a teacher happy Thanksgiving, I wouldn't care. But that's not what it is. I'm just saying be careful."

"I'm just saying I've got it under control."

"Do you, though?" I glared back at her. "Okay," she held up her hands in defense before dropping them back to the wheel. "I'll drop it. I'll see you tomorrow night, right?"

"Yeah, my parents were thrilled when I told them I would be spending the weekend with you instead of being all alone."

She parked in front of my house and turned to face me. "So you'll be at my house. The *whole* time?"

"Samantha…"

She just nodded and faced forward again. It was only a moment before she was turning back again. She was never one to hold in her opinion. "I don't get it, that's all. I don't understand it at all, Carter. You do get that plenty of guys have wanted to date you these past years, right? You could have had a pick of a lot of them. Most girls would have loved to have them. I just don't see the point in doing this to yourself. Is this even real?"

111

"What do you mean, is it even real?"

"I don't know. There's just stuff out there. You know. Cases about students and teachers."

"We've been over this. That is not what this is. You seriously think he's like that? *I* want *him*, Sam. You think I want to want him? I don't. You think I don't know this is insane and can never work? I do. I do even more than you know. And yet for some unknown reason, I can't help it." I blinked hard and looked down at my hands before looking back at her again. "Have you ever looked at someone when they're not doing anything special, when they're just sitting there, and felt your heart swell? They aren't even doing anything and you can literally feel inside of you how happy just looking at them makes you. Or have you ever seen someone's smile and thought that there was never anything more perfect than that?"

She looked at me dumbfounded. "No…" she finally said softly.

"I hadn't either. And it's not a feeling I'm used to. I'm scared. I'm really scared. Because caring about people that much? Well, all it's ever going to do is get you hurt. I don't want to get hurt. But I also can't just give up on this. I *can't* even if I know I need to."

She rubbed a hand over her face and gave me a tired expression. "Please just be careful."

I gave her a close-lipped smile. "I will. I'll see you tomorrow."

*****

"Looks like the snow is finally slowing down," Samantha's father said as he sat back down in his chair in the living room.

"Tim, can you pick up your plate, please?" her mother called as one of the twins went barreling into the kitchen. A moment later there was a bang

112

followed by the crash of glass shattering. Cassie started wailing a second later. This was Thanksgiving at the Greene household. By the time I had made it back to the kitchen, Sam was already sweeping up the two broken glasses, Mrs. Greene had a hold of each twins' shirts, and Tim was just standing with his plate, dumbfounded.

"Cassie crying," he said when he saw me enter the room.

"Thanks Timmy, I'll grab her." I smiled at him as I stooped to pick up Cassie who was sitting in the very center of the room. She stopped wailing as soon as I had her in my arms and proceeded to pull on my hair with her sticky fingers. In less than five minutes, the glass had been cleared, the twins were sent to their room, and Tim had moseyed back in to the living room to sit with his dad. I had Cassie giggling by now as I pretended to drop her over and over before snatching her back up again. It was a game she never got bored of, no matter how tired I got.

"Thanks, girls," Mrs. Greene said as she put the last dish in the dishwasher. She turned to look at us and even though she dealt with this mayhem on a daily basis, she still looked completely put together. I guess that's where Samantha got it from. They had a knack for keeping themselves together and putting others back together. I wished I could be like that. She reached out and took Cassie from me. "What are you two up to tonight?"

Samantha bit her lip and looked at me. "Well, I was actually thinking I would head home for the night if that was okay. I have an English paper I kind of wanted to work on." Samantha let out a half laugh at my words.

"Sammie, you didn't tell me you had a paper due." Her mom was the only person she ever allowed to call her Sammie. She tossed me a look of death.

"I have until Monday. I'll do it over the weekend."

"Not Sunday night," Mrs. Greene leveled. "Hon, do you think the roads are okay for Carter to drive?" she called into the living room.

"It's really not that far, Mrs. Greene. I'll be fine."

She only shushed me with one hand while bouncing Cassie on a hip. "I don't see why not," Mr. Greene's voice came from the other room. "Snow's almost stopped. The plows have gone by. She knows how to drive in winter."

Mrs. Greene looked unconvinced, but she let me grab my stuff to leave. "Just take this with you. We never got around to eating it." She placed the pie plate in my hand, my sole contribution to the feast she had put on. With the multitudes of desserts she had baked, my apple pie had been easily overlooked.

"Thank you for having me. I'll probably be back before the weekend's over."

She gave me a one-armed hug in return. "Of course, sweetheart. Any time! You know that. Drive safe!" She waved one more time before closing the door behind me and Samantha.

Sam stood with her arms crossed over her chest in an attempt to ward off the cold. "Where does he even live?"

"Sam."

"I'm serious. What happens if you go off the road or something happens and literally no one even knows where you were going? I need to at least know where he lives."

114

Her argument made sense. I relayed his address, which she quickly punched in her phone to save. "You don't know that, okay?"

"I'm not stupid, Carter." She sighed at me. "I'm not entirely sure if you're all that smart, though." I didn't even dignify her with a response. "Doesn't he have family to go spend Thanksgiving with?"

"He said he might not make it if the snow was bad."

"So instead you're going to risk your life to drive in the snow," she countered.

"Your dad just said the roads are fine! I'm going to be fine."

"Isn't his girlfriend with him? You know, the one you said he was going to propose to?"

"They broke up," I deadpanned.

"He was going to propose to her. And he broke up with her just like that? For you? Don't you find that a little strange?"

"He didn't break up with her for me. It wasn't about me at all. You don't know what his life is like."

"You're right, I don't. But do you? Do you even know what you're getting into?" she cried.

"Yeah, Sam, I do. Now I've got to go. Because I need to know if this is all on me or if he wants this, too. Do you understand that? Will you let me go if I tell you it could all be over tonight?"

"What do you mean?"

"I told you it wasn't like those news stories you told me about. I told you I want him. I need to know if I'm being stupid or if he wants me too. So tonight I'm going to figure it out. Maybe I'll be back here tonight. Maybe I won't. But either way, I'm going to him now, okay? I'll see you later." I was done with this argument, even though I knew she could continue it for another hour strong.

Her grumblings could be heard even as I pulled my car door open and she was still standing on the front walk. "Just, please be smart. And text me when you get there!"

"Yes, Mom!" I called back. I couldn't see her, but I knew she was rolling her eyes at me from the doorway. Right before I pulled my door shut, I could have sworn I heard her call out 'good luck'.

I texted Samantha once I had parked next to Noah's car in the lot outside his apartment. She answered me within a minute, telling me I should really think about what I was doing. But I already was thinking about it. I had thought about it on the whole drive over. I thought about it still as I walked up to his door. The last time I was here, I had been with Sarah and Keaton. Though he hadn't seemed happy about the arrangement at the time, it wasn't like I showed up uninvited. This was entirely different. Maybe I was making a mistake. Maybe I had him all wrong. But there was nothing to do but try one last time. So I raised my fist tentatively and knocked.

Noah

I turned the volume down on the football game and listened again, sure I must have heard wrong. No one would be knocking at my door this late on Thanksgiving. But there it was again, more forceful this time, so I pushed myself off the couch.

My breath stopped when I pulled open the door. There she was, her eyes such a demanding green against the creamy white of her face, her blonde hair laced with snowflakes. And in her hands she held a pie plate. A smile overtook her entire face as she scanned me over, from my bare feet, to my open flannel, to my mussed up hair. "Hey," she crooned.

"Hey," I breathed once I recovered from the shock of seeing her here, at my apartment. "How...What...What are you doing here?" I stammered.

"It's Thanksgiving," she replied as if it was obvious. As if I should have been expecting her. "You can't spend Thanksgiving alone. And it snowed, so you couldn't go see Keaton. So you get me instead. If that's okay. I know you're the better cook between the two of us, but I brought pie." She lifted the plate between us. Her smile faltered as I failed to form a response. "Well...can I come in?"

"Yeah, uhm, yes. Of course." I stepped aside and she brushed by me, her arm skimming my own and causing me to suck a breath in. Every nerve in my body was on high alert from one touch and I closed my eyes tight, wondering if I was dreaming. Then I peeked my head back into the hall to make sure no one had seen her before shutting the door behind us.

"What are you doing here, Carter?" I asked as I turned back to face her. She had already placed the pie down on the counter and was standing in the middle of the room, sucking the air out of it and setting me on edge. I'll be damned if I wasn't happy to see her here.

"I told you, I didn't want you to be alone on Thanksgiving."

"Cub."

A tentative smile reappeared at my nickname for her. "I need you to know, I understand. I understand why you've been the way you have been. I understand why no one can ever know about it. But like I told you at my house, I can't stop, Noah. There's something about you. Something about us...I know you know it, too. We can't just ignore that. I missed you. And as much as you don't want to admit it, you missed me, too."

"I see you every day." I tried to reason. I didn't even acknowledge anything else she had said. I did know there was something here, something that kept pulling us back to each other even when I fought so hard to be good. Something that made me ache to hold her. It was absolute torture to see her sitting in the back of my class every day and not be able to touch her, to even speak to her in the way I wanted to. I was too afraid that everyone would see how much she affected me if I even came within a foot of her, so I tried my best to keep my distance but the walls of the classroom had been starting to feel like they were closing in on me each day.

"That's not what I mean." I knew what she meant. All I could think about these past days had been what had almost happened in her house. How much I wanted it to happen. I should have never let her in. Because I knew if she didn't leave now, she wouldn't be leaving for a long time. She stepped into my space and her eyes were killing me. They made me want to bend, they made me want to break every rule I knew.

"Don't." She took a step closer despite my warning and the cinnamon and apple smell swirled around me. My eyes fell shut. "Carter, I swear to God if you come any closer..."

"What, Noah? What are you going to do?"

Her smell was stronger now and my breath was ragged. My jaw tightened and my hands balled into fists by my sides. I could do this. I had told her to leave enough before, I could do it again. I would be jeopardizing everything if I let this happen. We had gone way too far, she knew this wasn't okay. I had enough self-restraint. I just had to open my eyes and tell her she needed to go. But then, oh my God, her lips. The lips I had been mesmerized by for weeks, the ones I had wondered what would feel like against mine since that night at her house, were suddenly on me. She suckled at the base of my throat and I couldn't help it, I groaned. And then they were climbing higher, up my chin, skating across my jaw which remained clenched, inching closer to my mouth. But just as she was about to press her lips to mine, I gained control of myself.

"No!" I growled, pulling myself away from her, thudding into the door behind me. My eyelids flashed open to see her quickly hiding the hurt and confusion I had just replaced in her eyes.

"Stop pretending like you don't want this. You want me, too!" she yelled at me. For once she was not going to be deterred by my words. She had found that sense of confidence she claimed she didn't have. I breathed out hard and threw my head back against the door. Good God, she made life difficult. "You do want me...don't you?" I heard her ask with doubt laced through her voice. I hated how I was just another reason for her to doubt herself. Didn't she see what she did to me? Didn't she see how I couldn't think straight with her around?

"Say something," she pleaded, but I couldn't. I couldn't say anything. "Oh my God...you don't want me. You don't feel what I feel." I felt her back away from me, felt her heat leaving my chest, her scent dissipating. I could let her go. She could go on thinking I never wanted her. This was my easy way out after all the difficult times I had tried to keep her at bay. This was the chance to let it all go. It would be okay if she never loved me. That's what should happen. That's what she needed. But I realized in that moment, that's not what *I* needed.

"Carter," I finally whispered as I lowered my eyes from the ceiling to her face.

"Just move, I'm going."

"No, Carter..."

"I'm sorry. I'm sorry for everything. I thought...well, you know what I thought. I don't know how I read you so wrong. I'm so sorry. I need to go. I need you to move." She wouldn't meet my eyes and her hands were tugging on her sleeves incessantly and I found myself wanting those hands on me. On my chest, my shoulders, in my hair, anywhere. I needed her in my arms like I had never needed anything in my life. So when she reached for the doorknob behind me, I snatched her wrist in my hand.

"Look at me." My voice was harsh; I had no control over myself at this point. Everything was instinct. She immediately complied and whatever she saw in my eyes startled her. She almost looked scared. But then I had her other wrist in my hand and suddenly our roles were reversed. Her back was pressed against the door, her wrists trapped in one of my hands and the fear I had first seen in her eyes a second ago was mixed with something else now. It was mixed with the desire I was sure was swimming in my own eyes.

Before I had a chance to regret what I was doing, my mouth was on hers. I was swallowing her gasp of surprise and pressing myself as close as I could get, eliciting another moan from her. I was pretty sure her little noises had become my new favorite sounds just as her taste had become my favorite flavor. I kissed her slowly, making up for how I had made her doubt me. I kissed her top lip, then her bottom lip, then each corner of her mouth. I kissed her as softly as I could.

And then I finally snapped, giving in to what I had wanted from the moment I saw those big, green eyes staring back at me on the beach. I teased her mouth open with my tongue and let it tangle with hers before gently biting down on her lower lip. I felt her struggling to free her hands from my clasp but instead of releasing her, I went about torturing her in the only way I ever should have. My lips eventually left hers and she gasped for air as I placed light kisses all around her mouth, but never once covered it with mine again.

"Noah…please," she whimpered, sounding so much like that day at her house. She squirmed against me, fighting to free her wrists.

"Do you not like this?" I whispered as I kissed a path down her neck.

"No," she stubbornly panted, but the beat of her heart and the arch of her neck told me otherwise. I chuckled again as I finally released her hands so I could cradle her face in both of mine. My thumbs brushed over her cheeks tenderly as she stared back at me and her eyes told me she couldn't believe this. I had never seen them so bright, even in the half light.

So alive. So happy. The desire swirled in them drew me in and I molded my mouth to hers again. Her hands fisted in my hair and she arched into me, pressing herself closer.

"You drive me insane." I whispered the next time our mouths separated. She let her head fall back against the door as I kissed along her jaw to whisper in her ear. "I'm done staying away from you." I continued back down to her collarbone. "I can't do it anymore."

I felt the answering vibrations of her moan against my mouth. "Don't," she breathed into me. "I'm sick of you fighting me." She pulled my head back up to her and kissed me hard. Her hands tangled in my hair, then down my neck, across my shoulders and down further. It was like she wanted to feel every part of me and I gladly allowed that.

When her hands came up to push my flannel off so that I was left in just a t-shirt, I took the opportunity to take a step back from her. I wasn't sure how long I had kept her pressed up against the door. I could kiss Carter McMillan for hours and it wouldn't be enough. If it was anyone else, I would have already had them laid down on my bed. I would have been thinking further ahead. But not with her. Something about her was different.

"What?" she asked as she struggled to catch her breath. I shook my head as I leaned back in to brace my arms against the door on either side of her head, caging her in.

"We need to slow down," I breathed into her. My forehead rested against hers and her exhales mingled with mine. I couldn't remember the last time my heart had beat so fast. Her lashes fluttered closed and I leaned forward to press my lips against her closed eyelids as softly as I could. The answering gasp of surprise she gave caused me to chuckle. When she reopened her eyes to stare back at me, I saw a hint of that doubt back in them.

"You want me, though...Right?"

It was my turn to let my eyelids drift closed. Instead of answering her with words, I kissed her again. This time it wasn't rushed and intense and full of every desire I had held back for months. This time it was deep and tender and I felt her sag into me, completely relying on me. When I finally pulled back, she dipped her head into my neck and folded herself into my arms. "Thank you," she whispered into me. I wrapped my arms around her and pulled her into me even more, if that was at all possible.

She was like a wounded body part. She was a part of me. I knew I should have just cut her off, but I couldn't handle the thought of losing her. There was no turning back now. I should have realized it the moment I met her.

"I'm sorry. You're telling me you have no food. And it's Thanksgiving?" Carter groaned as she rummaged through my fridge later that night. We had finally made it further than my front door and at some point she had pulled on one of my sweatshirts over her long-sleeved shirt. She was swimming in it and I couldn't help but laugh every time she tried to push the sleeves up to her elbows in order to use her hands.

"I didn't plan on having Thanksgiving here." I leaned into the counter and gave her a bemused look when she turned to me with a glare and placed one hand on her hip. She tried to look so intimidating but I had never seen her look more like a cub than she did right now.

If she asked me why I chose to call her Cub, I would say there was no reason, but that wasn't true.

Even though I had always fought it, I had thought of her as mine ever since the first day I had seen her. I wanted to protect her because she was so small and looked so sad or frightened. Almost like a baby animal. Then the more I got to know her, the more I realized just how strong she was. How when she wanted something, nothing would stop her. It made me think of a little lion cub.

"Why are you looking at me like that?" she demanded while she fought to push my sleeves up yet again.

I laughed and stepped forward, carefully taking her arm and rolling the sleeve so it would stay. "You amuse me, Cub." I grabbed her other arm and repeated my ministrations before turning to study my own refrigerator. She huffed and leaned into my side and my body tensed for a minute, still not used to allowing her so close, to allowing anyone so close.

"I really don't have anything, do I?"

"Some master chef you are," she scoffed at me. Then she was pulling away and venturing further into my apartment. I trailed behind her, watching as she took everything in. Different pictures of Keaton I had. Ones of my sisters, my parents. She made her way into my room and skimmed her fingers along the spines of the innumerable books lining my shelves. It was weird, watching someone take in everything that made up your life. It made you think about each thing differently, wondering how they were seeing it. Again, I had that feeling like I was an immature teenager worried about what a girl thought of me.

She spun the globe I had in the corner of my bedroom and picked out the dots I had marked all over it. "What are these?"

"I used to want to travel."

She noted my use of the past tense. "Used to?"

"Things changed once I had Keaton."

"But now?"

I shrugged. "Now I need Keaton back."

"I'm not going to get in the way of that, you know that, right? I just want to be by your side while you try to get him back." Her eyes were earnest, needing me to know how much she meant that. I smiled back.

"I know. I always knew that. It's just easier to try to keep things black and white." She opened her mouth to retort, but I already knew what she was going to say and beat her to it. "We're grey, though. I know." Her smile met mine and she stepped over to my bed before giving me a questioning look. I answered with a half nod and she took a seat, then scooted back against the headboard and pulled her knees up to her chest, taking in the room around her.

Just seeing her on my bed had me wanting things I hadn't thought about in a long time. It made me nervous and excited all at once. This was insane. I still couldn't believe she was here. I couldn't believe I was actually crawling over to where she was sitting right now. That I was actually leaning in to kiss her again, pulling her hips down so she was laying with her head on my pillow as I stared down at her. *Her head was on my pillow.* Just thinking that sentence, seeing her here, made me smile.

She giggled beneath me. "What?" she asked, her hand reaching up to trail down my jaw to my chest. I didn't answer, just watched her, my eyes jumping from her blonde hair splayed out over the pillows to her dark eyes, her swollen lips from all my kisses.

"I'm scared, Carter." I whispered as I hovered above her, holding my weight on my arms so I didn't crush her. I knew what it was like to grow up too fast.

125

Just like she said, I had given up the things I loved. I was scared if Carter was with me, she would give up the things she loved. I would make her grow up too fast. She would be sucked into my mess, when it was clear she had enough to deal with on her own.

"Of what? Not getting Keaton back?" I shook my head, though that was in the back of my mind, too. It always was. "Of what then?"

"Of this." I leaned down and pressed my mouth to hers and she arched up to greet me. I allowed myself to get lost in her. Forgetting all the fears I had, forgetting every single line I had crossed tonight. Instead, I just focused on the feel of her mouth on mine, the taste of her lips, and the sound of her sighs. My hands traveled from her hips, up her sides, pushing my sweatshirt up with them so I could feel the goosebumps I was causing to erupt all over her skin. Her own hands skimmed down my back, lightly scratching, and I had to fight back a groan. She felt good. She felt way too good and I needed to stop.

"Carter…" I gasped when I finally pulled myself away from her. How was it that tonight was the first time I had kissed her? The first time I ever really touched her? I felt like I had been doing this for years. Her chest was heaving as I gazed down at her and tempting me to just lean in again, let whatever happens happen. "We need to stop."

Her eyes flicked open, drawing me in again, every emotion written in them clear for me to read. She wanted me as much as I wanted her. "Why?" she mewled.

"Because. We're not having sex tonight, Cub." Her eyes widened and her mouth popped open in a gasp and it was the cutest, most comical look I had ever seen that I couldn't help but laugh.

"Noah!" she hissed. The blush on her cheeks was adorable.

"What?" I asked through my laughter. It was insane. I could go from having the most serious conversation with her, to getting so caught up in her I almost lost control of myself, to laughing in all of ten minutes. She drove me insane. She reached up and slapped my chest angrily. I recoiled away from her hands and sat up. "Ouch! Why are you hitting me?"

I caught both her hands in mine as she attempted to hit me again. "If you thought we were having sex tonight, I would be extremely disappointed in you." She tried to give me a stern look but it didn't work on her and I just grinned in response.

"I obviously didn't think I would be having sex with you on Thanksgiving, Cub." She huffed at me and her hands jerked in mine but I just pulled them closer to my chest. Pulled her closer. "Actually, I didn't even intend to spend Thanksgiving with you. That was all on you." I smirked and then feigned shock. "Carter...did you come here to have sex with me?"

"Noah!" She ripped her hands from mine before I could react and resumed her attack until she was straddling me and I couldn't help but laugh.

"I'm kidding! Jeez, woman. You're gonna bruise me." I caught her hands again and this time wrapped them around my neck to anchor her to me. She followed my lead and threaded her fingers through the hair at the base of my neck. I let her tip my head back so she could lean in and brush her lips against mine. A whisper of a kiss. But she left her mouth there so that her exhales brushed over my lips in soft waves that made me want her like I had never wanted anything before.

127

"I didn't come here for sex," she whispered.

I grinned against her. "I know, Carter. I know."

She squirmed on my lap and I had to suck in a quick breath before she stilled again and I looked back into her eyes. She was torn on what she wanted to say, I could tell. "I don't want you for sex. You know that, right? That's not what this is about." I nodded, my forehead bumping into hers. "Good. Because, well, not that I don't think you're attractive or anything..."

"You better think I'm attractive." I smirked.

She rolled her eyes at me but her lips turned up in a smile. "Of course I do. Obviously you know I do. It's just, that's not why I want you." Her fingers trailed down from my temples to my chin, rubbing against the hint of stubble that had grown throughout the day. I let my eyelids flutter closed at her touch, soft as a feather. She traced back up to my forehead, then over my eyebrows, down my nose, and paused on my lips. "I've never wanted anyone like I want you. I've never wanted *anything* like I want you. Is that wrong?"

I shifted and laid us down, her head resting right above my heart as I wrapped my arms around her. "No, Carter. That isn't wrong."

She shifted so she was clutching me tighter and didn't say another word until I was just starting to drift off. "Noah?" she whispered.

"Mmm?" I muttered back. I flicked my eyes open as I felt her fingers trail over me. I was transfixed by them as they crept over my shirt, cataloging the lines and ridges of my body beneath the cotton. The shivers I kept experiencing had nothing to do with being cold.

"Thank you." She murmured, placing a light kiss on the hollow beneath my throat. "Thank you for finally letting me in. For letting me see you like this. This is all I ever want from you. It's all I need. You know that right? You don't have to give me anything else. I just want you to hold me like this, let me listen to your heartbeat, let me talk to you about everything. I just want you to know…I'm happy. You make me happy. We'll figure this out…together."

DECEMBER
Carter

"McMillan!" I was just about to step into Noah's class when Mr. Olsen's voice cut through the crowded hallway. I watched Noah's head flick up at the sound of my last name and his smile grew, although it was a secret smile. One just for me that held everything that had happened in the past weeks. I bit my lip in response before backing out of the doorway and making my way towards Mr. Olsen.

It had been three weeks since Thanksgiving. Three weeks since Noah and I had been together, if we could even call it that. It was weird because when it was just us, he was completely different. I was starting to catch more and more glimpses of the boy he used to be before he was forced to grow up so soon; before he was forced into so much responsibility; before he doubted himself. He was still in there, buried deep inside. Carefree and alive. His laugh was my favorite sound in the world. If it was the only thing I heard for the rest of my life, I would be happy. The amazing thing was, I was the reason behind that laugh. Whether it was his throaty chuckle when he knew he was saying something that would get me riled up, or his full out, head thrown back, eyes crinkled laughter, I was completely in love with it. There were so many things I was falling in love with because of Noah Sweeney.

For now, I came to stand in front of Mr. Olsen and smiled up at him. He was my history teacher freshman year, back when I wouldn't say a word to anyone. Somehow though, I had managed to form a connection with him. Maybe because I was just really interested in history and he picked up on that in the papers we had to write for class, so he'd ask me to stay after sometimes and discuss them. I looked up to him a lot, almost like an older brother because he was probably only a few years older than my own brother as it was.

"Let's take a walk."

"I really shouldn't. I don't want to miss any more class. I kind of slacked off at the beginning of the year." I gave him a shrug like I really wished I didn't have to go to class even though that was a lie. Any time I could get with Noah, I wanted.

"Oh, I'll write you a pass. I'm sure Mr. Sweeney will be fine with it."

I bit my lip and looked over my shoulder at Noah's door while the bell rang overhead. A second later, I heard his voice calling out for everyone to settle down. "Okay…"

He smiled that ever-calming smile again and led the way down the opposite hall. "How have you been?"

"I'm good, you?"

"I've been well. I haven't seen you a lot this year. Have you been getting excited for college?"

I shrugged. That was the million dollar question these days. Everyone needed to know where you were going, what you wanted to be, if you were nervous, excited, ready. It was overwhelming and honestly…I didn't even really care. That probably sounded bad. The truth was, all I knew for sure was that I wanted to be happy. I wanted to be happy and alive and out of this town where the guilt and anger hung over me like a cloud for what happened with Johnny. I didn't want to see Mariah's face anymore. I didn't want to sit in the same classes with her to be reminded of who I used to think she was. I had always wanted to get out and never look back. That had been the plan. That's why I wanted to photograph the world. Because it was beautiful and it was constant. It didn't lie to you. It was just there. It was everywhere so I would never have to stay in one place for too long.

I realized now that for the first time, I wasn't so sure about what I wanted. I didn't want to leave Noah. I didn't want to travel forever and never settle down. I wanted to have a life, not a different place every month. For the first time in years, I realized that I wanted to be loved by someone. I wasn't worried that he would turn out to be a monster. I trusted him. I hadn't felt like that to anyone but my own family and Samantha. The thing was, I wasn't even afraid.

"Carter?" Mr. Olsen's voice shook me from my thoughts and I glanced up at him.

"I'm sorry, I guess I just have a lot on my mind."

"I can see that. Anything you want to talk about?" He gave me a hard look, like he was trying to figure out what I had been thinking, and I didn't like it. I had relied on him for the past three years. He was a genuinely good guy and I knew he had taken me under his wing because he felt it was part of his job; to make sure his students were happy.

"No, I'm good."

"You know I worry about you."

I gave him a smile. "I know. I appreciate that. I need you to know though, I'm okay."

He studied me a moment longer. "You do look good. A little preoccupied, but better."

I smiled to myself because I *was* better. I liked smiling all the time and laughing and actually meaning it. "I am."

"Good. I just wanted to make sure. Now get to class before I get you in trouble." He pulled a pass from his pocket and handed it to me, letting me know this was a planned check-in. I smirked and took it from him.

Noah's eyes traveled over me as I placed the pass down on his desk and I gave him a wink while my back was still turned to the rest of the class. His cheeks immediately blushed and I had to fight hard to contain my laughter as I made my way back to my seat.

"Goddamn, McMillan. If I knew you could smile like that I would have fallen in love with you three years ago." Nate commented as I threw my bag down and sat between him and Samantha. I couldn't help but laugh and punch him lightly.

"Shut up, Nate. You didn't even know me three years ago."

"I would have made it my goal to get to know you."

"Nathan!" Noah's voice cut through any small discussions that had been going on and instantly silenced them so that everyone turned to face us. I hated a lot of eyes on me. Noah knew I hated people focused on me, so what was he doing? I squirmed uncomfortably in my seat. "I am trying to teach a lesson, but clearly your conversation appears to be more important."

I looked down at my desk, unwilling to catch Noah's eyes aiming to the back of the room. I could feel Samantha's gaze boring into me but I refused to look at her as well. "Honestly, Mr. Sweeney...which would you be more interested in if you were me?" Nate started with an easy drawl and I immediately knew this was not going to be good. "The gorgeous girl sitting next to you, or the hundred-year-old poem we're supposed to be reading?"

"Out." Noah deadpanned and any giggles that had started at Nate's comment immediately ceased. I snuck a peek at Nate to my left. He looked genuinely shocked underneath his cool mask. Mr. Sweeney was known as the laid-back, young teacher. This was not a reaction anyone would have expected from him. It wasn't a reaction even *I* would have expected from him.

"Come on, Mr. Sweeney…"

"Get out. Now." Noah raised a hand and pointed to the door. I had never seen him so angry. I had seen him frustrated and confused and happy and serious, but never angry.

"Jeez, Sweeney. I thought you were supposed to be the cool teacher." Nate swung his bag onto his shoulder and then leaned down to whisper in my ear. "I don't care who the guy is that's got you all smiley all the time McMillan, but I damn sure wish it was me." Before I could even respond, he planted a kiss on my cheek and stood up to stroll out lazily. I kept my eyes locked forward on Noah the entire time, watching as he threw his fist, which had been clenched tight through the whole encounter, into his desk with such force I swore it must have bruised his knuckles. However, it wasn't the smack of flesh on his desk that I heard. It was the resounding thump of a huge textbook hitting the floor right beside me that caused me to almost fall out of my seat in shock.

"I am *so* sorry!" Samantha gushed from next to me as she stooped to pick up her English book where it had toppled off her desk. "You all know I'm a klutz." She laughed, even though that was the opposite of the truth. She was the most graceful person I knew. No one in the class would dare disagree with Samantha Greene, though. So instead they just smiled as Nate made his way towards the door, laughing at Sam's mishap. Everyone was so focused on her, no one was facing the front of the room except for me. I was the only one who watched as Noah ran a hand through his hair, mussing it up even more than usual, and then gripped the back of his neck before shaking out his arms and clearing his throat.

"Alright, that's enough. Settle down." His eyes flicked to the clock on the back wall and he must have realized there was no point in teaching now. "Talk quietly amongst yourselves. We'll pick up here tomorrow."

My eyes stayed glued to him as he paced back to his desk and started typing in his computer. Samantha shoved my arm, causing me to turn my focus on her. "What the *hell*, Carter," she hissed. "I literally just saved your ass. Stop drawing more attention to him."

I swiveled in my seat to fully face her. "What?"

"God, you are so blind." The bell rang just then and the class filed out until it was just me and Samantha left in the room. She walked swiftly to the door and I assumed she would walk out to leave me with Noah so that I could figure out what the hell had just happened. Instead, she yanked the classroom door shut then stormed back to where I stood by Noah's desk.

"What were you thinking?" She practically shouted at him.

"What are you talking about?"

"Don't play stupid, Sweeney. You just almost screwed up, big time. Hell, you did screw up. You want the whole damn school to know?"

"Jesus, Carter...she knows?" He swiveled to me and had the gall to act angry towards me. Before I could even defend myself, Sam jumped in.

"Of course I know! I've known from the very first day. Why do you think I sent you to find Carter in the Special Ed building months ago? You don't

135

think I bought for a single second that it was all to get her to come to class, do you?"

"You can't tell people about us." He growled, but I wasn't sure if he was directing that statement to me or Samantha.

"Oh, because I'm the one you need to be worrying about? You just basically told your entire class!"

"Sam!" I hissed.

"She's right. God, she's right, Carter." His hands came up to grip the back of his neck as he spun away from us. His fist flashed out to punch the white board in front of him and both Samantha and I jumped. When he turned back to face us with his back leaning against the board, there was so much raw emotion in his eyes I could barely take it. Hurt and anger and fear and jealousy. "He said he would love you, Carter. And then…Goddammit, he touched you. He *kissed* you. And I'm supposed to just sit here and watch it?"

My heart felt like it was splintering at his words. I remembered how I felt when I knew he had been with Whitney, and that was back before we had even become…whatever it is we were. I couldn't imagine what he was feeling. I just always assumed I cared more for him than he did for me. But hearing his words, I was slowly starting to realize that maybe he needed me like I needed him. I didn't have a chance to respond to his question. Samantha did for me.

"Yeah, actually you are. Because you're her *teacher*, Mr. Sweeney."

"I'm your teacher, too, Samantha. You would do well to watch how you're speaking to me."

She only laughed but there was no humor in it. "You really think you can pull the upper hand on me right now?" I knew her quick temper well, so before she could say something she'd regret, I cut in.

"Alright, everyone needs to stop. Just stop for a minute." Noah's hand ran through his hair, his nervous habit in full force. Sam just folded her arms over her chest and glared at the two of us as if we had committed some crime. Maybe we had. Was what we were doing really that bad?

"Noah, I'll see you later."

"What?" His eyes found mine and once again they were unreadable. His moment of weakness was gone.

"I said I'll see you later."

"You're just going to leave right now?"

"We can't exactly discuss this here," I hissed.

He reluctantly agreed and just as Sam went to pull open the door, he spoke. "Sam." She turned to face him with a bored expression. "Thank you."

She nodded and pushed out the door, not even slowing her steps for me to catch up. "Sam, talk to me," I pleaded.

It wasn't until we had almost reached her car in the student lot that she finally looked at me. "I don't even know who you are anymore."

"What do you mean?"

"I mean I told you this was an idiotic idea! Stupid! So much more insane than any moronic thing I've ever done in my entire life!"

"I know…" I agreed quietly.

"But you don't! You clearly don't or you wouldn't be doing this! What just happened in there?" Her hand raised to point back towards the school buildings. "That's not okay. If anyone even suspected anything, you would both be screwed. Do you understand that? I don't care if no one ever got any hard proof. A rumor is all they need. A rumor to destroy any reputation you've gained. A rumor to destroy his career. Got that?"

"Sam…"

"No, you don't get to Sam me right now. You get to listen to me. I wanted you to smile. I wanted you to laugh. I wanted you to go out and have a good time and live a good life. I wanted you to be a normal teenager. This is not what I had in mind. You know how you told me about that love crap? Well you want to hear the truth? What no one ever has the heart to tell the true romantics? There *is* right and wrong. There *are* rules in love. There are people you aren't allowed to love. You're not allowed to love him, Carter!"

I stood frozen, unable to form any words to contradict her. I had no defense to anything she wanted to throw at me. She yanked her back door open and pulled out her gymnastics bag and slung it over her shoulder before facing me yet again. "End it, Carter. Just end it now before you're in too deep. Before you pull him in too deep. Because I don't want to try to piece you back together when this all blows up in your face. I couldn't even piece you back together the first time. Just know, I won't be there to pick you back up if this goes bad."

Finally, I found my voice. I found that confidence that Noah had slowly been showing me I had. "How many times do I have to tell you, I never asked for you to fix me! I didn't need to be fixed then and I sure as hell don't need to be fixed now. I can't end it. I'm already in too deep."

She just rolled her eyes as if she could never possibly understand my words. Maybe she truly couldn't. Either way, I had clearly taken too much of her time for the day because she pushed past me and headed back towards the gym, leaving me standing alone in the snowy lot. I was worried that I had been pushing Samantha further and further away the closer I got to Noah. I didn't realize how quickly she would turn her back on me. Maybe she was right, in one sense. Would I really lose any hope of a normal life if I kept this up? But then again, did I ever have hope for a normal life?

I took another compulsory glance down the hall before lightly tapping on Noah's door. It was immediately yanked open before I even had a chance to drop my hand. His arm came out to snake around my waist and he pulled me inside so fast I felt dizzy. Then the door was shut again and I was pushed up against it, back in the same position I had found myself in on Thanksgiving night. His hands came up to cradle my face, so warm against my cold skin, and he held me in place before dipping his mouth to mine. He kissed me hard, as if he hadn't seen me in days. By the time he pulled away, my knees were weak and I was breathless. "What was that for?" I asked when I was finally able to speak again.

"I'm sorry," he said as he paced back towards his couch. "That's just all I could think about doing since the moment I saw that punk lean in to whisper in your ear in class."

I giggled and made my way over to him on unsteady legs. "Did you just seriously call Nate a punk?" He raised one eyebrow at me as I curled up beside him on the couch. "Does anyone actually use the word punk anymore?"

"I'm starting to think that you're a punk, too." He reached out and poked my ribs so that I squirmed away from him.

"You love that I'm a punk," I grinned at him as I caught his finger in my hand and brought it up to my mouth to place a kiss on the pad of his finger. He watched me with rapt attention as I flipped his palm over to trace each line with my index finger. Before long, he had pulled my mouth back to his and pressed his lips to mine, making me forget everything else, making me forget even my own name. When he was satisfied with erasing my memory, he shifted me off his lap and back onto the couch, that stupid grin I loved to hate plastered on his face. My cheeks heated in a blush at how easily affected I was by him.

"I'm sorry...it's just I want to kiss you every time I see you. And I can't. So I have to make up for lost time." I was sure my face was beat red at this point so I blinked quickly and looked away before he could see how much I loved hearing that confession. "I'm also sorry I was so out of control today. I should have never been like that. That could have been horrible. It can't happen again, Carter."

He placed his hand back in mine and I began tracing over his palm again, regaining control of my breathing and thinking about what he had said. "Why were you like that?" I asked and looked up at him again, folding his fingers over mine.

He took a deep breath like he didn't want to admit whatever it was that was in his head. "I don't like how the other guys have been looking at you lately. I watch them as they watch you in the hall as if they're just now realizing you exist. I don't understand how anyone could have ignored your presence. I can't ignore you even though Lord knows I tried my hardest to pretend you didn't exist."

"Wow, you just know all the right words to make a woman swoon, don't you, Sweeney?"

He flicked my arm with his free hand and gave me that look like he was completely exasperated with me, even though I knew that wasn't the case. "You are a punk."

"And you need to know that I never wanted those guys to realize I existed. I'm happy with it that way."

"Well they know you exist now and I don't like it. I don't like Nate, either."

"You do like Nate. He's hilarious and he's a good kid and he's smart. He actually enjoys your class, you know."

"I really don't need you listing off every good attribute the kid has," Noah grumbled. "You should just be with him."

I pulled away to look him in the eye, even though I knew that would get me nowhere. They were hard as stone, the dark grey not giving anything away. "Noah..."

"Come on, Cub. We both know I'm no good for you. You need someone like him. I'm sure he could make you just as happy."

"I need you," I whispered, admitting it for the first time.

"Why? Why me and not him?"

"You're different."

"That doesn't answer the question," he deadpanned.

"What do you want me to say? You want me to say you're different because...because...I love you? I love you and I've never loved anyone like I love you and I sure as hell don't love him? Is that what you want me to say?" My words tumbled over each other on their way to get out. I couldn't believe I had just admitted that I loved him. Out loud. To him. This was bad. This was very bad.

He stared at me for so long I had almost decided I should stand and leave. That was a stupid thing to say. I was just about to get up when he spoke again. "Why do you love me?"

Yes. Because that's what you want to hear when you tell someone you love them, I thought to myself. I sighed heavily. "I love you because. Because I do." He just crossed his arms and cocked his head to one side. I threw my hands in the air in frustration. I never expected him to say he loved me back, but he could have at least let the whole thing go without making it worse. Instead, he was clearly waiting for me to give a valid answer, as if he were going to grade it like it was one of the argumentative essays for his class. I closed my eyes and tried to find a way to put my feelings for him into words.

I loved him in the purest way possible. I loved him without even knowing I did. I had never stopped to think of why before, probably because I was more preoccupied with attempting to convince myself *not* to love him. I finally opened my eyes to find him still staring at me intently, his arms still crossed. "Fine!" I huffed. "I love you because you're different than anyone I've ever met before. Because you're so much more than you let anyone see. I love you because you let *me* see it. Because you're kind and compassionate but annoying and rude. Because you like some of the same things I do, but even more that I don't. Arguing about them with you is one of my favorite things to do. I love you because you challenge me. You challenge me to live life. To be happy. To remember what it felt like to be free. I love you because you're as messed up as I am but you have this confidence that I wish I had, even when the world has given you every reason to doubt yourself. I love you because you're showing me how to have that confidence, too. I love you because of you."

I stared up at him once I finished, wondering if I could take back all my words. Not because they were untrue, but because I didn't know how he would react to them. I could never tell what he was thinking and it drove me insane. I looked at him, silently cataloguing every feature of his face, wondering if this was it. If I had gone way too far. But then his eyes lightened and he smiled at me. His real smile, the one where I could see every single one of his teeth and he reached out to grab my hips and drag me towards him. Once I was close enough, his long fingers reached up to trace a line from my temple to my collarbone that I could still feel even as he rested his hand on my neck, cradling it carefully as if I would break under his pressure.

His smile widened even more, if that was at all possible. "You never said you loved me because of my amazingly good looks." He said it as a joke, because that's how we dealt with serious situations, but in the very backs of his eyes I could see how much that meant to him. There was something there from the past that haunted him. Maybe that was the reason he had asked why I claimed to love him. He didn't want to be just an attractive face again.

Tentatively, I lifted one hand and placed it over his heart, feeling the erratic thump beneath the fabric of his dress shirt. I gave him a half grimace. "Personally, I think your 'good looks' are a bit overrated." It was a lie of course, he knew it as well as I did, but he threw his head back and barked a laugh before staring at me hard. Harder than he ever had before. For the first time ever, I wasn't worried about what he would see in my eyes. I had just laid every feeling I had for him bare. Then, without warning, he crushed his lips to mine and I knew. I knew, right, wrong, complicated, impossible… it didn't matter, there was absolutely no way I could ever let this go.

Noah

"It's freezing," she grumbled and pressed herself closer to my chest. I didn't think she could get any closer, but she kept finding a way. My arms ran up and down her back in an attempt to warm her up. She was right; it was freezing. But it was only about to get colder for her. I had a feeling she wouldn't mind, though. "Can we please just go back inside? I'm tired and cold and this is weird and spontaneous and all, but can we postpone whatever this is until a warmer date?"

I chuckled and her little hands found their way under my jacket and pressed against my skin, shocking me with how cold they were. "I could postpone it. But I want to do it now."

Today was the first day of winter break, and it came as such a relief. I had felt fear before, plenty of times. When I first walked into that apartment to find Kelly and Keaton. The weeks that followed, seeing her in a hospital gown with those dead eyes while countless tests came back showing nothing and so many treatments failed. The moments after my parents had told me if I agreed to taking care of Keaton they would never approve of it; they would distance themselves completely. The months, years, since then where I wondered what the hell I was doing with Keaton. How I was possibly going to make it work. How my parents could really just abandon their own grandson. Their own son. When the social workers had told me they were taking Keaton away from me. So yes, I had felt fear plenty of times before. But I had never felt fear like I had these past weeks being with Carter. Fear that I was going to mess up, which I almost had. I still couldn't believe how close that had been, how I had completely lost control because of *jealousy*. I was never a jealous person. I

145

was never one to let my emotions show. Carter was changing me, and it was terrifying in both a good and bad way. When she admitted she loved me the other night, it terrified me. I was scared of how happy it made me. I was scared of what it meant for us.

Just then, I heard the sound I had been waiting for and it shook me out of my thoughts. It was faint at first, but growing steadily louder. I had no doubt it was Keith. Who else would be out at midnight at the end of December? He was a good friend just for doing this. Not that it hadn't taken some serious pleading on my part. Carter didn't realize what it was at first. Either that, or she didn't think it was for her. But eventually the rumbling was too loud to ignore and she lifted her head from my chest and turned to peer over her shoulder.

Keith swung into the parking lot and pulled up right in front of us, idling by the curb. I couldn't hear Carter's gasp of shock over the motorcycle's roar, but I could feel it. When she turned back to face me, her eyes were huge in the streetlight. "Noah!"

My grin widened. "Merry Christmas, Cubscout."

"No…no way."

I chuckled as I untangled her from me and took her hand in mine. "Keith…this is Carter. Carter, this is my buddy, Keith. He was my roommate in college and he very kindly offered to help me check off one of your little boxes." I reached out to shake Keith's hand and he gave me a look that told me we both knew he hadn't exactly signed up for this voluntarily. But he looked past me to give Carter a winning smile. Then he reached behind him and held out a helmet to Carter.

Just then, I heard the church bells begin their chime of midnight. "That's your cue, Cub. Ride on the back of a motorcycle at midnight, right?"

She turned back to me once she had placed the helmet on her head and I bent down to buckle it beneath her chin, purposefully letting my fingers brush against her skin which caused her to suck in a breath. I smirked. I loved how affected she was by me, how affected she always had been by me. It was exhilarating. "I can't believe you."

"I know, I'm the greatest thing that ever happened to you," I joked with a cocky smile.

She reached out to slap my chest and rolled her eyes but didn't deny it and I knew what she was thinking about. That time in the diner so long ago when she had claimed to hate me and I said that was the opposite of the truth. I was kidding then, but maybe I had been right all along. Now, her eyes were telling me I was right.

"I don't know what to say." She lifted up on tiptoes to reach my lips, not giving me a chance to reply. I kissed her back hard. It took everything I had to pull away and give her a light shove towards Keith and the bike. I watched as she swung on behind him, cautiously wrapping her arms around his middle like he instructed. A stab of jealousy hit me even though I knew it was completely irrational.

"Take care of her, Keith." I saw him roll his eyes and give me a thumbs up before he revved the engine and took off out of the parking lot.

I would be lying if I said I wasn't worried the entire time she was gone. I trusted Keith; of course I trusted Keith. I had trusted him with Keaton all through college. But there was just something about Carter that had always made me feel like I needed to protect her. Sending her on a motorcycle in the middle of winter didn't exactly fall under the category of protecting her. The look in her eyes when she realized what I had done for her, though? That was definitely worth the worrying I was doing now. I wanted to put that look in her eyes for the rest of her life. I stilled. Did I really just think that? I was thinking about forever with her? No. No way. There was no way. I couldn't even say 'I love you' to her.

That was one thing I couldn't bring myself to do. I had crossed so many lines with her. But one thing I wouldn't let myself do was tell her I loved her. That would be it. That would be everything. Maybe it was stupid, but somehow that was where my moral compass drew the line. I couldn't love this girl.

Finally, the door to my apartment was thrown open and in the next second Carter had launched herself into my arms. She was freezing, her lips felt like little ice cubes as they pressed over every inch of skin she could reach. Her arms around my neck were so cold it was almost painful and I could feel the chill seeping off her clothes and through my own where her legs wrapped around my waist and she pressed into my chest. Each time her lips lifted an inch from my skin, she whispered the words "thank you" over and over.

"God, you guys are sickening and I'll be damned if I'm not jealous of it." Keith's deep voice reminded me we weren't alone and I slowly let Carter slide down to stand on her own, but I couldn't wipe the happy smirk from my face. "Spare room?" He asked and lifted up his overnight bag. I nodded and he made his way to the room that had been his our sophomore through senior years of college. It was weird to hear him refer to it as the spare room and not his own room now.

"Hot chocolate?" I asked as I made my way into the kitchen and pulled out a mug for Carter. She shook her head but slipped around the counter towards me nonetheless. Her arms came to wrap around me from behind as I poured a cup of coffee for Keith and I felt her cheek rest against my spine. That feeling of home? The one I had only ever gotten from my sisters and Keaton? I felt it more than anything with her. She was becoming my home.

"Thank you," she murmured for what had to be the hundredth time. "That was...I don't even know what to say. You're incredible." She placed a kiss between my shoulder blades and I turned in her arms to face her.

"Well, you do have a lot of life goals, don't you?"

Her eyes smiled at me in the semidarkness. "I do have a lot of life goals. Thank you for helping me check them off."

"Of course." I ducked my head to press a kiss to her still-cold lips but before it could go any further, she pulled away.

"I think I'm going to bed for now. I'll let you have your guy time with Keith."

"You don't have to-" I started.

"I know," she cut me off. "But I want to."

"Goodnight, Cub." She smiled at her nickname and slipped out of my arms, almost crashing into Keith on the way to my room.

"Thank you again, Keith." He only nodded at her and swung onto one of the bar stools.

"That mine?" he asked. He didn't wait for my response, just leaned over to slide the mug from my grasp. "Thank God, because I think my entire body is frozen solid by now. I'm not even sure if I'm still a man anymore."

I chuckled and leaned into the bar opposite him. "Thank you. Seriously, I know it was a stupid request. A bike in December. But thank you."

"Yeah, yeah. Whatever I can do to help you get laid."

My eyes immediately rolled. "It's not like that."

Keith took a long swig from his mug, even though I was certain it should be burning his mouth. "Well from what I saw when I walked in here, it sure looked like that."

"It's not what it looks like." I snapped.

"So then what is it really like?"

"I'm not talking about my relationship with you."

His eyebrows raised at my defensive tone. Of course he would be surprised. He used to know almost everything about me. No one ever knew everything, but he was pretty close. That was why he knew my limits. He knew when to stop pushing for information because it wouldn't get him anywhere. He lived with me the whole time I had Keaton and yet he didn't know the whole situation. Maybe that was a mark of a true friend. Someone who doesn't need to know everything to still have your back through it all. He was the only true friend I had for all these years.

"Alright, I'm intrigued. The guy who puts on the perfect mask has yet another secret."

"Shut up, Keith. Keaton was never a secret."

"And Carter is?"

"I never said that," I groaned.

He gave me a smug look in return but let me off the hook for now. "Whatever, man. It's better than Whitney." He had never been shy about his hatred for Whitney. Every time she stayed over included at least one fight between the two of them. "But hey, where's my little buddy?"

"Sarah's."

"He's at Sarah's for Christmas?"

I shrugged. "I'm heading up there later I think. Stay the weekend."

"So he's with her full-time?"

"For now. Just while I get a hang of the new job. I don't know." My hand came up to push the hair off my forehead more. He had moved out by the time the social workers came to evaluate the situation. He didn't know Keaton was removed from me. It was easier to tell him that he was only with Sarah until this job was secure. It made it easier for me to believe that as well.

"Maybe it's a good thing." I leveled him with a stare. His hands came up in defense. "All I'm saying is you look good, Sweeney. You're not so stressed. God, you used to stress me out with how much you worried about that boy. But now, I don't know. You sounded different on the phone…and here? You're laughing. You're smiling. And it's not for Keaton. You know what I'm saying?

"When I was here, you were living for him, everything you did was for him. Now, you're back to that kid I met freshman year. Maybe it sounds stupid, but you're living for you now. You're not acting like a thirty-year-old dad."

I paced away from him because honestly, I didn't want to hear it. I wasn't supposed to be living for me anymore. I was supposed to act like a thirty-year-old dad. I was supposed to have Keaton. The whole point was to live for Keaton to make up for how I had lost Kelly. Instead of doing that, I had failed. I had been forced to ship him back to that awful place I had saved him from. A place I hadn't even stepped foot into since I had pulled him out of there. I hadn't gone back there, I wasn't sure if I could. Now he was living there and I hadn't even been able to muster the strength to go see him there. My hand raked through my hair.

"You know why I was that way?"

"You took care of Keaton."

"Yeah, but do you know why?" I knew he didn't. No one but Carter did. Here I was, ready to tell someone else. It was crazy because even though the two of us had to be some of the most messed up people, somehow we were finding a way to make each other better. I might have been her teacher, but that girl taught me more than she would ever know.

Keith stayed silent during my story. It wasn't as long as it had been for Carter because he lived parts of it. He just didn't know Kelly. "Why didn't you ever say anything?"

I shrugged my shoulders. "Didn't want to talk about it I guess."

"So now?"

"Now I've been shown that the only way you can get over some things is to accept that they happened and realize that you can still live a life without letting your past control you." Before I knew it, I found myself standing in the doorway to my bedroom. Carter had already fallen asleep curled up in one of my favorite sweatshirts. It looked better on her anyways.

Keith leaned into the opposite side of the doorjamb. "Pretty smart girl you found." I glanced at him and he just stared back at me so I bit my lip and nodded. We both turned back to watch her as she slept, more content than I had ever seen her. She had an entire expanse of bed to sleep on and yet she chose to curl in a ball in the very center of it all. I chuckled to myself and I felt Keith's eyes flick between me and back to her. In that moment, I realized that she slept the same way she lived her life. Not all spread out or dramatic, demanding to be seen and loved. No, it was the opposite. She curled into herself in an attempt to stay hidden but still found her way unassumingly to the center of anyone who tried to care about her and proceeded to curl up and remain there.

The next morning, light streamed through my window and painted shadows across Carter's cheek as I gently ran my fingers through her hair. I wondered if she always slept this peacefully, or if it was simply because I was here. Not that I was so presumptuous as to believe that I could be the sole reason for calming her. But then again, she had done that for me. I never used to be able to sleep. For a long time, it was because sleeping with any newborn around is impossible. Then, once Keaton got older and slept through the night, I found that every time I closed my eyes I could see that apartment again. I could see the squalor, hear Keaton's cries, see his tiny ribs poking through, and feel how frail he was when I scooped him up out of the filth. It was easier to just keep my eyes open. So instead of sleeping, I would just study. Or read. Or flick through old movies and infomercials on TV. Anything to pass the time until Keaton woke up again and I could devote all my time to him, attempting to forget what he had gone through.

Now, I was going back there. For the first time in over three years, I was going to have to step back into that place. Sarah had kept the apartment. She had moved back into it once Kelly had been moved to the psychiatric hospital and I had refused any invitation she had given for me to go visit her there. If I ever needed to go to New York for anything, I booked a hotel. I used to go quite a bit, in the first couple years, to visit Kelly at the ward. Sarah always tried to get me to stay with her, but I couldn't bring myself to do it. Eventually, I couldn't even bring myself to see Kelly anymore. The more I got to know Keaton and got to see his personality develop, to see the little person he was becoming, it made it harder and harder to see Kelly. It hurt me to know she hadn't even given him a chance. She would never know the person her son became. And he would never have a mother. I got angry at her because I felt like she wasn't even trying. If she would just try, maybe she could come back to us.

"Hey…" Carter's sleepy voice completely startled me, even though my fingers had been moving through her hair this entire time. Her hand came up to stroke my jaw and my eyes took a second to focus on her face and not my distant memories. "That's not a good look. Is something wrong?" She struggled against my hold to sit up and I let my arm drop. "Noah, what are you thinking about?"

She picked up my hand from where it had fallen back on the comforter and started tracing the lines on my palm. It was something she always liked to do when we were alone. Tracing along whatever parts on me she could reach. "New York."

Her fingers paused at my admission. "New York? Why are you thinking about New York?"

I swallowed then looked back down at her. "I'm going there."

Surprise immediately flooded the dark green of her eyes. "When?"

"New Years' Day. For that weekend before we go back to school. Sarah and her fiancé Sean are taking Keaton for Christmas at Sean's family's home in Pennsylvania. It's the first Christmas he hasn't spent with me. I fought it, but Sarah said there was no way he could spend the entire holiday with me while she was away. She was right, of course. That didn't mean it makes me feel any better. He belongs with *me*. I'm the only parent he knows. How can they think this is right?"

My voice cracked and I was angry at myself for being so weak. I was so angry. Angry at Sarah, even though I knew she was just trying to help me; to do the right thing. Angry at the government for pulling that little boy from me. Angry at Whitney for ever thinking this would be okay. Carter didn't speak, there were no words she could say now to make me feel any better, so she just held me while I broke apart inside.

"I know I can't focus on that. I just need to focus on getting through this year and then everything will go back to normal...whatever that was." I chuckled. "Sarah felt bad. She offered for me to spend New Years' with them since they would be back in New York and school doesn't start until after that weekend."

When I paused, Carter could see my internal struggle and she scooted around so she was facing me instead of curled into my side. Her fingers flexed in mine and I realized I had tried to run a hand through my hair unknowingly. It was a nervous tick I had never been able to break. Her free hand came up to comb through my hair for me and my eyelids fluttered at the soothing touch. "What's wrong with that?"

I reached out and played with a lock of Carter's hair, twirling it around and around my fingers, stalling. "I haven't been to New York in two years. I haven't been to that apartment since I went there and found Kelly and Keaton in that mess. I don't want to see that place again. I don't want to be reminded of the worst day in my life. In Keaton's life." I felt like there was a weight sitting on my chest, just waiting to crush me completely at the mere thought of that apartment. "I'm not sure if I can do it. I don't know how I'll react. I don't think I can do it alone."

Her eyes widened at my implication. "What are you saying?"

My eyes flickered from the top of her head, down over her nose, her lips. I had broken so many rules with her. So many lines had been blurred, so many totally erased. What was one more at this point? "Carter, I want you to go to New York with me."

JANUARY
Carter

Noah had told me on our ride to the city that Sarah and Keaton would be out when we got there and that Sean would be at work. He said they had done this on purpose. Sarah must have known he would need to see that apartment for himself before he was expected to celebrate Christmas there the next day. So we were apparently going directly there before checking into our hotel. If I was at all nervous, it was nothing compared to Noah. He got increasingly more quiet as we made our way deeper into the city until he became completely unreachable despite my best efforts to pretend like this was totally normal. Eventually I gave up even trying to reach him and just toyed with the end of my sleeves, watching skyscraper after skyscraper blur past us.

When he finally parked behind an inconspicuous-looking building, the sun was already starting to dip behind the city. The days were short still and the wind whipped against my face as I stepped out and walked around the back of his car to reach him. He stared at the building with completely unreadable eyes and it reminded me of all those early days with him when I thought he would never let me in. But then his hand reached out to take mine silently and he set off towards the door with purpose, towing me along in his wake. If this wasn't such a hard thing, I would have taken the time to revel in the fact that his skin was touching mine and we weren't in the confines of his apartment. As it was, I clutched his fingers tighter, hoping to be strong for his sake.

The inside of the building was more modern than I had expected from its exterior. It had probably been renovated and made to be a hot spot to live, with a historic exterior but chic interior. The lobby definitely screamed that this was a place for well-to-do people, which made sense I suppose. Kelly had been a successful model after all, and Sarah was a doctor now. Of course they could afford to live in a nice place. Noah, naturally, saw none of this. We could have been walking through a bombed-out city for all he noticed. His head didn't even lift from watching the carpet where his feet were stepping. He barely even looked when he reached out to light up the number four on the elevator.

When he did finally look up from watching his own footsteps, he stopped so suddenly it threw me off balance. His hand was still clutching mine, even tighter than before, while I stood next to him and watched his jaw tick. Then I swiveled my eyes to face what was causing him so much difficulty. We were facing the door of apartment 406. To me, it looked like each of the other rust-colored doors we had passed on this floor. To him, it clearly meant something different.

When I couldn't take the silence anymore, I tentatively cleared my throat. "So this is it?"

He didn't answer, just licked his lips and pulled his hand from mine in order to reach into his pocket. He pulled out his set of keys and I noticed that it took him no time at all to locate a small gold key on the ring. Even though he had said he hadn't been back to this place in over three years, he still had the key. It made my heart ache for him. He stepped forward and eased it into the lock. I heard the click when he turned it, and his eyes squeezed shut so tightly it was painful to watch. Like he was trying to erase whatever image was haunting him. Then he turned the knob and pushed it open, but made no move to step inside. His breathing was shallow, as if he had just stepped off a treadmill and I could see the tremors running through his entire body.

I tentatively walked to his side again and placed a hand on his arm. "Noah? You're scaring me."

My voice startled him out of whatever nightmare he was reliving and his eyes found me. That color of wet denim I remembered from the first day in his classroom was back, drinking me in as if I was a life raft. "What?" His voice shook and I could see him struggle to fix that. Then both hands came up to cradle my face so tenderly my heart swelled. "No, Cub," he crooned. "I don't want to ever scare you. It's okay." I could tell it wasn't just me he was trying to convince when he said everything was okay. His thumbs brushed over my cheekbones and I let him comfort me, his calming aura enveloping us. "It's okay," he repeated. Then he was turning away from me again, facing the apartment and stepping through the open door.

I trailed behind him, not sure what was hidden behind this door. I hadn't prepared myself for this. From what little Noah had told me of this place, and the pain it caused him, I expected it to be dark, grimy, desolate. What I was met with completely shocked me. The last of the day's sun shone through the windows at the back of the room, which was painted a warm coral color, making the whole place look like it was on fire in the best way. Plush pillows invited you to sit on a huge couch in the living room to our right and a whole play area had been set up behind it, complete with a huge train set and Lego castles. The carpet squished softly beneath my feet as I followed Noah slowly into the room and took in all the pictures on the walls which were artfully placed. It was clear this place was a home.

"Noah…" I came up behind him again and wrapped my arms around his waist cautiously. He was stiff beneath my touch and didn't turn to face me. "It's beautiful."

I felt him take a deep breath and then he shifted so he could put his arm around me and tuck me into his side. "Yeah. Yeah, it is." The calm in his voice didn't reach his eyes and his muscles were still tense against me. It hurt that I had no idea what was going through his head. I had no idea how to make this any less painful, because to me this place was wonderful. He stepped out of my arms and made his way down a short hallway straight ahead. I watched as he paused at the first door and actually winced before turning the knob. He stood in the doorway a long time, his eyes screwed shut in pain, his jaw tight and I suddenly felt warm tears trickling down my cheeks. I had never seen another human shoulder so much pain so silently. He had been harboring this for years, on his own, never letting anyone else in. I couldn't imagine what that did to a person. I knew what it was like to relive a scene over and over again, but even I couldn't imagine what being in this place must have been putting him through. I watched as he stepped through the doorway to whatever room it was that was currently breaking his soul and I let out a quiet sob for him. I knew he needed to do this alone.

It was a long time before he came back to me. The sun had fully disappeared by now, the living room no longer looked like it was set on fire, and my sleeves were very much stretched out at this point because I hadn't been able to stop tugging on them since he had gone in that room. My dad would have snapped at me if he had seen me now, complaining that I was ruining my shirt. He used to hate when I tugged on my sleeves as a little girl, but I couldn't help it. I always needed to be doing something with my hands, especially when I was nervous.

"Hey…" Noah's voice was low, gravelly, and I startled out of the trance I had been in to see him crouching directly in front of me. His hand reached out and a thumb brushed across my cheekbone. "What's wrong? Are you okay? You've been crying."

I chuckled and it sounded watery, bogged down by the tears I had shed for him. Of course he would worry about me right now. When he had so many other things on his mind, he could still worry about me. It made me fall a little bit more in love with him. I leaned forward so both my hands could cradle his face with those beautiful dark blue eyes staring back at me, trying to find a way to fix me. All I wanted was to be able to fix *him*. I had no words for him right now. None of them would sound right. I wanted to tell him how amazing he was. How strong and caring and beautifully wounded he was, but I knew it wouldn't come out right. So instead, I leaned in to kiss him. I told him everything I needed to say without words, letting him know just how much I loved him. He kissed me back with everything he couldn't say, and I believed he loved me, too.

*****

"I'm sorry. About this afternoon. I'm sorry you had to see me like that." We were sitting on the bed of the hotel he had booked for us and despite the late hour and the absolutely mentally draining day we had, I felt wide awake.

I swiveled to face him more and reached out to place my hand against his cheek. "No. Never apologize for that, Noah. I want to see you. I want to see *all* of you. Please stop trying to hold back from me so much."

161

He gave me a soft smile and pulled me into his lap, wrapping his arms around my back and I laid my head against his chest. "I don't want to make your life any more difficult, but I fear I did that the moment I came into it."

I shook my head against him, but didn't look up. I was enjoying listening to the sound of his heart beating a steady rhythm against my ear too much. "It wasn't much of a life before you came into it. I want difficult with you so much more than wandering through life barely living."

He huffed against me, but one hand came up to stroke my hair lovingly. "You want to be crying in an apartment because I'm so messed up it's painful to watch?" His voice was so harsh it was almost unrecognizable. My heart hurt for him.

"I want to be there with you for all of life's messy moments. Because I know what it's like to have to go through the messy moments alone. I know what being alone is all too well." I looked up to stare in his eyes so he couldn't doubt me. "I don't want to be alone anymore."

He watched me for a long time, measuring my words, drinking me in with his eyes as if he was making a tough decision in his head. "I never want you to be alone. I'll never leave you alone, Carter. I can't."

His mouth met mine and he kissed me in a way I had never been kissed before. Soft and sweet and slow, but full of promise. My hands tangled in his hair and I tugged gently, causing him to groan in response. I wanted more from him. I wanted all of him. So when he shifted to lay me down and stared at me with eyes mixed with a question and desire, I nodded. He leaned back and I took the opportunity to pull his shirt over his head before quickly pulling his lips back to mine, my hands exploring every inch of his bare skin I could reach. I gasped when his lips traveled lower and he found his favorite spot on my neck to suckle while his hands started inching my sweater up higher and higher until he lifted off me so he could toss it somewhere far away from us. Instead of immediately coming back to me, he stayed sitting up while I lay panting beneath him.

"Carter..." He was breathing as hard as I was but I could see the internal struggle in his eyes. "I don't know..."

I sat up too, my arms snaking around his waist and pressing his bare skin to mine so that his eyes fluttered shut against his will. "I do." My lips closed over his chin and he let out another groan that caused me to grin, knowing I did that to him. Then I leaned forward and let my lips trail over his chest until his eyes flashed back open and he grabbed my upper arms, trapping them to my sides as he took control again and laid me down.

"You're sure?" he panted. "You're really sure you want to do this? You want me? As messed up as I am?"

"Noah...I love you." I had never meant something more than I meant those words. His lips crushed to mine, but only for a minute before they started traveling down, lower than they had ever gone so that I was squirming against him by the time his hands reached the button on my jeans. He looked up at me one last time with hooded eyes and I bit my lip and watched as he slowly began to peel them off me.

When he had finally finished pulling them off, I held my breath while he sat back for a moment taking me in. In books, the guy always says how perfect the girl looks. How her skin is a perfect, glimmering tan. How her legs go on for miles with not a single blemish. I, on the other hand, was far from flawless. I had scars marring my legs, my skin was a ghostly white color, I was nowhere close to the porcelain-looking girls most guys dreamed of. A part of me screamed to cover myself; to say I wasn't ready for this. Noah was too perfect. He was a Greek god in my eyes and I was just a simple girl, but before I could do anything he leaned down and his mouth met a long scar by my ankle. I gasped as I felt his tongue dart out and make its way across the length of it.

His voice was husky when he spoke. "What's this from?"

I could barely form the words with his lips still mere inches from my skin. "My brother and I were playing in the woods when I was five." I sucked in a quick breath as he feathered more kisses along the scar. "I was running to catch up to him and didn't see the old barbed-wire fence."

He kissed it once more, then dragged his tongue up my calf to the next oval-shaped scar. My eyes rolled back in my head, overwhelmed by his hands and mouth on me. "And this one?"

"On a trip to Africa with my parents. I was seven and wanted to play with the puppies. Except those aren't dogs you play with there. I'm sure he didn't mean to hurt me." The scene I was remembering in the dusty African village was immediately forgotten when Noah's lips sucked on the scar again before he leaned back and his fingers took the place of his mouth.

"So he knew just how amazing you taste." His words paired with that smirk in the semi-darkness caused me to squirm beneath him and my normal sarcastic snap back at him was lost in my throat. His eyes lifted from the scar to my face and he must have seen the need in my own eyes because a hungry look

164

came over his face in an instant. It caused all the air to rush out of me in a single plea.

"Noah," I hadn't even finished his name before he was crawling over me, his mouth colliding with mine. There was no more holding back between us, no more second-guessing. We had done that for far too long now.

Noah

If I had my way, we wouldn't have left the bed at all today. I hadn't gotten enough of Carter; I don't think I ever would. Holding back from her had been pointless. I had known that from the moment she came into my life, but that hadn't stopped me from at least trying. Last night I had crossed the biggest line when it came to a student-teacher relationship, yet I found it hard to even feel guilty about that. All I could feel right now was happiness. In a trip I thought would break me down, I was able to feel happiness and it was all thanks to the girl laying next to me now. I looked down at her head on my chest and felt my heart swell just seeing her there, remembering our night. Allowing myself to be loved by her when I had felt far from lovable.

My happiness grew when I crawled out of bed at the sound of someone knocking on our hotel room door and opened it to see Keaton. He immediately barreled into my legs, wrapping his little arms around me as much as he could. Sarah must have just gotten him a haircut, because it was much shorter, fluffier even, than the last time I had seen him. He looked like he had grown so much, though I knew it was just because I was so used to seeing him every day that going this long without him had felt like a lifetime. "Hey, little guy," I cooed, scooping him up in my arms as quickly as I could. I tossed him in the air before catching him again and crushing him to me. He was still giggling as I tucked him under my chin and his arms wrapped around my neck tightly.

"I'm not little any more though, right? I'm a big boy now. Auntie Sarah even got a big boy bed for me!"

His bright blue eyes were so full of excitement it made my heart feel completely full for the first time in a long time. "I saw! You *are* a big boy. You've gotten so big, it's crazy!" I saw a flash of his bedroom at the apartment again, but I quickly pushed it out of my mind to focus on him. It was so hard yesterday to walk in that room and see he was actually staying in it again, even if it was painted a baby blue color and toys littered the floor and his big boy bed looked extremely cozy and safe. I would never be able to erase the image of that room when I first found him there.

"I can count to ten now!" He immediately rattled off the numbers and I praised him extensively. "And I know my alphabet!" I set him down on his feet when he wriggled in my arms, even though I didn't really want to put any distance between us, and he sang out the alphabet as he wandered further into the hotel room.

"Hey." Sarah finally stepped forward to give me a huge smile and pulled me in for a long hug. "You look good, kid." She was half a foot shorter than me, but she still reached up to ruffle my hair as if I were a child.

"You, too," I commented as I held her at arm's length. "You look happy."

She smiled even bigger. "I am happy. Spending the holiday with Sean's family was great. Keaton loved them. I'm even more excited to extend my holiday with you, though. And Carter?" She craned her head to look further into the room.

I had called her to let her know that I would be bringing Carter with me, and instead of being shocked or disapproving of my continued relationship with a student, she had been happy for me. She couldn't wait to see Carter again. I guess they had really hit it off when she had handed Keaton off to Carter to watch in October. "Yes, Carter was still asleep…" I trailed off when I heard Keaton's voice coming from around the corner.

"Hey! You're the girl with boy name! Carter!" I hurried to catch up with him, very clearly remembering that Carter had not exactly been fully clothed when I had left her in bed. When I came around the corner though, she was sitting up on the edge of the bed in my long-sleeved shirt that had been tossed haphazardly on the floor the night before and her jeans that I distinctly remembered dragging down her legs last night. Remembering that brought a smile to my face immediately and I had to mentally shake myself. My child was in the room; I needed to get my mind out of the gutter.

"Keaton! How have you been, buddy?"

"I've been good. Guess what? I have a whole other Lego set here and I've been waiting for you to visit because you are the best Lego builder and I need your help. So we should go do that. You *are* coming over, right? I mean, you're here in New York, so you must be coming to visit me." I loved the sound of his voice, I had missed it so much. Of course, he still had trouble saying some words, but he had gotten so much more talkative since this summer. He was growing so fast. I also loved the way Carter was smiling at him right now.

"Oh my goodness. I don't know about that, you goon. I think *you're* the best Lego builder I know, but it would be an honor to help you build some more. And as a matter of fact, I am coming over to visit you because we missed you *so* much." She reached out to tickle his sides and he giggled, squirming away from her hands. She laughed along with him and it was the most beautiful sound in the world, the combination of her tinkling laugh and his little giggle. He turned and ran back to my side, pulling on my hand so that I squatted down to be on eye-level with him.

"Me and Carter need to go play Legos now. Come on, Noah. You play, too. Let's go." He took my hand in his fingers and pulled me over to where Carter was sitting before taking her hand and tugging her up. "Let's go, Auntie Sarah. I need to bring them to my Legos."

Sarah laughed at his antics before scooping him up from between Carter and I. "Not so fast, small fry. I have some plans of my own, you know." She tapped his nose and he made a face, reaching for me instead. Sarah rolled her eyes at his preference, but handed him over to me and I pulled him close. "So I was thinking, you and Keaton spend the day together. You deserve it." She smiled at me and I attempted to convey just how grateful I was for her in a look. She had no idea how much this meant to be. No matter how much I had been distracting myself, not having Keaton with me at all times always felt like I was walking around with half a heart. "Me and Carter can take the day, go shopping, have some girl time. Then meet back at the apartment around five for dinner and presents? Does that sound okay?"

I looked at Carter, asking with my eyes if she was okay with that. It wasn't exactly what she had been anticipating, I was sure. A day alone with my always over-exuberant sister. I wouldn't even be near her to make her feel comfortable, and I knew just how closed-off she always was, even if she had never been that way with me. This would be completely out of her comfort zone. "I don't know, Sarah...Maybe we can all do something-"

"Oh, no! That sounds like fun! I would love to go shopping with you, Sarah," Carter gushed. I could tell from her overly sweet tone that she was less than thrilled by this arrangement, but I didn't know why she was going with it.

"Great! Well, I'll let you guys get ready. Keaton and I will be down in the lobby waiting for you. Come on, Keaton." I set him down and he dragged his feet over to Sarah with a pout.

"But I wanna play Legos…"

"Hey, little man I'll tell you what. Why don't me and you go ice skating today? And then tonight we can play Legos. How does that sound?"

His face immediately lit up. "Really?"

"Really. But you have to go with Auntie Sarah for now, okay?" At my words, he all but sprinted out of the hotel room with Sarah following behind him chuckling. When the door slammed shut behind them, I turned to Carter. She had her back to me and was pulling my shirt over her head, reaching for her bra. The sight of her bare skin had me itching to wrap my arms around her and bring her back to bed, but I knew we had no time. Plus, I needed to figure out what the hell she was doing agreeing to Sarah's plan.

"So what was all that about?" I followed her lead in getting dressed for the day and unzipped my suitcase at the end of the bed, pulling out a clean sweater. She turned to face me after she had clasped her bra and I fought to keep my breathing steady.

"What do you mean?" Her hand brushed mine as she reached for her own sweater and I saw the skin on her arm erupt in goosebumps as soon as we touched.

"You didn't have to do that. I know you don't want to go wandering around a city with a person you barely know. I won't even be there to be your support system."

She took her time watching me pull my jeans up and slip my belt through the loops and I smirked as I caught her staring. Her cheeks blushed and she pulled her sweater over her head to hide her face for a moment. "Noah, that's your sister. I want to know her. More than anything, I want you to have the time you deserve with Keaton. If that means I need to learn how to be a more open person, well that's something I deserve, too."

After yesterday and how she had been there for me. After last night and how she had loved me in spite of it all. After this morning and seeing how she was with Keaton. And after this, hearing how much she loved me that she was willing to put herself in what was an uncomfortable position because she knew how much time with that little boy meant to me...well after all this, I was so close to letting it all go. Letting her know just how much I felt for her. Yet for some reason, I couldn't bring myself to say those words. I wasn't even sure why I couldn't, so I just let myself feel it. And I let Carter feel it too when I pulled her into my arms and kissed her deeply. "Thank you," I whispered against her lips.

My day with Keaton had been perfect. It was everything I needed and for the first time in a long time, I felt so full of hope. Hope that everything would work out. Somehow, this would all work out. I could somehow manage to have a life with Carter and Keaton in it, because I had never been happier than I was right now.

We went ice skating at Rockefeller Center, then grabbed a hot chocolate and watched different people rushing back and forth on the cold sidewalks. It was a thing we always used to do when I would bring him to campus for classes with me. Whenever we would sit to eat at one of the school cafes, or we'd be sitting before class, I would make up different stories about the different people that passed by us. Different lives that we would never know, but we could speculate on and make up. Now, he was old enough to make up his own stories about the different passersby. It made our old pastime that much more exciting. So far, he had told me about a man whose sister had made him eat dog food for breakfast as a joke and that's why he had looked so cranky, a girl whose mom had accidentally let her pet goose escape and that's why she was in such a rush, and an old man who had lost his rocking chair.

We had also made a stop into a huge toy store, where I told him he could pick out anything he wanted. He had immediately dragged us to the Lego section and picked out a huge Star Wars set. The box was almost bigger than him, but he insisted on being the one to drag it up to the counter for the cashier to ring up. In between, he told me all about life in New York. He was absolutely loving it. Sarah had enrolled him in preschool here and he had all sorts of new friends, but he said his best friend was a boy named Quinn. He also complained about a girl named Nikki who apparently never left him alone and had these stupid braids in her hair every day. I chuckled at how upset he was by the way she wore her hair and told him that sometimes girls that didn't leave him alone were a good thing. Carter refused to leave me alone, and I wasn't sure where I'd be if she had just given up on me a long time ago. I'd be a lot more miserable, that's for sure. All I would have been focused on was the fact that I was missing Keaton this whole year. Instead, she had reminded me how great life truly was, even though it could get messy. It hurt a little that Keaton loved New York so much. I wished he had missed me like I missed him, but at the same time all I ever wanted was for him to be happy. If he could be happy here, that's all that mattered for now.

Sarah and Carter were already at the apartment when we arrived and Sean was just finishing up dinner. Walking into this place was still extremely difficult, but I had to pretend I was unfazed for Keaton's sake. He wouldn't understand if I had a breakdown, and I never wanted him to have to understand. That was a pain I never wanted him to know. I was so focused on trying to hold myself together in front of him that I didn't even notice Carter come up to wrap her arms around me and lean her head on my chest. I pulled her to me like she was a life raft and I was sinking under the waves. I wasn't even able to notice that sadness that was buried in the deep green of her eyes, didn't pick up on the worried glances she kept tossing my way all through dinner, couldn't see that something about her day with Sarah had changed her in some way. The difference in her went completely unnoticed by me and she never went into detail about her and Sarah's day, even long after we had returned home from the city.

FEBRUARY
Carter

"How long have you lived here?"

"Since my sophomore year of college. Why?"

I sat up from where I was lounging on the couch and took in all the walls around us. White. Every single one of them was white. I watched from the corner of my eye as he put down the essay he had been grading while chewing on his pen and frowned at me. "Why do you have that look on your face?" he asked.

I turned and faced him, unable to hide my smile. "What look?" I asked innocently.

"The one where you're judging something. Like when I order bacon with pancakes."

I made a face. "Hate to break it to you, but bacon still doesn't go with pancakes."

"Bacon goes with everything," he deadpanned. I laughed and shook my head, knowing he could not be swayed. "So what is it that you're judging now?"

"Nothing..."

"Except?"

"Your walls are white."

He wrinkled his nose and glanced around us. "You're judging my walls right now?"

"And your door a little..." I admitted. His eyes flitted to the door of the apartment with its shabby black paint. Before he could get offended, I hurried on. "I'm just saying...you've lived here for that long and you're still living in a white-washed apartment. It reminds me of a hospital, that's all." And I had seen my fair share of hospitals. Enough to know I liked to stay away from them. They reminded me of the days after Johnny's accident. When I was the only one who actually sat with him or tried to talk

174

to him. His parents simply followed doctors around demanding answers. They were often accompanied by some man in a dark suit. I never fully understood who he was or why he was around. Mariah never once came. Not when he was in the hospital, not when he got transferred to the rehabilitation center. I ground my teeth at the thought but pulled myself together enough to focus back on Noah.

"Right, right. No big deal. My home just reminds you of a hospital." I wondered if he had the same negative thoughts towards them as I did, only with his sister in the bed and not Johnny. "I think my bedroom is painted."

"Your bedroom is grey," I replied disdainfully.

"What's wrong with grey? It matches everything."

I shrugged my shoulders. "Not exactly cheery."

"Why would you want a bright bedroom? It's where you sleep."

I pursed my lips at him. He had a point. "The guest room isn't even painted. Keaton stays in there."

"So?"

"So, he's a kid. Kids like fun rooms."

"You're an expert on kids now?" He raised his eyebrows in a playful challenge. I didn't respond, just leveled him with an unamused look which caused him to laugh. The sound caused a soft smile to come to my face.

"All I'm saying is you need some life in here." I laid back down with my head in his lap and he gazed down at me steadily. I wasn't so scared of his stare anymore. I wasn't scared to lay myself bare for him. Especially when his eyes were this color, a pale blue today. It wasn't a color I saw often.

"You want to paint my apartment?"

"Can we?" I knew my entire face had lit up but he only smiled.

"I'm not painting the whole apartment. Not in winter when I can't even open the windows to air it out." My face fell and his long fingers reached out to stroke from my temple down my chin and my eyelids fluttered at his touch. "But I think the kitchen could use a different look."

"Really?" I sat up again in my excitement. He laughed and pulled me to him so I was sitting in his lap facing him.

"Why do you want to paint so much?"

I sighed and rested my cheek against his shoulder because it was always easier to talk if I wasn't so distracted by simply looking at him. There were a few reasons. I hadn't painted anything in so long, it was another of the things I had lost interest in over the past years. "My brother used to love it. You know how most people paint a room but then leave it like that for the next ten years?"

He rested his chin on top of my head so I felt it when he talked. "Yes, as you can see I'm one of those people." I barely heard the chuckle he let out, but could feel the vibrations of his chest against mine.

I smiled and continued. "Well, he was never like that. Every year, his room was something different. It wasn't just one color, either. No, he'd make entire landscapes. You felt like you were in the Caribbean by how well he painted it one year. The next year, you'd be on top of Mount Everest. Then on a ledge at the Grand Canyon. I have no idea where he got that talent from. It was absolutely incredible. I'm sure it still is. His whole house is probably like that in Utah.

"He would paint my room for me, too. Anything I wanted. He even let me help, though I was probably messing it up more than helping. I got the easy job, like the base color. We always had a base color. Most times it was blue for the sky, but not always. That's what I got to help with, just painting on the base color like you would with a normal room. Then he would add everything that would make it come to life."

"Sounds amazing." Noah's fingers weaved through my hair as I talked and I sunk into him more.

"It was. I would sit there for hours, just watching him. Maybe that's why I like to watch you cook." I pulled back enough to look at him and smiled. "That's kind of like art. I always wished I had something like that. A skill. Something I excelled at."

"Carter, you're good at so many little things. And I've seen your pictures. They're breathtaking."

I made a face and leaned against him again, talking before he could argue with me further about my so-called talents. "I think the painting was actually the reason I got into photography in the first place. He could take a picture and paint the world from it. I wanted to actually see the world and take a picture of it to keep with me."

"I wish I knew your brother," he whispered after we had stayed silent for some time.

"Come with me to Utah," I blurted without thinking.

"What?"

I sat up straight to watch his face. Already, I could see some of his walls coming up, closing me off. I hurried on before he could completely shut me out. "After graduation. You won't be working. It's just me going. We'd be okay then."

"Slow down, Cub."

"Why not?"

"Let's not talk about this right now." I could feel just how tense he was against me. Sometimes I felt good. I felt great even. I knew he loved me, even if he wouldn't say it. But then there were times like this. Where he would shut down and I didn't know who he was anymore. I didn't know what would happen with us.

"Why can't we? Why do we never talk about it? Any of it?"

His arms left their spot wrapped around my waist so one hand could brush through his hair and he looked away from me. "Because if we do I'll be reminded of how messed up this is." I flinched away from him at his words, curling into the opposite end of the couch. His eyes reflected the hurt I was feeling as he looked back at me, across the space I had put between us. His hand skimmed over his jaw, which was clenched tight. Finally, he spoke again in a low voice as if he was speaking to a wounded animal. It was a tone I knew well, but hadn't heard in quite some time. "Cub...I didn't mean that."

"Yes, you did," I snapped.

"It's just not easy, that's all. That's all I meant by that." I eyed him warily. "Come here." He held his hand out to me and the childish part of me wanted to fold my arms over my chest and stay far away. The me from the past five years wanted to put up more walls because I was suddenly terrified of how close I was allowing myself to get to him. Instead, I silenced both those parts and took his hand, letting him pull me back into position in his lap. I was learning to trust. Even if it did get me hurt.

He took my hands and placed them on his shoulders, then held me by the waist again. "I'm sorry."

My fingers skimmed over the silky feel of his dress shirt he still had on from class today. It was untucked now, the tie shoved in his bag long ago, the top two buttons opened so I could see the white cotton of the shirt he wore underneath. He made it hard to concentrate and he didn't even try. "But you won't come to Utah with me."

He sighed. "We'll see when the time comes."

I bit the inside of my cheek but chose to pick my battles. I knew when he was done giving out information. This was one of those times. So instead of pushing further, I trailed my fingers from his shoulders down to the next button on his shirt and toyed with it, popping it out and buttoning it back up. His hands slid up my sides until he tipped my chin up and forced me to look at him again, but by now I had tucked my disappointment away.

"I'll talk to the landlord in the morning. To make sure we can paint. Okay?"

I nodded and stood, picking up my coat from the chair. He trailed after me to the door. "Hey..." I turned before I pulled open the door. "I'm sorry."

"Don't worry about it."

His eyes smoldered and the face he made at me told me he didn't believe my words, but he let it go anyways. "I'll see you tomorrow?"

"Yeah." My hand came down on the doorknob, but he grabbed my hips and turned me to face him.

"Carter..." he breathed, as if saying my name pained him. As if being this close to me could burn him. But it was a burn he wanted. His lips pressed to mine and there was nothing sweet about it. It was raw and consuming and in a matter of seconds I couldn't tell what was up and what was down and what body parts were mine and what were his. Finally, when I didn't think I could take any more, he nipped my bottom lip and slowed, bringing us down from a high, giving me a taste of sweet. He set me back on my feet and I realized the whole time, he must have been holding me up. Then he took a step back, letting his fingers trail down my arm until he no longer had a hold on me and I felt completely bereft.

He smirked at me as I blinked, trying and failing to ground myself again. I hated how he knew how worked up he got me and yet he always seemed completely unaffected by me. It was unfair. "Goodnight, Carter."

I lifted one hand up to touch my swollen lips and his eyes sparked in amusement. "Night," I whispered and slipped out into the hall.

*****

"I'm just confused, that's all." We still hadn't talked about the other day. We were pretty good at that; finding ways to distract ourselves from the truth of our situation. So for now I kicked my feet back and forth from my perch on the counter and watched as paint from his brush dripped onto the ripped pair of jeans he was wearing. I had never seen him in them before, but from the way they were hanging off his hips, I wasn't complaining.

"It needed something different. You're the one who said that."

"You're painting it a very pale yellow... How much different from white did you want?"

He turned from scrutinizing the wall and gave me a halfhearted glare. I smiled back cheerily. "There's gonna be stuff. Once I'm done. You'll see."

I hopped down from the counter and slowly came up behind him. I leaned my chin on his shoulder to see the wall from his point of view. When I had come over the other day, the kitchen had pails of paint sitting on the floor already, the whole area draped in sheets to prevent any spills. It was his way of apologizing for his reaction to me wanting him to come to Utah, and I accepted it. Although his choice had been such a pale color that I was a bit disappointed. My disappointment didn't last for long though, because I had found that watching him while he worked was rewarding enough for me. It wasn't long before I had put down my own paint brush in favor of the lovely view I had from the counter.

Now, I turned my head to whisper in his ear. "I think it looks great so far. Maybe you should take a break." My hands came up to wrap around his abdomen and carefully unfastened the lowest button on his flannel shirt. Then I pulled back enough to place a careful kiss right between his shoulder blades. When I lifted on tiptoes to trail kisses further up his spine all the way to the base of his neck, I heard the air hiss out from his clenched teeth.

"How attached are you to that shirt?" He spit out the next second.

I paused my suckling on his throat to give him a quizzical look. I was wearing a plain black long sleeve, nothing special. "Uhm..."

Suddenly his hands were on me, pulling me around so I was in front of him, my back pressed against his chest as his hands pulled my hips back into his. I now knew why he asked as yellow hand prints marked my upper arms and hips. My head fell back against his shoulder and I groaned as his lips found their way along my throat to my collarbone. His paint ridden hands made their way from my hips up my stomach, painting a vibrant trail in their wake. "Noah..." I whimpered.

"The jeans..." He murmured back. I was happy to hear he was as out of breath as I was. "How much do you like the jeans?"

"I could use a new pair." I panted.

Just like that I was spun again, my back slamming into the freshly painted wall as he caged me in, his lips starting a new assault on my skin.

At first I was so surprised by the new, unforgiving surface of the wall on my back and the way his body was pressing into mine, that all I could do was surrender to him. I moaned as his hips ground into my own and he nipped the column of my throat, which I knew by now was his favorite part of my skin. His hands were under my shirt now, the sticky paint helping them slip up my body to my bra, where he traced over the cups lightly as I arched into him. His fingers moved around to find the clasp and he paused in question. "Yes." I practically begged. In the next second, it was unclasped and my shirt went flying over my head. His hands were everywhere, exploring and kneading and driving me insane so that I was rocking into him without even knowing what I was doing.

Finally, I gained enough control to realize I was at a total disadvantage. He still had on way too many layers of clothing. My fingers made quick work of the buttons on his flannel and I slid it off over his biceps. He ripped his t-shirt off in the next second and my time on the offensive was over. My back went slamming into the wall again, the paint squishing satisfyingly behind me and making it easy to slide over. When his mouth left mine to travel lower, I sank my teeth lightly into his shoulder.

"Jesus, Carter." He moaned, every muscle tightening against me. My hands were already traveling lower, finding their way to the button of his jeans and freeing it. His hands caught mine and held them captive in the next instant, preventing me from making any further moves.

"No." He panted. "Not like this. We can't." He was having trouble stringing words together and I reached forward to kiss his chest right over his heart. "Jesus." He repeated, his head dropping to my shoulder.

"Yes. We can." I whispered as I kissed my way further down his washboard abs. We had done slow and sweet that first time. It was amazing. But I needed him. I needed him now.

I woke up with a start and immediately panicked. Something was touching me. Wrapped around me. But then I realized it was just Noah and I couldn't say if he was the one wrapped around me or if I was wrapped around him. One of my legs was tucked between his, one arm thrown over his stomach while his arms held me tight, as if his muscles never relaxed, not even in sleep.

I remembered what Keaton had said about him never sleeping and I wondered if it was true. I thought I knew why he was the way he was. Why he was so responsible, uptight, reserved. He had to raise Keaton and he didn't need anyone's judging eyes on him. But there was something else. There was a fear in him and I hated how I couldn't erase it.

For now, I wiggled out of his grasp and stood at the foot of the bed gazing down at him. He was perfect. So much more perfect than I would ever be and I wondered how in the world I had gained his attention. How was I the one he would risk everything for? Because wasn't that what we were doing? Risking everything?

I was so stupid. I had fallen for a teacher. Never once did I think it was wrong or disgusting, though. Despite what I had known my whole life, this wasn't wrong. Nothing that felt this good could be wrong. It wasn't that I was worried about. I was worried that if anything ever got out, it would destroy Noah's career. It would destroy his chance to get Keaton back, and there was no way I could live with myself if that ever happened.

Instead of focusing on all the bad that could be thought of in our situation, I grinned as I took in the yellow spattered all over him. Flecks in his hair, streaks across his biceps. Even the sheets had their fair share of yellow because Noah had insisted we were more civilized and had brought me to bed yesterday afternoon rather than keeping me pinned to the newly painted wall.

I slowly backed out of his room and pulled the door closed behind me. Even the knob was covered in yellow paint that flaked off under my hand. I made my way over to the bookshelves in the corner of his living room by his desk. I vaguely wondered how someone so young could have so many books, but I didn't stop too long to read every title. Just enough to know they were the classics with authors such as Defoe, Swift, Dickens, and Brontë. Then I went to stand by the window on the other side of his desk. It looked out over the river, the streetlights reflecting off the quick water and casting a warm glow on everything despite the snow that coated the walkways. I trailed my fingers over the glass, feeling the cold bite into them before I pulled Noah's sweatshirt around me tighter.

He had two frames on his desk. One of Keaton smiling over his shoulder at the camera while he held a fishing pole that was bigger than him. Another was of Noah with his arm thrown over the shoulders of a girl who looked so much like him I had no doubt it was Kelly. But this wasn't the Kelly I had met in the mental ward. This girl was gorgeous. Obviously, I should have known she would be gorgeous. She had been a model after all. But this...this was just breathtaking. She wasn't so skinny it was disheartening like too many models were. She didn't have an air that she was looking down on anyone, no hint of superiority was in the picture at all. She just looked free. Alive. She looked like everything I always wanted to be but never had been. She looked like Noah in those rare moments he let me see when he let go of everything. I wondered if this was how they had always been. Back before she moved to New York. Before drugs and Keaton and mental hospitals. I wondered if she would ever be that girl in the picture again. I wondered if he would ever be that guy again. From what I had seen myself and heard from Noah, I somehow doubted it.

My stomach growled, jolting me from my thoughts and I remembered why I had originally wanted to get up. I wandered back to the kitchen, which was in shambles. The paint can was still open and I smiled before stooping to replace the lid on it. Then I laughed quietly at the mess we had made of that one wall. Good thing the fridge would be hiding that terrible paint job once it went back into place when the paint was dry. For now, it was sitting in the middle of the kitchen so I found my pie I had brought right where I left it, completely forgotten. He had liked the pie I had made for Thanksgiving so much, I had decided to make another one for Valentine's Day. We clearly hadn't gotten around to eating it yesterday.

I didn't want to go opening and closing all his drawers in an effort to find a fork, so instead I picked off a piece of the crust with my fingers and bit into it. Then I continued picking pieces off until I could get into the actual apple slices. I was just licking the cinnamon-sugar goo off my fingers when I felt Noah wrap his arms around me from behind.

"You do know I own these things called plates. And forks." He whispered in my ear. I only stuck out my tongue at him before swirling my finger in the goo again and wiping it across his neck. He jerked back in response, but I stepped forward before he could wipe it away and licked it off slowly. He rewarded me with a deep groan before pulling my lips to his. How many times had I kissed Noah? Yet he still managed to take my breath away every time. There were no words. I completely lost myself.

"On second thought," he breathed when he had finally pulled away from me again. "I hate forks. Plates are overrated, too." I giggled and before I could react, he had scooped me up and sat me on the counter next to the pie plate, settling himself between my legs so that we were eye-to-eye. "I'm so happy you made me another pie," he murmured, tugging the pie closer towards us.

I watched as he dipped his long fingers into the pie, carefully plucking out one of the apple slices and biting into it. I watched his lips close around it and his eyes drift shut in pleasure. Once he swallowed, he gazed back at me with happy eyes. "And you said I'm the better cook out of the two of us?"

"Pie's about the only thing I know how to make."

"Is that why you always smell like apples and cinnamon?" he asked casually before reaching for another apple slice.

"I smell like apples and cinnamon?" I snatched the apple slice out of his hand just as he went to place it in his mouth and he scowled at me. I couldn't help but smile as I swallowed. Then he pulled me to him again, exploring my mouth with his tongue before pulling away all too soon and giving me an all-knowing smirk.

"You taste like it, too," he admitted, causing a blush to heat my cheeks immediately. "Always. Not because you stole my apple just now." I couldn't help but laugh and he smiled as he watched me. His eyes didn't scare me now. He didn't intimidate me anymore. Not like this. Not when it was just us.

"Noah?"

"Mmm?" He popped another apple slice in his mouth.

"Kelly...do you think she'll ever be like the girl in that picture you have again?"

Noah

Suddenly the apple didn't taste so sweet anymore. I finished chewing slowly while I studied her, wondering where this was coming from. "What do you mean?"

"I was just looking around when I got up and I saw that picture of the two of you on your desk…it's not the same person anymore. I hardly recognized her."

I was caught off guard. She hardly recognized her? She had nothing to compare Kelly to. The only thing she should have got from that picture was that Kelly was gorgeous and we shared quite a few of the same features. "What do you mean, it's not the same person anymore? You wouldn't know."

Her eyes grew large in the glow from the light over the kitchen stove and I saw the panic there. Panic that I had caught her in something. It made me sick to my stomach. "I know." Her voice was so small I knew she had done something wrong. She knew it, too. I backed away from her, putting space between me and the counter I had placed her on. "Noah…"

"What did you do?"

"I just wanted to understand." She hopped down from the counter and tried to take a step towards me again. I just retreated further, distancing myself. I didn't know what was standing in front of me anymore.

"Carter, what did you do?" I demanded. It was a voice I had never used on her before and I saw its immediate effect. She recoiled from the anger laced through it and a part of me was glad because she stopped trying to get close to me. I didn't want her touch distracting me.

Her eyes dipped down to the floor, the tiles still covered in old rags to protect it from dripping paint. She couldn't even look at me when she spoke. "I went to see Kelly."

Immediately, I sucked in a sharp breath. Shock; complete shock. And betrayal. How could she? When she knew I had never even been back there since it all happened. Questions swirled in my head and I could barely focus long enough to figure out what I wanted to know first.

"When?"

Carter's green eyes flashed up to meet me, trying to read whatever emotion was on my face. I knew it was completely blank though, I was too good at hiding what I felt. That was confirmed when I saw her face fall, unable to guess what was going on in my head. "After New Year's. When Sarah and I went shopping. We also stopped at the institute."

My head spun. After New Year's? When I was in a state of bliss that I had finally found someone who saw all of me and accepted it, who let me see all of them, she was secretly doing something she knew would upset me? How could she do that after the day we had spent together? After that *night*? The betrayal I had felt inklings of grew to a steady burn now. "Why?" My voice cracked on the way out and I hated it for that, I hated showing even a hint of weakness. "Why would you do that?" Now it sounded angry again, I saw her blink back tears at the harsh tone.

"I thought I could help. I thought if I could understand better, I could help you more. That she could want to see Keaton. If I told her how well you both were doing." Her words tumbled over each other in a rush to get out. To convince me this had been a good idea.

I turned my back on her and my hand raked through my already messed up hair, catching on paint that had dried there and I was immediately reminded of how different things had been in this kitchen less than 24 hours ago. "Keaton is *never* going to that place. Ever." I demanded. I whipped around to face her again, made sure she could see the resolve in my eyes. I apparently hadn't been clear enough before when it came to anything relating to Kelly. "Do you understand me?"

"Yes." Her voice was barely audible and her lower lip trembled.

"No. Do you really understand me? Are you listening to what I'm saying? You don't get to decide anything about Keaton's relationship with his mother."

"I didn't mean that. I wasn't deciding anything!" Her teeth ground together as she learned to stand her ground with me. "I needed to see the situation for myself. So I could fully understand. And tell you that she needs you!"

"Shut up." I didn't shout. I didn't need to, the calm in my voice did more to silence her than any yell could. "Shut up right now. You don't know anything. Don't try to tell me that because you saw her for...what? One visiting hour? That you know more than I do. That you know what can fix her. Nothing can fix her, Carter! Don't you understand? I've made peace with that and you're trying to tear that apart."

"That's not true. That's not what I meant to do." Her voice was so small it didn't sound like her. I couldn't look at her now. I didn't want to see her now.

"Just go back to bed, Carter. Please." I couldn't have this fight now. I didn't have it in me to even know what to say. I heard her footsteps begin to retreat slowly before she paused. I didn't turn around to see why she waited and after another second I heard her finally leave and my bedroom door close.

Immediately, I crouched down with my head cradled in my hands. I didn't trust my legs to hold me up much longer as all the images from being back at that apartment resurfaced. When I had been there last month, it took everything in me to block out images of Kelly. It was bad enough I kept picturing what that place looked like the last time I was there; what Keaton had looked like there. His room had completely ruined me the day Carter and I had gone there alone. But I had handled it. I handled it because I hadn't thought about my sister at all. My hero. I refused to even go down that hallway further than Keaton's room the whole time I was there. I didn't want to see that again.

Yet here I was, crouched on my cold kitchen floor in the middle of February and I could have sworn it was late June in New York City and I was cautiously tip-toeing through the squalor of the dark hallway.

My hair was way too long, it was sticking to the back of my neck in the summer heat. I didn't pay any attention to the first closed door in the hallway. Kelly never used that room, it was like a closet. "Kel?" I called out, but there was still no answer. I wondered if she was even here. "Kelly, it's me. Noah. I swear to God, if you pop out and scare me like this is some way over the top joke I'm going to kill you. I'm hungover and not in the mood after that train ride." A nineteen-year-old me reached the last door in the short hallway and it was open a crack. "You better not be in there with a guy, because if I walk in on my sister having sex I'm going to be scarred for life." No one answered, so I pushed the door open.

The smell hit me first and I vomited. "What the hell, Kelly." I looked up again and my eyes adjusted to the dark of the room, almost complete blackness from the thick curtains that were hung over the huge windows on the back wall. That's when I saw her. Spread out on her side across the king-sized bed in an absolute mess. She was wearing only a bra and panties, her hair was matted to the side of her head thickly, as if it hadn't seen a brush in weeks. Her skin was so pale it looked almost translucent and all the bones were clearly visible, in her wrists, her cheeks, her shoulders. She looked like a living skeleton. And then her eyes opened and I swear they took up half her face, the size of saucers, void of all color and emotion. I stumbled back and hit the wall, buckling over so that my hands met my knees, but my eyes stayed fixed on hers. It was almost impossible to look away. The skeleton that had replaced my sister, my hero, opened her mouth, but no sound came out. I gasped, tasting salt from what must have been my own tears running down my face. I knew I needed to do something but I had no idea what. Her mouth gaped wide again, but still no noise reached my ears. I finally tore my gaze from her and focused on taking deep breaths in and out.

This wasn't real. This was just some awful, drunken nightmare. I really needed to lay off the drinking. I was going to wake up and stumble to Keith's dorm and he would be sitting there laughing his ass off when I told him about my weird dream. We'd both get a good kick out of it and then we'd drink some Gatorade and plan the next night's shenanigans. Right. This was a dream. So just wake up. Come on, Noah. *Wake. Up.*

Then I heard my name and my head snapped up so fast it hurt. The sound of it gutted me, like I was hearing nails on a chalkboard. I never wanted to hear that sound again. But then the skeleton spoke once more. "Noah," it croaked. This was no nightmare.

That was enough to snap me out of my frozen state. I needed to do something. *Now.*

"Shit, Kel. Shit, shit, *shit.*" I stepped forward, over wads of clothes and God knows what. "What have you done." I side-stepped a pool of what I thought was vomit and almost emptied my stomach again. "Okay, this is okay. It's okay." I gagged and swallowed hard the closer I got, my eyes scanning the room for something that could help me. "It's okay. I'm going to help you. I've got you now."

I stood in front of the bed, my arms outstretched, but if truth be told I was scared to touch her. *Clothes.* I thought. She needed clothes. I turned around and located the door to her closet, making my way over there in search of some clean clothes. I found a pair of shorts and a sweatshirt, which I grabbed even though it was ninety degrees out. She could use the extra padding. Then I hurried back to her and braced myself before pulling the clothes on her. I felt like I was dealing with a wild animal, I had no idea who she was. *What* she was. "What have you done, Kel?" I asked again, knowing she wouldn't answer. "What have you done?"

As gently as I could, I leaned over and scooped her up. It was like picking up our old barn cat, Simon. That's how much she weighed. If it was at all possible, my heart broke a little more. I swear I was going to break her just by holding her, she was so frail. I hadn't known I was still crying until I watched my tears splash down onto her face, which was still staring straight up at me. My tears cut lines through the grime on her face and I coughed to cover up the fact that I was gagging at the sight. Her eyes were still the size of saucers, pits of despair, so I looked away from them fast. I felt like if I looked too long, she could suck out my soul too, because it was clear hers had left her. A sob cut through me as I edged my way back into the hall of the apartment.

It was cleaner out here, the air not so putrid. There were less piles of grime that I had to step over while I carried her towards the door as quickly as I could. I needed to get her out of here. Far away from this place. We would never come back. Ever. I had almost reached the door when the skeleton finally moved. The bones in her hand wrapped around my wrist and I gasped, almost dropping her. When I dared to look back at her she was looking at me so intently I couldn't breathe. "Kel, what's wrong?" *What wasn't wrong?* I thought to myself.

"Save him," the skeleton croaked.

"What?" I gasped. *Him? Who the hell was he?*

"Keaton," the thing in my arms gasped, the voice of nails on a chalkboard ripping me to shreds. "Save him, not me."

"Who is he, Kelly?" The creature's saucer eyes were beginning to shut again and I was scared they would never open again. "No, no, no, Kelly. No. Just tell me who he is. Where is he, Kel? I'll save him. Whoever he is, I'll save him. I promise." She didn't answer but the bones that had been clutching my wrist released and she pointed over my shoulder. I swiveled to look and found that she was pointing at the first door in the hallway. I knew before I even went that whatever I was going to walk into in that room would not be good. It would completely wreck me, more than this whole trip had. That room would destroy me. I knew it before I started to ease the skeleton of my sister down to the floor, resting her bones against the door so I could complete her request. I would save him.

"I'll be right back, okay? Just stay with me, okay? I'll be back with him. I'll save him. Then we'll all leave, okay? It's okay...it's okay."

I was still muttering that over and over to myself when I finally pulled myself from my memories and realized I was still crouched on the kitchen floor, my head still in my hands. "It's okay...It's okay...It's okay..." I repeated to myself over and over again. I sat on the cold tiles for quite some time, long enough to see that the grey morning light of winter was beginning to creep into the apartment. A chickadee called out in the cold air beyond the window and I looked up to watch a few snowflakes drift past. I finally lifted myself, stepping around the mess left behind from painting, and made my way as quietly as I could back to the bedroom. I didn't even look at the bed, not wanting to see Carter. I didn't want to look at the face that I had trusted and feel any more betrayal in my life. My eyes stayed focused on the carpet as I shuffled over to the closet and pulled on some jeans and a worn-out long sleeve.

I didn't bother leaving a note, just shoved my wallet and keys in the pocket of my coat and left. Snow fell soft on my head as soon as I stepped outside. My steps hitched, but I turned away from my car in favor of the path by the river. Enough snow was coating the sidewalk already that I left a trail as I picked my way down the route I used to take every day to get to campus. It was still early, no one was out and with the snow falling, everything was hushed so that the whole world sat silent. I both welcomed the quiet and despised it. With everything in my life, I had grown accustomed to chaos so when the world went quiet, it was disconcerting to me.

Without even realizing it, my feet had taken me to the soccer field on the outskirts of campus. I hadn't been back here in quite some time, but I still knew the way without even having to think about it. What felt like lifetimes ago, I had chosen this college for one thing really and it didn't have anything to do with its teaching program. My freshman year, I was on the starting lineup for the soccer team, something that was unheard of, and I loved every second of it. Of course, that was the first sacrifice I made after taking in Keaton. Six in the morning practices were replaced by six a.m. diaper changes. I took a seat on one of the home benches and stared out at the field, thinking of just how different my life could have been if I never got that call from Kelly's manager. If it really all had been a weird dream that day.

"What's up, lover boy?" I almost jumped out of my skin at the sound of the voice and whipped around.

"Keith, what the hell?" He was standing a little behind the bench I was sitting on with his hands on his hips as he gasped in lungfuls of the cold air. His face was red, and it was clear he had just finished up a run by the way he was dressed. "What are you doing here?"

"I'm staying with Sasha for the weekend," His girlfriend had been a year behind us so she was still at school here. "And then I saw a sad, grey lump of a human out here on the old stomping grounds so I had to check it out. What are you doing here anyways? It's Valentine's weekend. Aren't you supposed to be holed up with the girl?" He brushed off the spot next to me on the bench and took a seat. For a second, I felt like I was back in a team huddle freshman year with Keith sitting next to me. Keith might not have been a key player that freshman year like I had been, but he was the only other freshman on the squad and we had immediately hit it off, which is how we came to be roommates my sophomore year. Even though I had to drop the team, he still kept me somewhat connected to it.

I huffed at his description. I was not a sad, grey lump. Then I watched as my breath puffed out in clouds in front of me. I had forgotten it was still Valentine's Day this weekend. It sure didn't feel like it anymore. "Yeah, well. Things don't always go as planned."

"Don't tell me you broke up with the love of your life…"

I glared at him out of the corner of my eye. "She is not the love of my life." Even I could hear the lack of conviction in my voice, though. It scared me a bit.

"But you really broke up?" He swiveled more to face me, rubbing his hands together in an attempt to keep warm.

I shook my head. "She went behind my back, knowing how much it would bother me."

He paused after I had spat that reply, letting it sink in. "I don't know, man. That doesn't sound like the girl I met a few weeks ago. She was crazy about you."

"Yeah I wasn't expecting it, either."

"Did she mean to hurt you, though?"

"Does it matter?" I didn't want to listen to Keith's logic. He was the most illogical person I knew, that's what made me love him. I wasn't expecting some deep insight from him.

"Of course it does. It makes all the difference in the world. What a person does isn't the problem…it's the reason behind why they did what they did that really matters. If she did it to hurt you, drop that chick. But if she did it for a good reason, I think you at least need to try to see her side of things.

197

There's always more than one side to something." He stood from next to me and started stretching out his legs, making sure he didn't get sore later. I didn't speak for a long time, just leaned forward with my elbows on my knees and watched him stretch, thinking about what he had said. When he finished, he turned to me. "Listen, if you don't want to head back to your place for the day, I'm sure Sasha wouldn't mind. She hasn't seen you for a while. Come back with me to her place. If I beg a little, throw in some puppy-dog eyes, I can get her to make us eggs and bacon. What do you say?"

"Oh, no that's fine, Keith. Thanks for the offer, though…"

He made a face at me and shook his head. "What you forget is that I know you, Sweeney. I know how you turn down offers all the time. So I refuse to accept that. Let's go." He held out his hand to me and raised his eyebrows, knowing before I did that I would agree.

MARCH
Carter

"Carter McMillan! My girl!" Nate's over-exuberant voice bounced over to me as I was stepping into the gym. I quickly plastered on a smile, the one I had perfected over the years of hiding within my shell. The one that said, "everything's okay, I'm okay, I swear I'm normal" but underneath, I was a wreck. Noah still hadn't spoken to me. He refused to look at me in class, and I refused to participate, not that he noticed, of course. I had barely been able to sleep after we had argued, but I must have eventually dozed off because when I woke it was light out and a few inches of snow coated the ground outside the window. The apartment had felt cold, and not because of the season. I didn't need to call out to know he wasn't there anymore, but I had anyways. I even peeked in Keaton's room, knowing I wouldn't find him there, but still feeling the need to check. He hadn't even left a note and I had a feeling he would be gone for a long time. I didn't realize it would be weeks.

I left countless messages. Apologizing, telling him I could explain, needing him to talk to me, begging him not to do this. Not to give up on this. He hadn't returned a single call or text. I stopped trying a week ago. I knew how to deal with being alone. I could manage to do that again. Except last time, I hadn't been completely alone. I had Samantha then and I didn't have her now. That's why I found myself walking into a packed gymnasium on a Saturday morning. It was the state gymnastics meet today, her final meet of her high school career. I felt like such an awful friend, I had been so caught up in my relationship with Noah I hadn't even been there for her while colleges were beating down her door to have her tryout for their teams. I didn't even know which ones she was seriously looking at.

At the moment, Nate's arms folded over me in a hug and I did my best to return it. "I wasn't expecting to see you here!" he crowed once he had released me, but continued to hold me at arm's length and studied me. I wanted to shy away, close myself off yet again, but I forced myself to smile a little bigger. Nate made a face at me, but then shrugged it off and threw an arm around my shoulders. "Well, come on then. We're sitting up here." *We're.* As if I was actually a part of his friend group.

"Do you always come to these?" I asked as we made our way up the bleachers a few rows to a group of his friends, most of the kids we sat with at lunch mixed with some more girls Sam was friends with.

"Yeah, I've been to each one this semester." I swallowed the guilt I felt rise up, knowing I hadn't been to a single one. I wondered if this whole group of friends had always come, even in the past years when I hadn't missed a meet. Maybe they had and I was just so closed-off I didn't notice. Now, they smiled and waved as Nate and I sat on the edge of their row in the bleachers and watched the different gymnasts go through their warm-ups. "You okay, Carter?"

I turned to see Nate watching me with concern clouding his deep brown eyes. They reminded me of a Golden Retriever's eyes. Now that I thought about it, Nate kind of reminded me of a Golden Retriever. The thought made me smile, even if it was a small one. The first actual smile that had happened in weeks now. "Yeah…no…but sure."

"You've been sad again these past few weeks. You seem distracted. Did you not get into your dream school or something?"

I guess that was a valid question, it was that time of year. Everyone was either excited over acceptances, disappointed from denials, or stressed as they attempted to decide between schools. I had gotten accepted to a couple of schools, but what was key was that I had been offered an internship with National Geographic. It was the dream. The only person I wanted to share that news with, other than my family of course, was Noah. He was also the reason I was torn on what to do. I couldn't tell him that, though, even if we had been talking. I was too afraid it would scare him away. I wasn't sure how I was going to hide it from him, he always saw right through me.

"Hey...I didn't mean to upset you." Nate's hand closed over mine and I realized I had been toying with my sleeves incessantly again. I had been doing it even more than usual this past month. "I shouldn't have said anything."

"No, no...it's okay. I got in to wherever I applied. I'm just not sure yet."

He smiled back at me but didn't release my hand. For once, I was okay with it. I needed someone to hold onto me lately. "Congrats! That's awesome. I'm sure you'll figure it out, you've got time. I got into a couple schools too, even had some offers to play ball at a couple different places."

I smiled for him. "That's amazing, Nate. Do you know what one you're going to choose?" It was nice to turn the focus on something other than myself.

"Well, not really, no. My dad's very overbearing in that part of my life. Very focused on what place has the best baseball program and all that. Which isn't very good because my mom doesn't even want me to play in college. Says it will take away too much time from my education. So basically, I just sit in the middle of them fighting over what I should do and I get no say." He grimaced and I gave his hand a light squeeze.

"What do *you* want? Isn't that all that matters?"

He shrugged. "Is it? I don't think I want to play in college. At least, not as a varsity team. I'd like to just do it somewhere as a club sport. Not because I think I need to focus more on academics like my mom says. Just because I miss when the sport used to be fun. It hasn't been fun for me in a really long time. My dad just forces me to play year-round, year after year, and I can't even tell you the last time I enjoyed the sport of baseball. Isn't that sad?"

"I'm so sorry…"

"I take it you don't have overbearing parents like mine?" he chuckled.

I shook my head. My parents were currently in Prague doing another article for their magazine. They would be gone for another three days, then home for ten before they headed off to Bangkok. "No. My parents are very hands-off. I don't mean that in a bad way!" I hurried to amend. "They just travel a lot, and they used to take us with them when we were very young, then when my brother and I were in school they would take turns on who stayed home with us, and now they just leave me a lot. It's okay. I understand, because they're still amazing parents even if it is from halfway across the globe. They're extremely supportive of anything I want because they took the unconventional route, too. Whatever makes you happy, right?" I chuckled a bit because of just how unhappy I currently was.

"I wish I had that…" The longing in his words made my heart hurt just a little bit more. Everyone truly was going through their own battles and you could have no idea. Nate, my own personal Golden Retriever, battled every day and I would have never even known it.

"Wow." A high voice interrupted our conversation at that moment and we both quickly looked up. It was Samantha, looking breathtaking in her leotard. She fit every bit of captain-of the team and the entire school. "Didn't think I'd see you here today." She glanced at me with raised eyebrows. She was in her bitch-mode which was enough to send most people cowering, but I was well-acquainted with it. I had never found myself on the receiving end of it since I had first met her but it didn't bother me. I deserved it.

"I wasn't going to miss your last meet here."

"I wouldn't have been surprised if you had. Hey, Nate." Nate stayed silent but nodded to acknowledge her greeting. She tossed the rest of the group a smile and thanked them for coming before turning to lope off. I quickly scrambled out of my seat, not nearly as graceful as her, and rushed to catch her.

"Sam, wait!" I wasn't looking where I was going as I leaped off the bleachers, straight into Noah's chest. His hands came up to grab me so I didn't fall flat on my ass and my body immediately erupted in goosebumps, my heart racing a mile a minute from a single touch. "I-I'm so sorry," I stuttered, completely out of breath just by being in his space. I tried to take a breath in but was immediately overwhelmed with his scent, like a forest right after it rains, and my head swam. For a moment I swore I saw his dark eyes lighten, but then they were a storm of grey and indigo and black and his fingers uncoiled from around my arms after he had made sure I was secure. "I'm sorry," I whispered. I meant it for so much more than just this moment.

I saw him swallow thickly before he took another step back, giving him enough room to run a hand through his hair. I noticed how it was beginning to curl at the ends, like he hadn't cut it in a long time. "It's okay," he whispered back. He stepped to the side further. "I think I saw Samantha head out that door." He pointed to his left.

"Oh...Oh, right. Thanks." I swore I was more eloquent, but I never failed to be flustered when it came to Noah. "Okay, well, I guess I'll see ya." I awkwardly shuffled around him, taking one last look over my shoulder as I headed out the gym door. I hoped he may still be watching me, but just like that very first day on the beach, he was already gone.

"Sam!" I called out, as I hurried down the staircase that lead to locker rooms. She was just about to turn into one when I reached the last step. "Sam, just wait a minute."

She stopped but didn't turn around. "What, Carter?"

I closed the distance between us and waited for her to turn, but she didn't so I just decided to talk to her back. "Listen, I'm sorry, okay?" God, I was sorry for so many things lately. "I'm sorry I missed all your meets this year. I'm sorry I missed Timmy's birthday. I'm sorry I don't know what teams you've tried out for. I'm sorry I suck as a friend. I'm sorry I was never the best friend, that I never knew how to be that."

She finally turned around to face me, but her face gave away nothing. "I never wanted you to be that typical best friend, my God you think you would have known that by now. I was happy with that. What I'm not happy with is the fact that everyone around us thinks you're some miracle child awakened from the dead lately; laughing in a lunch room, saying hi to friends passing in the hall, but the truth is you've dropped the one person who was there for you through those dead years."

I flinched from her words, from the complete accuracy of them. "I didn't mean to, Sam. You know I didn't. It's just hard, you know the situation. You're the only one who knows how hard the situation is."

She laughed without humor and tossed her ponytail over her shoulder. "It shouldn't matter the situation."

"You're right. I'm so sorry. I promise I'll be better." Her face seemed to soften a bit. "It's not going well right now anyways." I gave her a self-deprecating shrug but her eyes flashed.

"Really?" she spat.

I blinked, shocked at her sudden resurgence of anger. "What?"

She barked another laugh. "So you're coming back to me after the dick breaks your heart? Really? That's how you think this works? Why don't you try to get your shit together on your own this time, Carter?" I didn't even have time to think of a response before the locker room door slammed in my face. I felt a hot tear roll down my cheek and I quickly batted it away before scrubbing my face with my hands. That wasn't how I was hoping this would go at all. I pulled myself together as much as I could, plastered on my "everything's okay" smile, and headed back up the stairs and back into the crowded gym.

"Hey, did you catch Sam?" Nate asked as I took my seat next to him again, even though I didn't want to be there anymore.

"Yeah, I got her just before she headed in the locker room."

"Good, I'm glad." He smiled at me. "Oh, I almost forgot. Sweeney said you dropped this when you bumped into him." He pulled a ticket from his pocket and handed it to me and I took it hesitantly. My ticket was still in my back pocket, there was no way it would have just fallen out from running face first into Noah.

"Thanks." Trying not to look too obvious, I flipped the ticket over and attempted to see if anything was out of place. And that's when I saw it, scrawled so tiny in the corner that if I hadn't been specifically looking I would have never noticed it. *Lake. 6.*

Noah

I was already sitting on one of the larger rocks right above the water when I heard the gravel crunching under her tires. Her headlights swung over me and then flipped off. The ignition cut and I heard her door slam, followed by the soft padding of her footsteps. When they finally came to a halt right behind me, I heard her suck in a deep breath before letting it out slowly.

"It's beautiful," she said on the exhale.

"Every time," I replied, thinking back to how I had explained this place the very first time I had brought her here. The ice had just thawed out completely last weekend, so the water was high but smooth as glass tonight. The sky was turning to a deep, deep blue with hints of purple streaking through it as the sun began to dip below the trees. This sunset was darker than the first we had watched together here, colder, but just as beautiful.

Carter took a seat on a rock to my left, keeping distance between us still. I wanted to close that distance. I wanted to hold her, feel her heart race when my fingers touched her, have her mouth on mine, have the scent of cinnamon and apples make my head fuzzy. She was my wounded body part; it was true. I had thought I could cut her off, cut off what I believed to be an infection, but she was a part of me.

"Noah, I'm so-"

"Sorry," I finished for her. I turned my head to face her, watching the wind whip her hair around her shoulders. She didn't even attempt to keep it in place. She was such a beautiful mess it was hard for me to look at her. "I'm sorry too, Cub."

"Wh-why? There's nothing for you to be sorry for, that was all my fault and I know it was wrong and if I could undo it I would and I swear I never meant any harm in it I didn't mean to hurt you I just wanted to understand better you had been so upset at that apartment I didn't mean to pry I just wanted to help and-"

I chuckled to cut her off and shook my head before looking back out over the water. "Shhh. Breathe." She took in a dramatic breath and I laughed at her antics. It felt like the first time I had laughed in weeks. Her returning smile almost blinded me. "Come here."

She didn't hesitate for a single second, the next thing I knew she was burrowing into my side with her arms wrapped tight around my middle. I snaked one arm around her and rested my cheek on the top of her head. We both let out a sigh at the same time. That feeling of home had returned to me. "I know. I know you would never do anything to intentionally hurt me, Carter. It hurt all the same, though. I'm sorry for running away from you. I just couldn't handle one more betrayal from a girl I thought I knew."

She swiveled in my arms, her deep green eyes probing mine. "I didn't mean to betray you! You *do* know me. You know me better than anyone. I'm still that same person."

"Shhh," I hushed her again and tucked her head back under my chin. "I didn't mean it like that. It's just after Whitney did what she did, that was one betrayal. Then after I heard what you had done, after that day and night we had spent in New York... Forgive me for overreacting."

"There's nothing to forgive." She planted a kiss right above my heart and I sucked in a quick breath, my desire for her unfurling.

"I want to say that you should have just asked me. Asked me to tell you exactly what happened.

Why I don't deal with it. Asked so you could understand better. But I know that if you had, I would have shut down. I would have gotten angry and defensive and told you nothing. It's not something I talk about. Ever. I don't ever want to talk about it, Carter." I pulled away to look at her. "Okay? I don't want to talk about any of it. I don't want to know what you saw. I don't want you to ask any more; you understand now. Is that okay?"

"Yes," she whispered into the dark. I nodded, pleased with her answer. I didn't need anyone to tell me that this wasn't the way to deal with your problems, but this was my way and for now I was okay with that. As long as I still had Carter by my side.

We didn't talk for a long time after that, just watched the water lap ever so gently at the rock we were sitting on and the sun continue its steady descent. When she finally did speak, it was in a joking manner. I had missed her teasing. "I can't believe you slipped that ticket to Nate of all people."

I smirked at her. "You told me he was a nice guy. Haven't you noticed I've been trying to give him another chance? Plus, he's not the brightest. I was pretty positive he wouldn't even think to look at it for a hidden message."

She punched my stomach lightly. "Of course you still manage to take a dig at him. Also, yes, I have noticed you being nicer to him in class. Kind of hard not to notice that when you've been completely ignoring me and paying attention to the guy who sits right next to me."

"Can't show any favoritism, remember?" I gave her another smirk and I was expecting her to come back at me with some smart-ass remark, but instead her lips were suddenly on mine. She was kissing me with every apology she had been trying to get me to hear for the past weeks, with every ounce of remorse she had, every bit of longing she had kept pent up. And I was kissing her back, God was I kissing her back. I had forgotten how much I loved kissing her, how she sighed into me, the way her body fit perfectly with mine when I pulled her into my lap. "God, I missed you," I finally groaned.

"God, I love you," she whimpered back after I had nipped her bottom lip and brought my forehead to rest against hers. Her hands were still in my hair, and she was toying with the ends. "It's long," she remarked, giving it a light tug. I tipped my head back as she ran her fingers through it some more and kissed her forehead, leaving my lips there.

"I need to cut it." I felt her smile in response and her hands left my hair to trail along my jaw line, rubbing against the growth of hair there. My beard had been coming in nicely.

"You've really let yourself go in my absence." I tipped my face back down so my lips met hers, not bothering to respond to her teasing. Instead, I went about teasing open her lips so that my tongue could tangle with hers. When she moaned into my mouth, I chuckled and pulled away again, giving her time to catch her breath.

"You don't like the beard?" She made a face at me, but her eyes were still filled with so much desire the combination was comical and I found myself laughing. "So no beard then?"

Her fingers combed through it and a growl bubbled up from my chest, causing her to giggle. "I don't even like it when you have stubble, Sweeney."

I made a snort of dissent. "Oh please, you can't keep your hands off me no matter what my face looks like."

She groaned. "You are so full of yourself."

"And you love it." When she nodded against me, her lips bumped into mine and I kissed them. Of course I kissed them, how could I not?

"So, did you ever catch up with Sam?" It had taken us a while, but we had finally managed to keep our hands to ourselves for more than a couple minutes and Carter was now sitting between my legs, her back leaned against my chest while my arms were wrapped around her. The sun had left us long ago, but I didn't have any desire to move anytime soon, even with the cool air blowing around us. I wasn't ready to move my little bubble of happiness.

She stiffened in my arms before even answering, so I knew whatever had happened between them had not been good. "Yeah, yeah I did. It didn't go well."

"What do you mean?" I pressed a quick kiss to her temple, unable to help myself with her so close to me again.

She sighed into me. "She basically told me everything I already knew. I kind of suck."

I laughed at her vague description. "You don't suck. Well…maybe a little…"

Her elbow came back and caught me in the spleen. "She said she won't pick me up if you break me."

I tensed for a second and then tried to brush it off. "I'm not going to break you, Cub." *But you might break me*, I added in my head.

"I really hurt her, though. She's like you. She pretends like she doesn't hurt, but I know she does. And I hurt her. I hate that I hurt her. I put you before her. I'm scared I want you more than a lot of things." Her voice trailed off in a pained whisper. I didn't like that she felt that way. I didn't like that *I* felt that way, because I wanted her so bad I was risking *everything* to keep her as mine.

"I never wanted it to be this way. I don't want you to give up anything for me."

"And I didn't want you to give up anything for me, but if anything were to happen..." She didn't have to finish that sentence. We both knew exactly what was on the line. Is that what love was? Knowing that every single thing could go wrong and diving in head-first regardless?

"I brought this for you." She reached into her jacket pocket and pulled out a piece of paper and handed it back to me. In the moonlight I was able to make out enough to see it was her list of life goals.

"Carter, you're giving this to me?" I gasped.

"Yes."

"No way. This is yours. I can't take it."

"I want you to. We'll do them together," she said adamantly.

I rubbed the paper between my thumb and forefinger, sucking in a deep breath. "Cub..."

"We do it together. Whatever happens, we find a way. We'll do them together."

We had fought so much lately, I didn't want to start another fight. I would hold on to this paper, I would keep it with me always because it was a part of her and I always wanted to have a part of her. But this was no simple situation. More than anything, this was just another weight on my chest, reminding me just how far I had crossed the line. Instead of focusing on that dread though, I tucked the paper into my back pocket and chose to focus on the feel of her in my arms, pressed against my chest. I placed another kiss in her hair and rested my chin on top of her head, watching the stars reflected in the water before us, wondering just how far we were going to take this.

APRIL
Noah

"Can we just walk? Please? It's nice out." She tugged my hand in the opposite direction of my car.

"Carter…" We didn't walk around here. I knew we were miles from school. I knew no teachers or students lived out here, it was really just a college town, but still. I didn't like to take my chances. It was one thing to walk around New York. This was a different story.

"Please? Isn't there a band playing downtown tonight? We could just stop for a minute to see them."

The sun made her hair blonder. I had forgotten how light it could seem and the spring air whipped tendrils of it into her face. I reached out to tuck them back behind her ear and she leaned into my touch. I couldn't say no to that. She saw it in my eyes and her face immediately lit up. "Thank you!" Her lips were pressed to mine so quickly I couldn't even react and then she was taking my hand and leading me down the sidewalk by the river.

"Isn't it beautiful?" she sighed as she swung our hands back and forth.

I shrugged my jacket closer to me. "Still kind of cold," I grumbled.

"Oh, lighten up." She released my hand in favor of wrapping her arms around my waist. "Better?"

"Carter," I warned, but threw my arm over her shoulders to pull her closer. "People could see."

Her lips found my jaw and I bit back a groan. "No one's going to see. No one knows us here."

I couldn't even argue further because we had reached the park downtown where there was indeed a band playing. Of course, no one had any clue who they were. Probably some kids from the college who

214

put together a group and played covers. From the way Carter's face lit up and she pulled me towards the stage, you would have thought they were some Grammy Award winning group.

"Come dance." She pulled me right up to the stage, which wasn't hard seeing as there were maybe two dozen people here.

"I am not dancing."

She turned and threw her arms around my neck. "You used to make me dance in the apartment all the time."

I laughed. "That's in my apartment!"

"So?" And then she was spinning away from me on the grass and shaking her hips and I couldn't help it; I had to laugh because a part of me couldn't even be sure this was the same girl who first caught my attention on the beach. That sadness that had drawn me in? It was gone now.

She was right, it used to be like pulling teeth to get her to dance with me in the apartment. I would have to act like a complete fool just to get her to do a simple twirl with me. Yet here she was, spinning with her arms wide, head thrown back in laughter. I had never seen her more alive than here right now. So the next time she opened her eyes and beckoned to me, I went and twirled her around until she was breathless. Then I pulled her close, even though I wasn't sure if the song playing was slow or fast, and I kissed her until she was limp in my arms. Maybe people were staring. Maybe I just didn't care at the moment.

"You're beautiful, you know that?" She just smiled but nothing in her said that she believed me. I let one finger trail down from her temple to her chin and tipped her face up towards me again. "You're so much more than beautiful, though. Don't ever let anyone tell you otherwise." There was a question in her eyes. Why would I be talking about anyone else when I knew all she wanted was me? I didn't let her ask it, though. Instead, I leaned down to press my mouth to hers, letting my tongue tangle with hers and allowing myself to forget who we were for a moment; forget that I was supposed to be the smart one, the one who always held back. When her fingers slid under my shirt to start counting up the ridges on my stomach, I grabbed her hands and pulled her away from the stage.

She gave me the most confused look when I turned the opposite direction of my apartment. I couldn't help but laugh because she looked so adorable and kissed the tip of her nose. "You do realize the whole point of this trip was to get something to eat, don't you?"

She stuck her lip out in a pout and it took everything in me to reign in my desire to take it in my mouth. Almost immediately, she was grinning at me again. "Can we go to the grocery store?"

"The grocery store? I thought we were going to grab take out?"

"Please? I want to go to the grocery store with you."

"First of all, you're the strangest woman I know. Secondly, you're very demanding today. Actually, you're very demanding every day."

Her grin grew. "So that's a yes?"

I shook my head at her in disbelief and tugged us down the side street that led to the local grocery store. "Why would you want to go to the grocery store? Most girls like to be taken out on a date. Not that we do that, either…"

"Am I like most girls?" I only raised an eyebrow at her as she released my hand to grab a basket on our way in. "I like normal with you," she admitted as I followed her down the first aisle. Her words hurt because I knew I could never give her that. "I like to know the simple things you do." When she looked up at me with those big, green eyes all I could do was give her a slight nod.

"So what are we getting?" I asked after a few moments of silence.

She gave me an incredulous look. "You're the chef out of the two of us. You tell me."

"Fair enough." I grabbed the ground sausage and hamburg I always used as we passed it and she eyed them wearily. "You're going to eat it and you're going to like it."

Her eyes widened and she had to bite her lip to keep from laughing. "I'm sorry," she finally giggled. "I feel like I just got yelled at for doing something wrong in class."

I laughed along with her. "And your reaction was to laugh? No wonder I can't control a class."

"You can control a class."

"I can't control you though, is that what you're saying?" That challenging look came over her face and I had to turn away before I did something completely stupid in such a public place. I pulled out a box of spaghetti noodles and dropped them into the basket. When I looked back up she was giving them her judgmental look paired with pursed lips. "What now? What's wrong with those?"

"I don't know. I just figured such a wonderful chef would make his own noodles."

"You're a brat and I'm never taking you grocery shopping again." I wasn't paying attention as I followed her laughter down the next aisle.

"How do you even know what to get?"

"Hm?" I glanced up at the shelves she was looking at and my feet stalled. Rows upon rows of baby food. Every muscle in me tightened. "Why are we here? Come on," I reached out to take her hand and lead her back to another aisle but she just kept walking, scanning the countless jars. All in all, I had probably spent hours in this very aisle, many times nearly pulling my hair out while Keaton banged on something in the cart.

"They all look the same, but they're all different. Right? How do you know what one's right?"

I sighed and walked further down the one place in this store that never failed to give me anxiety. "You don't." She turned and looked at me, not asking for more but waiting to see if I would continue. "Well, maybe moms know. Something about them always knowing what to do. I, however, missed that memo. So basically it was trial and error." I ran a hand through my hair as I remembered all the months trying different foods, praying Keaton would like the next kind I tried. More often than I would like to admit, it ended up on the floor. Or the wall.

Now, I raised my eyebrows at Carter. "You just never know. But you've got to keep trying, right?" She nodded, knowing my words pertained to more than just my situation with Keaton. "I hate this aisle, though. Can we keep shopping?" I extended my hand to her and this time she took it.

"I'm sorry. I just never knew there were so many options."

I smiled at her to let her know it was fine. "I'm sure when you have kids, you'll know exactly what food to get. I wasn't typical mom material."

"You did a great job with him. He doesn't need a mom with you and Sarah." There was still a hint of sadness in her voice and I had a feeling it was because she had seen what Keaton's real mom was like now. What I had said to her that night at the lake still held true, I hadn't brought up anything to do with Kelly since then. I didn't want to know anything. How she was, if she was better, worse, if she talked now. At the time I was angry. So angry at Carter for going behind my back. Lying to me. Doing what I had expressly told her I couldn't do. And so I told her I didn't want to know anything. I wasn't even sure why I didn't want to know. I guess because I had told myself I couldn't do anything to make her better and I should just focus all my attention on Keaton. But the more I thought about it, the more I needed to know. I hadn't seen her in two years.

When I lifted my eyes to meet Carter's, she saw the questions in them. "She didn't talk when we were there. The doctors say she's been better?" She was so tentative saying anything, I knew she was worried it would cause another fight. That I would fly off the handle again. But I could also hear the question in her voice. Better than what? Multiple suicide attempts in that first year? "You know Sarah visits her every other week…"

"Does it do any good?" I huffed, tossing a couple cans of crushed tomatoes in the basket beside the breadcrumbs. I saw her relax out of the corner of my eye, apparently seeing this would not cause another riff between us.

"I'm not sure." Her voice sounded small and that sadness was back in her eyes, but this time it was for me. Why she ever chose me to care about was beyond me.

I swallowed hard and forced a smile. "It's fine. Enough about that stuff for today." I took her hand and pulled her down the last aisle, snatching a box of her favorite brand of brownies. "Yes?"

"Is that even a question?" Just like that her grin was back, yet again seamlessly transitioning from a painful conversation to playful. I was still in awe of it.

"Let's go cook."

She tucked herself into my side. "You can cook. I'll watch."

I gave the sauce one last stir and took it off the burner. "Are the noodles done?" I had put her in charge of one thing; the noodles she had scoffed at for coming from a box. She hadn't been too pleased with the arrangement, but how hard could it really be to boil some noodles?

Before I could look to see what she was doing, something hit my shoulder and plopped onto my kitchen floor with a slap. I glanced down to see a limp noodle by my feet and then slowly traced back up her legs and torso to her innocent smile, hands neatly tucked behind her back.

"Did you just throw a spaghetti noodle at me?" I asked with one eyebrow raised.

She nodded slowly. "They're supposed to stick if they're done," she said dryly and bit her lip.

"You just threw a noodle at me..." I reiterated, still not fully comprehending but loving the look of mischief on her face. Her hands came out from behind her back with a whole wad of noodles dangling from them. I shook my head slowly.

"Carter..." Her eyes glinted back at me and before I could even react, a wet *smack* met my chest.

She barely had time to laugh, "They just won't stick!" before I was on top of her, reaching for the pan of red sauce on my way. She squealed, darting away from me, but not quick enough to get away from the warm goo I smeared over one cheek.

She danced further out of my reach with a squeal and picked up the bowl of pasta straining in the sink, quickly launching more handfuls at me. For a second, all I could do was stare at her green eyes standing out against the red on her face and her laughing smile and I realized I had never been more in love with someone in my entire life. But then more pasta slapped me on the neck and I quickly fished out the meatballs I had carefully crafted to throw at her.

When she finally ran out of ammo, she froze and I saw the panic pass through her eyes right before she tried to dart out of the kitchen. I caught her around the waist and hauled her into my chest, letting the sauce pan I had been holding clatter to the floor.

"Noah!" she giggled, slightly out of breath and still struggling in my arms. I tickled her sides and she squealed again and fought me harder. "Stop!" But I knew she didn't really want me to.

I was breathing just as hard as her from our little battle and I sank us down to the floor so my back was against the refrigerator and she was in my lap. She twisted to face me and placed her hands on my chest, no doubt forming two red handprints on my formerly white t-shirt. The kitchen was a mess. Pasta drooped from my newly painted walls as a result of her poor aim and my dodging abilities. Meatballs littered the floor and I was pretty sure one was squished under my leg at the moment. None of that mattered, though. All I could see right now was her. All I could feel was the rise and fall of her chest so close to mine.

I reached my hands up, my fingers dripping with thick, red paste, and traced her cheekbones, leaving a trial of sauce behind. Her eyes fluttered as her breathing picked up and my fingers brushed by her temples; smoothed the blonde strands back behind her ears. Then they traveled further south, the red still marking a vibrant path against the white of her skin, and I felt down the smooth column of her throat and across the sharp lines of her collarbone. Her eyes were fully closed now, her heart beating erratically against my palm and I reveled in the knowledge that I did this to her. My touch alone did this to her. I moved my hands north again to cradle her head and let my thumbs stroke her cheeks. Her eyes flicked open, drawing me the rest of the way in.

"I'm going to kiss you now, Carter." I breathed, almost too quiet to be heard over our beating hearts.

I didn't give her any time to reply before my lips closed over hers. She tasted like the spaghetti sauce that was coating her lips and I groaned at the delectable flavor. I felt her hands fist in my hair as she shifted in my lap, fighting now not to get away from me, but to press herself as close as possible. I took my time exploring her mouth until she pulled away to catch her breath before lapping at a point on my neck that was covered in sauce. I let my head fall back against the fridge as she placed openmouthed kisses down my throat and her hands worked at the hem of my t-shirt, pushing it up my abs until I finally got the hint and ripped it over my head.

I took her face back in my hands, pulling her mouth to mine while her hands felt over every inch of my chest and arms. "Jesus, Carter..." I panted when she pushed me back against the fridge so her mouth could replace her fingers on my chest. I needed more of her against me. My hands found her shirt and she leaned back enough for me to tug it over her head but just as I was about to lay her down right on the floor, I caught myself. "Why do we always find ourselves in the kitchen?"

I leaned forward to suckle the base of her throat, knowing it drove her insane while she tried to collect herself enough to respond to me. "Food turns me on."

"Carter!" I lifted my head but I couldn't help it, I was immediately laughing.

"I'm kidding!" She laughed with me. "You cooking turns me on." She tilted her head as she gazed back at me. "Actually, everything about you turns me on." I watched her eyes as she said it, watched the desire fill up in the deep green. Then as if to prove her point, she leaned forward and kissed me harder than she ever had before. Before I came undone, I pulled back.

"We're not doing this on the kitchen floor..." I said slowly.

She matched my tone. "One day, we're doing this on the kitchen floor..."

"One day." I disentangled myself enough to stand and pulled her with me, immediately pulling her back into my chest, feeling her bare skin against mine. It was too much. I hooked one leg around my hips and she took the hint easily, hopping up to wrap both legs around me and my hands came down to hold her up. She moaned as I pressed into her and her head fell back, giving me perfect access to her chest.

She finally brought her eyes back to mine to pant out the next words. "You better be a man of your word, Mr. Sweeney."

I backed towards my bedroom, carrying her with me. "Oh trust me, I am."

Carter

"Make it stop," I mumbled as I rolled over and buried myself in Noah's side. His chuckle answered me, his chest vibrating beneath my cheek.

"That's your phone, not mine, Cub."

I refused to peel my eyes open. "No one calls me."

"I call you," he countered.

"You're with me right now." The ringing eventually stopped, only to start up again a minute later. "Who calls this early on a Sunday?" I groaned.

"Well first of all, it's nine. So it's really not *that* early. Maybe it's something important." He hopped up from the bed and fished my phone out of the pocket of my jeans which were in a ball on the floor where we had left them, still covered in the remains of our uneaten meal. I smiled at the thought. We sure did have a knack for making a mess of things. Then he was handing the ringing phone to me and kissing my forehead before leaving me alone.

Mrs. Talcoma bobbed on the screen and I tentatively swiped my finger to answer. "Hello?"

"Carter?" It was a voice I had known since I was seven, back when Mariah decided we would be friends one day at recess. I remembered how she used to bark at her potential clients over the phone while she stirred a bowl of brownie mix for us. I remembered how she would snap at Johnny and Mariah to stop bickering. I was never too fond of her or her voice, but I had spent so much time at her house over the years, it was a voice I knew well.

I shook myself out of my memories to answer. "Yeah?" It wasn't like we hadn't talked since the accident. We did. We saw each other a lot. If Johnny didn't take the bus home, she would come pick him up at the special education building and would always say hello to me. I hadn't seen her that much lately. I wasn't sure if it was because she had stopped picking him up as much, or if it was because I hadn't spent as much time as I used to with Johnny. Suddenly, I realized how little time I had spent with him this year and I felt terrible. Yet another casualty of my obsession with Noah. First Samantha, then Johnny. I was horrible.

"Hello, darling. How are you?"

If she had asked me an hour ago, I would have said amazing. Heck, if she had asked me seven minutes ago, I would have said great. But now? Now I wasn't so sure. "I'm fine. How are you?"

"Oh, just wonderful. Listen, I was just wondering...if you weren't too busy that is, could you maybe come over here to chat?"

I froze, the phone clutched tight in my hand. Come over there? I hadn't stepped foot in that house since the accident. I refused to even drive down that street for three years. I couldn't bring myself to look at the spot where it all happened. And she expected me to go in her house? There was no way. I didn't want to face Mariah. It was bad enough seeing her at school, being in the same class as her this year, being reminded of everything. Being reminded that I should never trust anyone again. She hated me now. According to her, I was the friend who abandoned her at the worst time in her life. And all her little cronies believed her because every report that was made showed that Johnny had "tripped". No one knew the truth. Her parents hadn't been able to bear the thought of their princess daughter being portrayed as the monster she truly was in any of the papers. That was the thing about the truth; all too often it was hidden.

"Carter? Are you still there?"

"Y-yes. I'm sorry." I managed to stutter.

"So you'll come? This morning?"

"This morning?" I gasped incredulously.

"Or early afternoon? Please? I have a lot to get together in this week. It really is the only time I can spare."

Of course we all had to run on her schedule. I gritted my teeth. "Uhm...sure. I'll be there in about an hour?"

"Perfect! Thank you, sweetheart. Bye-bye now."

The call ended with a click and I let the phone slip from my clammy hand onto the bed.

Luckily, I had an extra pair of jeans stowed at Noah's apartment because my ones from yesterday had still been covered in spaghetti. As for a shirt, I had been forced to wear one of Noah's long sleeves and even though he claimed it was small on him, I was still swimming in it. I pushed my sleeves up for the tenth time before reaching out to ring the bell at the front door. A door I had entered countless times without even a knock.

Mrs. Talcoma pulled open the door now, looking as prim and proper as ever in her expensive clothes and lavish jewelry. It was sickening how this family felt like they could gloss over everything with a fake smile and some money.

"Carter, you look absolutely ravishing!" I glanced down at my baggy shirt that wasn't even mine and the ripped jeans. So *ravishing*. "I feel like I haven't seen you in ages."

"You haven't." I recoiled when she went to lean in for a hug. It was enough to remind her I'm not one to be touched by many people.

"Right, right." Pain flashed through her eyes because she knew I wasn't always this way. I ignored

226

any pity she wanted to give me. It was fake anyways. "Well, come in."

She ushered me into the huge entryway and I glanced up at the balcony above us and that same white door out of habit. Mariah's room. Sometimes I felt like I stayed there almost as much as I stayed in my own room. The Talcomas had always taken me in while my parents were traveling. I probably lived in this house as much as my own house all through elementary and middle school. I ducked my head quickly, forcing back any memories that threatened to arise, and followed Mrs. Talcoma in to the living room. I expected to see Johnny, as this had always been his favorite room, but he wasn't there. Instead, Mrs. Talcoma gestured for me to sit on one of the sleek leather couches.

"If you don't mind me asking, why am I here?" I perched on the edge of the leather and folded my arms over my stomach defensively.

"Right to it then, I see. Yes, well. I know you've been close to Johnny these past years-"

"I was always close to Johnny," I amended. In my head I added, *closer than you ever were.*

"Of course. Therefore, I thought it would be only right to inform you that we're moving."

"Moving? To where?"

"California."

"But that's across the country," I gasped.

"I'm aware of the geographic location of California. Thank you, though."

"Why? When?"

"Mr. Talcoma has a job out there now. I leave on Friday."

"Friday? Wait, you leave on Friday? What about the rest of the family? Where's Johnny?"

"He and Mr. Talcoma left this past Wednesday. Mariah is staying with her friend Jenny until graduation so she could finish her senior year with her friends."

I leapt from the couch. "He's already gone?" I practically yelled, but she wasn't at all phased. "You called me over here just to tell me he's gone? What was the point in that?"

"I thought you should know. Also, maybe you could try to patch things up with Mariah while we're away. So we can know she's okay and can have a little closure from you."

"You're kidding me…" This woman would never change. The only thing that had ever mattered to her and her husband was Mariah. This was never about Johnny. This wasn't a courtesy call. This was to make sure their daughter was okay. I paced away from her because she could not be serious right now. It was like that awful night so many years ago all over again. I could say anything, but they just wouldn't get it. Nothing but what they or Mariah said would ever matter to them. "It was his senior year, too!"

"Excuse me?"

"Johnny's! You do know they're twins, don't you? You said Mariah gets to stay here to finish out her senior year with her friends. What about Johnny? It's his senior year, too."

"You know as well as I do that it's different."

"It's not different at all. All I know is that you don't give a shit about him. Never have. Did you stop to think about what's best for him? Because I don't think any doctors would say uprooting him from the only place he's ever known and moving him completely across the country is good for him. But you probably wouldn't know that, would you? When was the last time you even took him to his doctors? A year full of tests and experiments but that was it, wasn't it? Are you even trying to make him better at all?"

I didn't know where this was coming from. I had hated this woman for years. Since that night when she had told me to forget everything that happened. That Johnny had tripped and that was all there was to it. Yet I had never said a word against her. She had always scared me in her pressed business suits. I wasn't scared anymore. Here I was, pacing up and down in a family room that never knew what family was. Yelling all the things I had kept in for so long.

"He is my son." She pulled herself up to stand so that she was towering over me in her high heels, but I didn't care. I just didn't care anymore. I was done being scared; of everything. "As a matter of fact, we're moving to California so he can be part of an experiment."

I froze. "An experiment?"

"A trial. It's new. The subjects get paid to test-"

My humorless laugh cut her off. "So it's not about Mr. Talcoma's job. And it sure as hell isn't for Johnny, either. You just referred to your own son as a 'subject'. What's wrong with you? It's all about the money with you people. I should have known. I can't believe you. You should be happy he's not dead! But I think deep down, you wished all along that he was, because that would have been easier for you. So, what? Now you want to put him in this experimental trial like a lab rat? If it doesn't work out, if whatever this is kills him, it doesn't even matter to you, does it? You get what you wanted and you get paid for it."

"How dare you!" She screeched. "Get out! Get out of this house!"

"Gladly." I slammed the door on my way out, remembering how mad it made her, and stormed down the front walk without lifting my head to watch where I was going. As a result, I crashed into someone. Hard. And a cell phone went bouncing into the grass.

"What the hell?" Mariah whined as she bent to pick it up. Then she looked up and saw who had caused this monumental mishap in her life and everything in her changed. "What are you doing here?" I had never heard more hatred packed into one sentence. There wasn't even a reason for it. I should be the one who hated her. I had a feeling that fear and hatred weren't all that different, though. And I was the only one who knew her worst secret.

"Leaving."

I made to move past her but she grabbed my arm. "I'm not kidding. Why the hell were you in my house?"

I wrenched my arm free from her claw-like grasp. "Is it even your house anymore?" She only stared at me, blocking my path until I would give her a satisfactory answer. "About Johnny."

"Stay away from him," she spat. I couldn't help it. I laughed. Did she think she had any right to say anything about him to me?

"You never knew, did you?" Her blank stare was answer enough. "These past years? I'm pretty sure I'm the only one who even talked to him. Who made sure he got a lunch every day? Who made sure he had a ride home or got on a late bus when his parents forgot about him? Who was his only friend? I was with him every day. Now your mom tells me you guys are shipping him off to be part of some experiment. He's already gone and I didn't even get to say goodbye!"

I fought to control my tears as it fully hit me that I may never see Johnny again. There was no way I would let Mariah see me cry, though.

"I don't believe this...you've been seeing Johnny behind our backs this whole time?"

"Your mom always knew."

"How dare you think you were welcome in any part of our lives?"

"Mariah, are you even hearing yourself right now? You almost murdered your brother!"

"Shut up!" Her eyes grew wide as she glanced at all the perfectly manicured lawns in this development. Checking to see if any well-to-do airheads actually heard the truth.

"You almost killed him, then denied it, and made me pretend like it never happened! And I did! I did exactly what your family wanted and I haven't been able to really live with myself until this year. How do you live with yourself?" I had never been this angry before. I had hid and I had suffered and I had kept my mouth shut. I was sick of keeping my mouth shut.

"He's your brother! You did that to your brother and you don't even care. So don't you *dare* get mad at me for being his friend for all these years. Apparently I'm the only one who has been on his side." I made to shove past her but then I realized I had so much more to say. "What is your problem with me anyways? I did everything I was told to do just to keep your family in better social standing. Pitied instead of having a daughter who was a pariah. Yet you still hate me. Why? If anyone has the right to hate anyone, it's me."

She looked me up and down slowly with an expression that said she'd rather be picking gum off her shoe. Then she got a look in her eye, one I had almost forgotten about. I used to see it whenever she said something that truly mattered, which wasn't often. "You've got it all and you don't even try. I hate that. I always did. You don't even see it or appreciate it. I had almost forgotten that's how you used to be. Then something changed this year. It all came back. All through high school, I tried to be on top. I actually tried. Then this year, my senior year, you're suddenly the one everyone's talking about. Like you came out of nowhere or something. A whole new person. Everyone else, even Samantha the golden girl, doesn't exist if the new Carter McMillan is in the room. Except you know what? It's not new. You just remembered who you are. You get whatever you want and I hate that."

"You're insane." I shook my head in disbelief. "You think I have everything? I had *nothing*. I had no one but Samantha and Johnny until this year. Now Johnny's gone. He's gone and I probably will never see him again and you don't even care. So you know what, Mariah? We're done here."

I almost made it to my car when I heard her sickeningly sweet voice once more. "Oh, Carter? Nice shirt." I glanced down at it in confusion and then back up at her smile that was anything but genuine. There was no way she could know it was Noah's. He never wore it to school. She was probably just poking fun at my lack of fashion sense. Even if that was the case, I couldn't help the unease that settled in my stomach for the car ride home.

I had tried so hard through high school to stay out of her way. I had succeeded, too. Until this year. One shared English class. One confrontation. That was all it took for me to wonder if this whole year had been a mistake. Maybe I had found myself, but in the process I had lost Sam. Even worse, I had lost Johnny, too and I might never be able to get him back.

*****

The following weeks, I tried to pull away from Noah even though in the back of my mind I knew that wasn't the answer to my problems. I attempted to throw myself into other things. I tagged along with Nate any time he asked. I showed up to some of his baseball games. I laughed along with Samantha's friends at lunch. I tried to catch Sam alone, but always failed. I tried to prove to her I still needed her in my life, no matter what else was going on with me. I tried to salvage the one friendship I could. But no matter what, I felt Mariah's stare on me every time I moved an inch. I still hadn't told anyone about Johnny leaving and the hole it had punched through my heart.

Nothing could truly make me feel okay again, though. Only Noah had been able to do that even though I had tried so hard to deny it. He was the only one I wanted to share my pain with. His eyes pleaded with mine each time I happened to catch his gaze in class. He called every night. Pretended that nothing had changed, tried to make me happy again. He never asked what had happened, but I could tell he was worried and I hated that I made him worried. I made it until the following Tuesday before I completely broke down. Maybe I wasn't as strong as I used to be. Or maybe needing someone took a strength of its own. I needed him, but I couldn't help the feeling that I needed more from him than he could give me. Maybe I *didn't* get everything I wanted, like Mariah had said.

MAY
Carter

He was pacing his room during his lunch hour right before my class and I took a minute to watch him before he knew I was there. I leaned against the doorjamb and tilted my head into it. I remembered the first day I walked in here and how he took my breath away. He still did. Then he turned and his eyes grew wide upon seeing me, but once again I couldn't read the emotion there. He didn't run to me or speak first, not that I would have expected him to do either of those things. Instead, he calmly walked towards me until he was directly in front of me and stretched up so he could grab the top of the doorframe above us. He towered over me, completely filling my space, yet not getting too close. Never too close. He watched me so cautiously, and I felt another pang of guilt for worrying him. For having him doubt my feelings for him. Yet here I was doubting his feelings for me.

I tilted my head to look up at him. "Hey."

His face didn't change, just continued to study me, but I saw the question in his eyes. "It's raining." I shrugged and struggled to give him a smile but it failed.

"I know, but that's not why you're crying." I reached out and caught his tie that was dangling between us and let my fingers fiddle with it. I was well aware of the breath he sucked in, the distance he tried to maintain between us even as I gave a little tug. The tears gathered in my eyes when I looked back up at him. "Can you pretend to love me for a minute?"

His entire body froze and I watched as his eyes scanned over my head, taking in the empty halls. I didn't give him a chance to protest before my hands were on his chest, pushing him off the doorframe and into the room. One hand reached down and weaved its way into his.

"Carter, what are you doing?" he hissed. What was I doing? This was stupid. In school? But I just needed him and I couldn't take another day of his questioning eyes in class without explaining.

I tugged him further into the room, into the back corner, and then I finally broke and buried myself into his chest and wrapped my arms around him as tightly as I could. He stiffened completely. "I just need you to hold me. Just for a minute. Please."

I felt his arms tentatively come up to cradle me, but he was still stiff against me, not the home I had come to expect and all it did was cause the tears to fall harder. "Carter, you have to talk to me. What happened?"

"I'm sorry," I hiccupped. It wasn't hard to slip out of his arms. I wish it had been harder. I wish he had wanted to hold me tighter. I turned away from him and leaned against one of the windows in here.

"For what?" His voice sounded as if he hadn't moved to follow me.

"This."

"Cub…"

"I don't break down in front of people. I don't let people in to see this. And I'm sorry for locking you out for so long, too. I guess I forgot that I don't have to face everything alone anymore." I paused and watched the rain splash down into the puddles beyond the window. "It's Johnny." I turned back to look at him, still in the same place I had left him. He didn't ask. He never did. Just waited for me to speak. "He's gone. They moved him to California. So he can be part of some experiment." My words were stilted through my tears.

He swore under his breath. "I'm so sorry."

"I didn't get to say goodbye."

"I know."

"I was horrible to him."

"What are you talking about?" He asked, still keeping his distance. It hurt. I didn't want any distance.

"This whole time with you? I've been learning how exciting it is to live and all the things I can do in the future. I've also been forgetting him. Just like I did with Samantha, except this time I don't have a chance to make up for it. I can't even tell you the last time I saw him. It's like I wanted to leave that version of me in the past and he was a part of that. How could I have been so stupid?"

"Hey, slow down. You didn't do anything wrong. You never did. Johnny's probably happy for you. Everyone is happy for you. They want to see you *live*, Carter. That list you've got? That's your life. That's what you're going to do. You know you're going to make it happen. I know you want to live, too. Life is so much more than just existing. Haven't you seen that these past months? You're *living*."

"What if I'm living wrong?"

"What do you mean? Where is this coming from?"

"Mariah."

"Mariah?" he asked. "What did she say to you?"

I tilted my head and looked at him; really looked at him. Then I scrubbed down my face with my hands, angrily batting away any remnants of tears. Wiping away my weakness. "She said I get everything I want. Without even trying. That's not true though...I didn't get you, did I? Even though I tried."

Something in his eyes changed, but I still couldn't read them. He took a half step forward. "I'm right here, aren't I?"

"But I love you." He opened his mouth, then closed it again, not bothering to come any closer.

I swallowed hard and nodded. I couldn't exactly tell him a part of me was breaking right now. I had spent this whole time believing he wouldn't say it because of our situation. Maybe I should have realized a long time ago it was more than that. "Right then. That's what I thought."

"Carter…" Instead of giving me an excuse, I saw his eyes dart to the clock on the back wall. Five minutes until the next bell. Our time was up.

"Don't bother. I'll see you soon, Mr. Sweeney."

I watched his jaw clench at my words and felt his eyes follow me as I fled from the room, but I kept my head down. I didn't even see Mr. Olsen until I crashed into him at the door.

"McMillan," he started.

"Not now, Mr. Olsen. I'm sorry." I grumbled as I shoved past him.

Noah

My head snapped up when I heard Carter's voice again and my eyes met Grant's over her head. I didn't think he was capable of anger, but the guy clearly was the master of disappointment. As he came into the room, I had never seen a stronger look of disapproval on someone's face.

"Noah," he said curtly. Like I needed to feel any worse about myself right now.

I straightened my tie and smoothed down my shirt, re-tucking it into my belt. Not that it really needed to be fixed, it was just something to do with my hands and I needed something to distract me from whatever had just happened. Grant's probing eyes told me it wasn't helping my case. When he closed my door and locked it, I immediately tensed. "Listen, Grant. I've got a class in five minutes."

"Then I'll be brief." I sighed and he took that as a cue to continue. "I got a visit from Ms. Talcoma after school yesterday."

I rubbed a hand over my jaw. "And why would she visit you?"

"I had her in class last year so she felt comfortable in coming to me. You know what she asked?" I didn't respond so he answered his own question. "She asked who she needed to talk to about a suspected student-teacher relationship."

I almost swore out loud, but I had become skilled in holding in my emotions. Grant eyed me hard but I knew my face gave nothing away.

"I think it's lucky she came to me. Moreover, *you* should feel lucky she came to me. I told her that was a very serious accusation to make so she would have to tell me the whole story. Apparently she's dating a boy who goes to the local university. He's in

238

a band and got the opportunity to play a show a couple weekends ago at the park in that town…"

No. There was no way. That one show. The one time I slipped and let us go out in public in town. No way.

"Noah, did you hear what I just said? She said she saw you. And Carter. At the show." I pinched the bridge of my nose and squeezed my eyes shut. I knew exactly what she had seen. I was remembering very clearly how carried away we had gotten while dancing to that music. "Goddammit, Noah. It's true, isn't it?"

"Listen…"

"No, you listen to me. I warned you. I told you to stay away. It's not hard. You're going to ruin her life if this comes out."

"Ruin her life? Have you seen her this year at all? I made her life *better*. She loves me."

He sucked in a breath at my words. "This is worse than I thought. What were you thinking? You're ruining your own life, too."

"You think I don't know that?" My hands fisted in my hair as I paced away from him. My breaths were ragged and it took several steps before I could even get out my next question. "So how long do I have? Before she tells administration?"

"She's not going to tell administration." My head lifted and a little flicker of hope ignited in me. Maybe we hadn't lost everything after all.

"What do you mean?" I couldn't dare get too excited.

"I told her that was such a serious accusation it would have to be investigated. If her information turned out to be true, she would know. If nothing came out, she was to keep her false accusations to herself."

"So we're safe?"

"Noah, I know what she saw wasn't made up. You just proved that to me. Yet I care about Carter. You've been my friend this year so I know you're not a bad person. You've just been stupid. It's time for that to end."

"What are you saying?"

"I'm telling you to end it."

"Grant…"

He held up his hands. This wasn't a negotiation. "Either you end whatever this is with Carter or I have no choice but to inform the school of the situation."

The bell rang just then, putting an end to this nightmare of a conversation. I had never felt so confused in my entire life. If I ended this with Carter, I would lose every ounce of happiness and confidence I had managed to gain back. But if I didn't, and this got out, I would lose *everything*. I would lose Keaton forever. There would be no way the courts would allow him to come back to me if a story like this were to come out. I'd lose any chance I had of securing this job. I may lose my entire career path. Everything I had worked for. I could go to jail. And after it all, I would probably still lose Carter.

"What's it going to be?" Grant's voice snapped me out of my thoughts.

"Just give me some time."

"Noah." Kids were lining the hall outside my locked door. Some peered in, wondering what was going on. I tried to catch a glimpse of Carter's blonde hair, but I couldn't.

"One day. To break up with her. Just give me one day."

I had no idea how I was supposed to do this. I had spent the past days pleading with her to talk to me, worrying about what had possibly gone wrong between us and how I could fix it. I hadn't known it had nothing to do with me; that she was blaming herself yet again for a situation with Johnny that was out of her control. More than anything, I wanted to be there for her now, because I wasn't there for her the last time it had happened. I wanted to tell her everything was going to be okay. Instead, I was being forced to do the exact opposite. I was going to shatter the new life she had built this year. I was going to shatter everything.

I texted her the next morning telling her to meet me at my apartment that afternoon. She didn't reply, but I knew she would come. I hadn't even taken off my tie yet when I heard her knock at the door. For a second, I just stared at it. I wasn't ready for this. I never would be. She had given me the perfect way out yesterday. I just didn't know if I would be strong enough to use it. I was really hoping it wouldn't come to that. Because if I did use it, I don't think I would ever be able to win her back.

She looked so small with her huge green eyes staring back at me when I pulled open the door. The sadness I saw creeping back into them was killing me. I loved this girl. I knew that. But I was about to destroy her. She brushed past me to stand in the middle of the room and I was reminded of Thanksgiving night. It seemed so long ago now, yet she still managed to make me feel like there wasn't enough air in the room. I closed the door behind us and clenched my jaw.

"You said we needed to talk," she said.

"Yeah…" I started, then stopped. Grant said it like it was so easy. End it. He didn't understand,

241

though. Before Carter, I probably wouldn't have understood, either. I ended plenty of relationships. I ended one this past year, and I had been with Whitney for years. So why was this so hard? Hadn't we known this was coming all along? But how was I supposed to give up the person who had taught me what love really was.

"Noah…"

"This needs to end." The words burned on their way out. I had said them to her before, but that was so long ago. Before I had fallen so far.

"What?" She recoiled from my words like she hadn't been expecting them at all.

"This. Us. It has to stop."

It was clear she had not been anticipating this conversation at all. She probably had thought I was going to apologize for not being able to comfort her in school yesterday, which is what should have been happening. It was what always happened. We got overwhelmed but we apologized and made up. We were really good at making up. Now, it took her a full minute to comprehend what I was saying instead. "What are you talking about? It's almost June. Graduation. We're going to be fine."

"You think that just because you graduate, we're going to be fine?" This part was easy. I had already questioned this on my own. I hoped it would be enough to end this.

"Aren't we?"

"Carter, you're leaving," I told her. It was something I had refused to acknowledge for a long time. Something we had just discussed weeks ago when I assured her we would find a way. "You're going to be all over the world. And this? This is my life now. If I keep this job, if I stay here, I get Keaton back. This is my life."

If I kept this job. It all came down to this.

"So I don't go. I can change my mind, you know."

"No," I growled immediately. I never wanted that, I never wanted her to give up her dreams because of me. I snatched up the worn piece of paper she had given me weeks ago that I always kept with me. Her list of goals, carefully written out in her scrawl. "Remember these?"

"We do them together! I told you that when I gave that to you!"

I shook my head. "Even after you graduate, it would still be weird. People would talk. We can't just do things together."

"Why?" She demanded. "Why can't we? Because I don't give a damn about what people say."

I knew what I had to say to her. The only thing that would make her truly give up. Let go of all of this. I needed to make her believe there was no use arguing. No hope. I looked her straight in the eye when I spoke so she couldn't question me at all. "Because I don't love you."

I watched the color drain from her face, watched the fire in her eyes completely die. I had done that to her. I had never felt so terrible in my life. All I wanted to do was wrap her in my arms. Tell her it was all a lie. Take her to my room and show her just how much I truly loved her.

Instead, I had to fold my arms across my chest to keep from reaching out to her and clenched my jaw.

"You don't mean that..." She finally managed to get out, but I could already hear the doubt in her voice. "You love me. I know you do. You just can't say it. Because of who we are. It doesn't mean it's not true, though."

243

I shook my head. "Carter, it's not because of our situation," I lied. It sounded so convincing, too. Like I actually meant it. "I just don't want you."

Her eyes blinked quickly in shock and she took a step away from me like she was afraid. Like I was a monster she didn't even know. She would be right. "So all of this was a lie? This whole time?" she spat.

I shrugged my shoulders. God, I wasn't ready for her to fight me on this. A few months ago, she wouldn't have. Now, her confidence was a force to be reckoned with and I could barely take it. Every word that fell from her lips physically pained me. Of course this all wasn't a lie. Being with her felt like waking up for the first time in years.

"You're not even going to justify me with an answer?"

"I don't know what you want me to say." My jaw worked back and forth and my hands balled into fists where she couldn't see them.

"I love you! You let me love you! All this time. You made me believe you loved me, too."

"I never claimed to love you. I never said those words."

"You didn't have to! When you love someone that much, you don't have to say it. You know it."

"Well I guess you misunderstood. I thought you would have gotten the hint yesterday."

She took more steps away from me and I didn't blame her. The harsh edge in my voice was scaring myself. "Yesterday was just a bad day. I've just been in a bad place lately, thinking about what Mariah said. We can fix this." I didn't answer her pleading, just gave my head a slight shake. Of course we could have fixed it if it had been just that. Of course I wanted to fix it. But I couldn't. "Noah, don't do this to me. Don't do this to *us*."

I swallowed hard. "There is no us. I'm sorry, but you should probably go now."

"I know you. This isn't you."

She knew me better than anyone ever had. Of course this wasn't me. "Just let it go, Carter. I'm sorry I'm not the man you thought I was." I wanted nothing more than to be the man she thought I was. "I can't keep doing this, though. It was a fun thing to do, but it's gone too far. I'm not willing to risk everything for someone I don't even love."

They were the worst words yet and I wanted to vomit just from saying them. Any urge to argue she still had left was immediately forgotten. She gulped down some air and blinked back tears that had started to well up in her eyes. I had never hated myself so much. I needed this girl like I had never needed anything in my life. Finally, she gave me a single nod and pushed past me to the door. I couldn't even turn to watch her leave because I knew if I did, I would be on my knees begging her to take me back in an instant.

I heard her voice just before the door clicked shut. "Goodbye, Noah Sweeney."

MAY – PRESENT DAY
Noah

"Mass General you said?"

"Mass General," Samantha confirmed. I nodded once and shoved out into the late spring morning where the sun seemed too bright for this. Didn't it know? Didn't it know the girl I loved was lying in a hospital bed in God knows what condition? Shouldn't it be pouring down rain or roaring thunder? But then again, shouldn't I have known?

How could I have been so stupid? How could I have done this? If Carter wasn't okay... The last thing I would have ever said to her was that I didn't love her. Everything from before seemed so stupid now. My career, Grant's threat, Mariah's accusation. What did any of that matter? I ruined the best thing in my life and if I couldn't get that back...I couldn't even think about it.

An hour later, I was swinging into the closest spot I could find and jogging towards the entrance of Massachusetts General Hospital. I must have looked as hopeless as I felt because an old nurse stopped in front of me just as I was beginning to scan the multitude of signs and arrows. "Can I help you?"

"Carter McMillan," I rushed out.

"I'm sorry. What was that, dear?"

"I need to see her. Now."

"Now calm down, sweetie. Let's bring you over to the front desk and see what we can find out for you." She grabbed my arm and walked me towards an information desk at an excruciatingly slow pace. Then she calmly went over to a computer and began typing in a few letters as I fidgeted and continuously glanced around me, taking in all the bloodied, bandaged, and pregnant people sitting in the waiting room.

246

"What was the name you said, sweetheart?"

"Carter. Carter McMillan. She was in a car crash last night."

"Are you family?"

I gritted my teeth. "No."

The old nurse gave me a sad look. "I can't give you any information unless you're immediate family."

"I just need her room. Just a number. That's all I need. Can't you give me that?"

"Well, dear, I really can't."

"You don't understand. I have to be there. She needs me. She needs me and I'm not there and I need to show her I'm here. She needs to know I'll always be here, because everything I said last night was a lie. I need her to hear that and know it's true. I need to say so many things. There's so much I should have said to her. Things I should have told her weeks ago. Hell, months ago. But I didn't because I thought I knew what was best. I thought I was doing the right thing. But I wasn't. It was the worst thing I could have ever done. I have no idea what I was thinking and I screwed up. I screwed up so many times with her, but I'm not going to screw up now. You're not going to *let* me screw up now. I *need* her. I need to see her. I need to hold her. So I need you to tell me where she is. *Please*."

I probably sounded insane, like I had no idea what I was even saying. Maybe this lady heard from crazy people every day so she was used to this. Maybe people were constantly asking her for information she wasn't allowed to give. For some reason, she must have seen something different in me because she sniffed a little and nodded her head at me ever so slightly.

"Now, it really wouldn't matter if I were to give you her room number or not, young man." I opened my mouth to argue but she held up a bony finger. "That's because when our *trauma* patients come in on the *fourth floor* at the *red wing*, no one is allowed to see them."

I ran a hand through my hair and slammed it down on the desk in frustration. The old nurse just continued to stare at me intensely. Then suddenly I understood. Trauma. Fourth floor. Red wing. She had told me without telling me. My eyes widened and I found myself running around the desk to hug the tiny, old saint. "Thank you. Thank you. Thank you."

"Go boy! Go find your girl!" She swatted me away and I was off running again, passing the elevator banks where people stood waiting for the next ride in favor of the stairs.

Up on the fourth floor, doctors rushed by on all sides. Patients were being wheeled by in various states of consciousness with tubes sticking out from every direction. Machines beeped from each door I passed. There were no other open hallways here aside from the one I came down now which led to another waiting room. Past the waiting room behind another desk, sliding glass doors were being opened with a swish by nurses hurrying ahead with key cards to scan.

I slowed down as I came into this waiting room. Almost every chair was taken by stricken-looking people. People who looked exhausted. People who knew the worst was coming. People who were praying it would pass them by in favor of someone else. I spotted Carter's parents almost immediately despite having never met them before. I remember her telling me they traveled a lot. I recognized them from the pictures at her house, from the same soft facial features she shared with her dad, the same insistent eyes that matched her mom. They were occupying two hard chairs in the very back corner, her mom looking incredibly small, as if this whole experience was shrinking her. I knew that if anyone could tell me where Carter was, it would be them. So before I could understand what I was doing, I was marching myself over to them. They didn't even look up when I stopped in front of them.

I cleared my throat and tried to think of something, anything, that I could say to them. Nothing came. "Mr. and Mrs. McMillan?" I started and faltered. I had no more words after that. No plan.

They slowly lifted their heads at my voice. Her mother looked completely lifeless and her father looked like he was barely holding on. "Are you another doctor?" he asked.

"What?" I looked down at my slacks and tie and could understand why they may have assumed as much. In the midst of my panic stricken brain, I came up with a very flawed plan. "Well, I just got here," I said, not exactly answering his question. "And Carter is now in room…" I knew it was a stretch, that if they analyzed this at all they would wonder why I didn't know her room number. From how they looked, I had a feeling no rational thoughts were in their brains, though. I knew I was probably violating a million rules, but hadn't I become used to that when it came to Carter? This was the only shot I had.

"447." Her mother supplied.

I breathed a sigh of relief. "Right. So I just wanted to let you know I would be going in with her now. Someone else should be out shortly." I really hoped someone would be out shortly, but they didn't seem to care either way. It was as if they had already given up. I tried not to dwell on that thought as I fell into step behind of pair of surgeons headed to the sliding doors. I almost made it completely undetected. Then the doors slid open and the surgeons in front of me started rolling the gurney through.

"Excuse me, sir... Sir, hold on one moment. Sir! You can't go back there!" The receptionist at the desk here grew increasingly more panicked, but at that point I had already squeezed past the surgeons and the gurney, shouting sorry over my shoulder to them as they stared in shock. Then I was sprinting, dodging other doctors and patients hobbling by with IVs clutched in one hand. My eyes scanned the room numbers of what seemed like a hundred doors until finally I was counting them down. 444, 445, 446. 447. I didn't pause to look back down the hall I had just come, I only threw open the door and rushed inside until my feet stopped and there was Carter. Except it wasn't my Carter.

The girl before me was smaller than Carter was, if that was at all possible. Her hair was not its beautiful mess. Instead, it was a disaster, shaved in places and tinted rust in others. A stab went through my chest as it reminded me of how her hair had looked with the spaghetti sauce streaked through it. Knowing it was blood that stained it now almost caused me to vomit. Then there were her arms, the arms I wanted nothing more than to have wrapped around me. I remembered grabbing them in our scuffle Thanksgiving night to keep her from hitting me. I remembered tracing up them with just my fingertips that night in New York as she shivered in anticipation. Now, tubes were snaking out of each elbow, wires coming from the fingers that used to catalogue every inch of me she could reach. Long gashes and black stitches marred most of the visible skin and I was scared of what she must look like beneath the thin blanket they covered her with. But it was her face I forced myself to focus on. Because however mutilated her body may be, her face had somehow remained unscathed except for one set of stitches along her left cheek.

"Cub…" I breathed, still rooted to the spot. This couldn't be real. She had been standing in my apartment fighting me just yesterday. "Cub, you've got to get through this. You have to listen to me, because yesterday-" I stopped.

Something was wrong. The beeps from the machines were coming slower now. I knew there was nothing I could do. Nothing I could say to stop it. Maybe she was already gone. She would never hear my apologies. She would never know I didn't mean a word I said yesterday. I was too late.

In the movies, in the books, it all shows you die with a flourish. Machines go crazy. Doctors come running in shouting at each other. The beeping is so excessive it gives you a headache and nurses prepare defibrillators to bring the patient back to life. But I guess that isn't the case. Because here in this hospital room, the beeps slowed until suddenly…nothing. Just silence. A long, flat, green line.

Then the commotion came. Nurses and doctors burst into the room and hands were all over me but I could barely feel them. I caught a glimpse of hospital security as they attempted to pull me, shove me, carry me out of the room. I should be fighting them, fighting to stay with her, but I didn't. Maybe a part of me had died with her because didn't I do this to her? Wasn't this my fault? I had broken her last night. Shouldn't I deserve this pain?

But she didn't. She didn't deserve any pain at all. I was angry. I was angry at the men and women in white coats and scrubs who were tugging me. I was angry at the security men. I was angry at these people who claimed to be doctors. They hadn't tried hard enough. They didn't save her. Wasn't that their job? To save lives? They couldn't do it. They couldn't do anything. They couldn't even wrestle me out of her room.

"She's dead!" I finally yelled. My throat felt raw, the voice that came out of it wasn't my own. "She died and you don't even care! You're useless!" I wrenched my arms free from their grasp and pointed back to the lifeless form that was Carter. "The girl I love is dead and all you care about is getting me out of this room!" The white coats were trying to talk back to me in soothing voices, but I couldn't make anything out. I didn't want to hear their apologies and lies. I didn't want their pity.

"Mr. Sweeney!"

"You know this man?" One of the nurses who was trying desperately to cling to my arm yelled back at the voice. It was Samantha. She was standing in the hallway beside Carter's parents with tears running down her face. I didn't know when they had gotten here, didn't know how much they had seen. Her parents looked even more defeated than they had when I first saw them. Ten minutes ago, I wouldn't have thought that was possible. Now, I understood. Her mother was sobbing uncontrollably. Her father just stared at me with dead eyes.

"Mr. Sweeney, stop." Samantha yelled again and I realized that this whole time I thought I hadn't been fighting, I had. My arms fell slack by my sides and I suddenly felt younger than I had in years; smaller than ever. The doctors and security guards loosened their grip, but didn't release me completely. Maybe they were scared of what I might do if they did.

Samantha left Mrs. McMillan's side and came to me. She tentatively reached out and took my arm. When I only flinched at her touch but didn't lash out, she tugged me out of the cluster and into the hallway. She kept her hold on me as we walked back towards the waiting room until my feet started working on their own again. The hallway seemed longer than it had before. Empty, even though people were still there. Lonely, even though Samantha was right next to me.

"Life sucks," I muttered to her. She just nodded and swiped at a tear that was about to fall off her chin. For the first time, I saw Samantha's perfect, tough armor completely gone. Her tears poured faster now, yet she didn't make a sound. I wasn't crying...not yet. It would come, I knew it would. For now, I was just mad. Mad at life. Because it sucks. It sucks because it ends. And what's even worse, you don't know when it's going to end. But we get told that all the time. We're all supposed to know. We've all heard it; treat every day like it's your last. Walk around happily and be nice to everyone and always tell people exactly how you feel. But that's not what happens. What happens is you get scared and you try to do what's right and you panic and say things you don't really mean.

Now I realize, when life ends, you can't take anything back. I was supposed to take it all back. I was supposed to take her back. After graduation. We could be us again, except better. I could show her exactly how much she meant to me. Let her know exactly what she did to me. But that's not what's going to happen now. I'm stuck with a million sorrys I'll never say. A thousand words I want to tell her I didn't mean. She'll never hear how much I love her.

And her last goodbye to me will play in my head until the day I die.

"Hey, what are you doing?" Samantha turned back when she realized I wasn't walking with her anymore. Somehow we had made it back to the main entrance and I pressed my back to the brick there and sank to the ground, pulling my knees to my chest. "Sweeney, let's go." She marched back to me and held out a hand, but I didn't take it. After a moment, she let out a sigh mixed with a sob and sank down next to me.

"You can't stay here."

"I can't leave."

"You have to." I watched as a couple strolled past us, him with his arm around her as she waddled by presumably to go give birth. I was finding it hard to believe that hospitals could hold any joy. One life started in the same place that another ends. It just seemed wrong.

"I can't. As soon as I leave here, it's real. She's gone."

Samantha gulped. "She already is gone."

I turned my head slowly to face her. Let her words wash over me and pierce into every inch of me. "I broke up with her last night." I had no idea why I was telling her this. She didn't look shocked as she stared back at me, though. She was probably incapable of feeling shock at this point.

"Why?"

"Mariah found out."

"Bitch," she spat. I only nodded and it took her a while before she spoke again. "So I guess no one will really care now. She's dead, right? That's kind of worse than sleeping with a teacher."

I liked how Samantha was never one to beat around the bush, even now. "No one's going to find out anyways. That's why I broke up with her. She didn't even know that Mariah found out."

"I'm confused and I really don't need any more confusion in my life, Sweeney." She flicked a pebble that had been resting by my foot and it went skittering along the concrete into the sunshine splashing into the parking lot. It was such a beautiful day. How could it be such a beautiful day?

"Mariah told Grant. So Grant, I mean Mr. Olsen, he gave me an ultimatum. End it with Carter or he would inform the school. So I told Carter it was over."

"You didn't just tell her what was going on? You didn't tell her why?"

I swallowed hard and our entire conversation flashed through my head, hurting ten times more than it did yesterday. At the time, I didn't think I could feel any worse. I had never been so wrong. "I didn't tell her the truth. She didn't need any more bad blood with Mariah now that she was finally getting over it all. So I just made sure it was over however I could."

"You're an asshole." I sat in silence for a second, but she didn't flinch or take back her words.

"I know."

She kicked a few more rocks away from us, then picked at some crumbling concrete. Her tears fell consistently, but she didn't do a thing to stop them or bat them away anymore. Finally, she pushed off the ground and stood up. "You can't just sit here."

I lifted my eyes to look at her and I was sure I must look as empty as Carter's parents had because there was nothing left in me. A girl laughed across the parking lot and my head snapped to look and suddenly all I could see was Carter at that concert with her hair flying around her and her mouth open in laughter and her eyes looking like sea glass in the bright sun and I just couldn't take it. The next thing I knew, I was leaning over to throw up in the garden that lined the side of the hospital. If I thought I had nothing in me a minute ago, I really had nothing now. I wiped my mouth with the back of my hand and fell back against the bricks with my eyes closed, but it didn't shut out any of the pain.

"Alright, no. Let's go. I'm not letting you stay here." She reached out and hauled me to my feet without my permission, but I had no fight left in me anyways. "Where's your car?"

"Good question."

"Dammit, Sweeney she was my best friend! I understand you guys had something but right now all I can think is that you broke her heart hours before she died. She was broken and she didn't even get the opportunity to get over that hurt! And that's on you! That's your fault! So you need to pull yourself together and get the hell out of here because if her parents find out who you are or if some friends from school come down to see her thinking she's alive, you can't be here. You made your choice. You chose your career over her so I suggest you stick to that choice and get the hell out." She stopped walking with me and stared at the ground between us. I could tell her that she had done basically the same thing, she had never made up with Carter, either. But I knew hurting her more was not the way to go. So instead I scrubbed a hand down my jaw and nodded, still tasting the bile in my throat. Then I pulled my keys from my pocket and pushed the unlock button until I found the flashing lights, parked haphazardly in the second row.

I didn't look back as I pulled out of the lot, I didn't have to. I felt like I was leaving my entire world behind even though I knew she was already gone.

*****

I heard a knock on the door but made no effort to move. Instead, my dead eyes just swiveled to the offending sound. It came again now, and I studied the black paint on the back of the door. We should have painted that. It really was hideous. Finally, I let my eyelids drift shut again. Whoever it was would give up eventually. The phone calls, the knocking, it all ended eventually. But instead of slowing and disappearing as all the other knocks had, this one just got louder. Faster. Harsher. Until a voice joined it.

"I know you're in there! Open up!" It took a second to register the voice. Everything took a while to register now. Almost like I was underwater and the distorted noises needed time before they reached me.

I didn't want company. The only company I wanted was dead. So whoever this was could leave. That would be nice. But the knocking didn't cease and for some odd reason I found my legs moving. They were stiff from disuse and I stumbled to the disgusting black door and threw it open, leaning into it heavily.

"My God, you look like shit." It was Samantha. She had changed since I'd last seen her. Her hair was back to normal, a new blouse was on. It reminded me I probably should have changed my clothes since then as well. But I hadn't. I wasn't even sure how many days it had been. Too many.

"You know where I live?" were the first words out of my mouth since the hospital.

"Obviously."

"How much *did* Carter tell you about me?"

"Enough to know where you lived in case she ever died," she replied dryly. I recoiled as if she had slapped me, but no slap could ever cause as much pain as those words. They were a reminder that this nightmare I had been living in was real.

"Sorry," she muttered after I failed to form some response. "I don't know how to deal with anything right now. Can I come in?"

When I didn't respond, she took it upon herself to walk past me. I didn't follow her, just kept leaning against my door, trusting it to keep me upright. I heard her sigh and come back to me. Her piercing blue eyes met mine once she was standing in front of me again and they softened upon looking at me. A part of me wanted to be offended by the pity I saw in her now, but a larger part was too dead to care.

"I'm also sorry about the things I said at the hospital. In the parking lot. I didn't mean them." I only raised my eyebrows and she hurried on, not that it really mattered. Samantha didn't say things she didn't mean. She had no filter. I didn't need an apology from her. "I don't know how you felt towards her, I'm not in your head, but I can assume. You didn't deserve what I said."

"It was true, though."

"Not everyone needs to be reminded of their truths." She watched me for a while longer, then grabbed my arm and pulled me into my own apartment, closing the door behind us. She walked me back to the couch, my permanent residence of late, and sat me down. I felt three, not twenty-three. Lost and confused like a little boy.

"Why am I here?" She asked after another long stretch of silence. "Oh, well, you know. I just thought I'd drop by." She answered her own question as if I had asked it. My eyes didn't meet hers, just focused on the patterns on the blanket sitting to my right. I felt a stab of pain as I remembered skimming my hands over Carter's feet as she sat under the blanket the first night she was here. When I told her everything about my past.

"Of course not," Samantha kept talking now. "I'm here because I don't know how to function anymore. And clearly you don't, either. You know you've missed two days of school? Plus the day you left to go to the hospital. You're a teacher. You have classes to teach. Actually, I'm not sure if you're a teacher anymore. You've probably been fired by this point. Olsen's been covering for you though, so maybe you're okay. Except he doesn't know a thing about English and I'm not sure how long he can placate Goldsworth. I overheard them talking Friday. Apparently no one's been able to reach you. So I figured someone had to make sure you're still alive."

She said the last line as a joke but then trailed off. Jokes about living and dying weren't all that funny anymore.

"Everyone misses her you know. It's only been four days, but it's insane. She always thought she was under the radar, all these years, but she really wasn't. This year she finally embraced that. I guess we can thank you for that. You know she's a really loving person? She's just afraid of it a lot. But she wasn't afraid of you and I don't know why. She picks people, very few, and she loves them like no one else ever could. Her family, me, Johnny, even Nate. But you know that, don't you?"

My eyes had slowly made their way from the blanket to Samantha's face, drinking in her words. I knew where she was going with this. Did she feel the need to hurt me even more than I already was? I wanted to tell her to stop. I understood. I didn't want to hear anymore. But she didn't and my mouth wouldn't open.

"She picked you. You know that. Lord knows why it had to be you, but it was. I'll never know that love. I'll never know the love she had for you. But you do." I closed my eyes tight against the pain but nothing would make it stop.

"She chose me too, in a different way. I was her best friend. And what did I do about that? Not a damn thing. When all she needed was my understanding and my support, I turned my back on her. I told her I didn't want anything to do with the two of you. I gave her up. I didn't love her back the way she loved me when she needed it most. Do you know how awful that makes me feel? I can never fix it-"

"I know." I cut her off, surprising even myself. "Trust me, I know exactly how that feels."

She stopped her pacing in front of me and stared back at me. Tears filled her eyes and dripped over her lashes. I watched as one fell off her chin to the carpet. "You never told her you loved her, did you?" she croaked.

I closed my eyes again, this time fighting to keep my own tears at bay. My throat burned in anticipation of them but I swallowed it back. "No." I had done the exact opposite. I had told her I didn't love her. I told her I had never loved her.

Samantha crumpled to the floor as if that one word from my mouth could possibly hurt her. She had no idea. She had no idea it was so much worse. "What did we do to her?" she asked me, as if I had any clue. I put my head in my hands, but my hands felt awkward, too big for my body. Everything felt wrong now. *I will not cry. I will not cry. I will not cry.* I repeated over and over in my head.

"Her funeral is tomorrow."

"What?" I sputtered, finally pulled from my thoughts.

"Yeah. It's supposed to be a 'celebration of life,'" she said with disgust mingled with her sorrow.

"Her parents didn't want to stand in line at a wake with everyone talking in hushed tones and crying at every hug. So they're doing a service at the church in town. You know...the big, airy one that everyone wants to get married in? Funerals and weddings all in the same place. It's kind of strange. Anyways, anyone can talk if they want."

"Tomorrow."

Samantha nodded. "Mr. Sweeney...she'd want you to speak."

"No," I immediately growled.

"Why not?" she snapped back at me.

"I can't get up there in front of a church full of people and talk about her. I can't even talk about her to you. I haven't even been able to change my clothes since I found out she's gone, let alone move. You expect me to say something great about her tomorrow? I can't even think lately."

She took my words in but then shook her head. "More than anyone, you discovered who she really was this year. You owe it to her for everyone to see that version of her."

I stood from the couch, stretching out my legs so I didn't wobble, and paced away from her. I didn't want to hear this. I didn't want to do this.

"I heard what you yelled at those doctors in her hospital room. She was the girl you loved and you should be one to speak about her."

I scoffed as I walked back to her and leaned on the back of the couch. "I can't just stand in front of that many people and tell them I love her! I couldn't even tell her."

"Now's your chance." She stood again from where she had collapsed on the floor, already pulling herself together to tell me what to do. She looked me over and made a face. "Just make sure you take a shower before the service."

"Samantha…"

"Have you even eaten?"

Now that I thought about it, maybe hunger had been adding to my pain. I hadn't been able to go in the kitchen. It reminded me of too much. There were promises there that would never be kept.

"Get something to eat, Sweeney! She wouldn't want you to starve." Sam started to stride into the kitchen, but I grabbed her arm.

"Don't."

"What?"

"Just don't." She gave me an odd look but seemed to know I meant what I said. I felt a little bad for being so harsh with her. How was she supposed to know the things that happened in that kitchen? Or almost happened. How was she supposed to know the words that were said?

"Okay…then what's the number to the closest pizza place? I'm not leaving until you eat. And shower."

When the pizza arrived, my stomach growled just from the scent of it and Samantha gave me a pointed look. "You really haven't eaten?" she asked. I shook my head and eyed the slice I plucked from the box. In seconds, my hunger won out and I devoured that slice and reached for another. She watched me the entire time. "Feel better now?"

"Is eating some food supposed to make me feel better about Carter being dead?" She blinked and I knew my words had hurt her just as much as hers had hurt me when she first arrived. Funny how certain things could bring so much pain to different people. "I'm sorry," I muttered.

She blinked a few times and took another bite of her pizza. I waited a few minutes before asking something that had been on my mind for a while now. "How are her parents?"

"How do you think?"

I nodded. "What about what happened at the hospital? With me?"

"Confused."

"Not mad?"

"No," she sighed. "Not really. She had been on life support. I found this out later, but an hour before you got there, the doctors told her parents there was nothing more they could do. Her parents gave them the okay to you know…pull the plug. They were given a chance to say goodbye. You must have seen them right after that. Then the doctors took her off life support. They all knew it was coming."

That explained why the machines didn't go crazy. They hadn't been panicking over a loss. They were just powering down. Their job was over.

She cleared her throat, focusing on the next thing. I guess that was her way of dealing with things. My time to process her words was over. "Shower and I'm gone."

"Sam, I can handle myself."

"Obviously you can't." She glared at me until I stood again and walked towards my bathroom. I went through the motions but none of it felt right. Wash, rinse, dry, get new clothes. But then I turned and saw my bed and it wasn't May anymore. It was March and Carter was laying in my bed, the late Saturday winter sun streaming onto her face.

"Life's tiring you know." She looked so small lying there at the time. So defeated even though she was still half asleep. At that moment, I had just laughed, thinking she was joking like she did most times. "It's just too much. Sometimes I just want to lie down, close my eyes, and never wake up."

Her words echoed in my head over and over again. The walls felt like they were closing in on me and my breaths were coming faster. I wanted to scream. Scream at her and shake her as if she was still laying in my bed now. No. No, you can't close your eyes. You can't fall asleep. I don't care how tiring this earth is. Don't you dare fall asleep.

My arm flew out and the lamp from my bedside table went careening into the nearest wall. The shattering of the bulb didn't drown out my yells, though. I hadn't realized I was actually screaming the words in my head. Maybe she could hear me wherever she was now.

I eyed the ceiling. "Is this what you wanted?" I roared. "It was just too tiring? Well, you can't open your eyes anymore! You're never going to wake up!" My hands fisted in the comforter on my bed and tugged until it ripped off and I threw it across the room, taking out a stack of papers on my desk. I tore the sheets off next, balling them up and pelting them at a frame on the wall. "You can't wake up!"

My legs gave out and I slumped down to the floor. "You can't wake up...You're never going to wake up again. I'm never going to see your sleepy smile again. Your eyes are never going to open again. I just need you to wake up."

Something hot fell on my hands and I realized that for the very first time since I found out what had happened, I was crying. Tears were pouring down my face and my chest was burning and breaking and I knew I had felt pain before, but nothing like this. There were no words that could ever fully describe this.

"Sweeney...Sweeney, it's okay." I had forgotten Samantha was still in my apartment and her hands tentatively found my shoulder now, giving it an awkward pat. It wasn't okay. It wasn't okay at all. She knew it wasn't okay.

"It's never going to be okay, Sam." I sobbed.

"Not now. But it will."

I didn't know how she could say that. How she could say everything with such certainty. I had gone through some terrible times. Times that made me question if there was a God. Question why life had to be so cruel. But nothing had broken me this much.

"Samantha, can you leave please?"

I heard her shift behind me, backing out of my room. She didn't belong here. I needed to learn to deal with this alone. I didn't need anyone else to see me breaking apart. "I'm sorry," she whispered from the doorway. "I'm sorry about everything. I'm sorry you couldn't love her like she deserved. But she deserves to be loved tomorrow. Please be there tomorrow."

I didn't answer her and after a minute, I heard the sound of my door closing distantly.

THE FUNERAL

I walked up to the church at five of five. It had taken me long enough to decide to come, I didn't plan on being here any longer than necessary. I had almost completely dismantled my apartment last night, making it look as destroyed as I felt inside.

A sea of black met me when I walked through the open oak doors and I had to stop. It was shocking. It looked like the whole school was here. Teachers, students, her family all in one pew up front with Samantha beside them. Everyone was here. For someone who thought she had no one, it was mind blowing to see how loved she was. I spotted Mariah in one corner and I clenched my jaw. She shouldn't be here. She didn't deserve to be here. To have the audacity to look like she actually cared...

A hand came down on my shoulder before I could do anything rash. I swiveled to see who it was, effectively shaking off their touch. It reminded me too much of all the hands on me at the hospital and my skin crawled. I gasped when I realized who it was. "Keith?"

"Hey, buddy. You do know you don't have to go through everything alone, right?" He reached out to pull me in for a hug and I let him.

"What are you doing here? How did you know?" I asked once we separated.

"You always thought I was morbid when I looked at the obituaries in the papers, remember? I always told you I like to know if there was anyone I needed to say goodbye to."

I nodded and gave a slight chuckle. I did remember giving him crap for that. I still thought it was strange. But today I was thankful for it. For giving me support I didn't even know I needed.

"You should have called."

"And said what?"

He bit his lip. "I don't know…Just so I could be here for you."

"You are here."

Just then a pastor stepped up to the podium and welcomed the already hushed crowd. Her parents may not have wanted the somber mood of a wake, but just because the sun was streaming through the stained glass here didn't mean the sorrow didn't press down on the shoulders of every single person in this church. I slid into a bench in the back, trying to draw as little attention to myself as possible, and Keith followed suit.

There were pictures of her all over the place. Bulletin boards covered in them. A big, blown up version of one of her senior pictures beside the casket. Even some landscapes that I knew she must have taken herself. I noticed how a lot of the pictures were from years ago. There was a gap until this year, like she hadn't been living until now. And then it was taken away from her. Right when she was ready to start again.

I couldn't hear what the pastor was saying. Maybe I just didn't want to hear it. He didn't know her. What could he possibly have to say about her? A bunch of nice things and sappy quotes that could apply to anyone? I didn't need to hear that. Her parents talked next. Or at least they tried to talk until her mom just couldn't anymore and her dad walked them back to their seats in the front row. He clapped a hand on the shoulder of a blonde guy as they passed. I gasped when the guy turned around and leaned into the podium. He looked so much like Carter, except where her eyes were green, his were too dark to even have a color associated with them. From here it looked like they could match the black that covered every inch of his body. There wasn't another color on him.

He glanced at the casket behind him. Then at the huge portrait beside it. When he turned back to face the front, he chuckled but there was no humor in it. His hand came up to skim over his short blonde hair and he shook his head as if he couldn't believe he was about to do this. I knew the feeling. I watched as his fingers flexed when he replaced them back on the podium; they turned white from holding on so tight. "Well," he started and paused again. "I thought the next time I would see my sister would be when she flew out to see me after graduation. I should have known, when it comes to Carter, plans always change." He glanced at the people in the front and they were all chuckling as tears streamed down their faces. "You see, I hadn't really seen my sister for a while now. I guess I missed what I heard was a really bad time in her life. I regret that. I should have been there for her. Made it better. But I wasn't there. I don't know that version of Carter. I only know what I believe to be the real version of Carter.

"She was the go-getter of our group. Always on the move. Always dragging us along with her, even when we had no desire to do some of the things she wanted. Growing up with her was exhausting. She gave us a hard time, she put us in our places, and my God she could be demanding when she wanted to be." One of the girls in the front row, I recognized her as the waitress from Sonny's Chicken Coop, chuckled here followed by more tears as she buried her head in the shoulder of the guy next to her who was silently sobbing. The boy at the podium wiped at his eyes and continued.

"More than anything, she laughed. And she made us laugh. She would spit out the most random things and all you could do was laugh at her. She was so quick. Smart. I'm sorry we all grew up and went our separate ways. We weren't around these past years when she needed us most. But we still need her now. Because she was the very best of all of us." He trailed off and looked over his shoulder at the casket. "She's still the very best of all of us."

He didn't bother wiping away his tears as he sat back down between his father and the girl from Sonny's. I watched as she curled herself into him and the guy beside her reached out to squeeze his shoulder.

Something scooted into the pew next to me and before I could turn to see who it was, I felt a tiny hand take mine. "Noah, don't leak. You never leak." I looked down to see Keaton's wide eyes looking back at me and the tears I hadn't realized were falling fell even harder. "What's wrong?" he asked.

I shook my head and couldn't answer him. Instead, I pulled him into my lap and wrapped my arms around him as tight as I could, burying my face in his unruly hair. I felt another hand on my arm and turned to find Sarah's sad eyes.

"I'm so sorry, Noah."

I loosened my hold on Keaton so he could sit back in my lap. "How…?" She tilted her head to Keith in response and he gave a shrug.

"I told you that you didn't have to do everything alone," he whispered.

"It's alright to let people in," she added. I looked up at the ceiling, fighting back more tears. It was a lesson I had tried to teach Carter. It was a lesson she had taught me. Sarah folded her hand into mine and I lowered my eyes to watch Nate step down from the podium. He didn't have any tears in his eyes now, but they were red like he had been crying all day. I felt a little bad I had missed his speech; I really did like the kid, despite always giving him a hard time. He had given Carter a friend. I knew he had shown her what it was like to just be friends with someone again, without them knowing everything. Without depending on them as she had come to depend on me. I could never thank him enough for that.

"Carter McMillan never wanted to know me, and that kind of pissed me off." I refocused up front when I heard Samantha's voice. I had always thought it was funny that she had the sweetest voice but absolutely no filter. It didn't fit at all, but on her it had no choice but to work. "I liked being at the top of the social food chain. It was fun. I was happy. Everyone knew me. Except for Carter. I never knew the happy-go-lucky Carter you knew." She looked at Carter's brother and cousins in the front row.

"I knew the Carter who had built titanium walls around herself and didn't let anyone in and refused to come out. I made that Carter my best friend. I tried to dismantle her walls, but I learned I wasn't strong enough. It was infuriating. I tried to show her what it meant to be happy again. Friends and parties and popularity. But you want to know what the funny thing is? She's the one who ended up showing me what happiness is. This year, she found her own way to dismantle those walls. She showed me what really living was. Dreaming and loving and happiness." Samantha's eyes finally found mine and locked on me.

"I didn't understand then. I wish I would have. I can't change that and I wish I could. So I'm sorry, Carter. But I do know someone who did understand. Who was there with her. Who made her live. And I am so grateful he taught her that. I think we can all be grateful he taught her that, because this year she taught us all so much more."

She kept her eyes locked on mine all the way until she sat back in her seat. I knew what she had done. She had said her apologies, but she had also led for me to speak. I just didn't know if I could do it. I had thought for hours last night into today of what I could possibly say, but nothing was good enough. How was anything supposed to be good enough after what I had done? I looked down at Keaton in my lap. Ran a hand over the stubble I hadn't had the effort to shave since the morning I broke up with her. I knew I should have shaved last night. She would have hated it if she could see me now. But that was in the past, just as she was. Forever frozen as the girl with the big, green eyes who captured my heart. I felt another tear drip off my chin as my eyes refocused on the casket up front and I realized this was never really a choice. Nothing about her was a choice.

"Hey, buddy? I've got to get up, okay?" I whispered as I shifted Keaton off my lap and placed him back in my seat once I stood. "I'll be right back."

Vaguely, I heard the pastor asking if anyone else would like to speak as I shuffled past Keith into the main aisle of the church. He paused when he saw me and nodded, then stepped down again. People turned, craned their necks, everyone wanting to know who else would have words to break their hearts a little more. Then the whispers started. I knew there were plenty of students here. Plenty of teachers. Maybe my boss. It didn't matter to me. It didn't matter one bit.

I kept my head down the entire walk to the front, refusing to meet anyone's eyes, refusing to even look at the casket up close once I got there because I knew I wouldn't be able to keep it together if I did. I tucked a hand into the pocket of my slacks and felt the worn paper there. Then I pulled it out and smoothed it over the podium just so I could have something to focus on other than the hundreds of eyes waiting for the words from my mouth. I fingered my growing beard and let my confusion grow. How had we gotten here? How was I supposed to do this? Why me? How had I made it to this place in her heart? That I was the one who knew her best? Did she want to see me do this? Because I didn't know if I could. Did she want to see me fail? I had failed in loving her and now I was about to fail again. I really couldn't do this. But then I took a deep, rattling breath in and did what she had taught me. To just do my best.

"Carter McMillan was a student in my last period class..." I began. I felt Samantha's eyes glaring at me and I met them head on.

"Carter McMillan was the only person I have ever truly fallen in love with. And I fell more in love with her every single day." I heard a few people gasp, shook out of their grief by my confession, but I continued.

"I could tell you a million things about her. A thousand things no one ever knew about us. But that's not what I'm going to do. Because that belongs to me; to us." I swallowed hard, a hundred moments flooding my brain. Her head thrown back in laughter, her hands covering her face in embarrassment, the challenging look she'd give me, the softest brush of her lips against my skin. "I'm not sure why she chose me, but I do know it's a privilege to have been loved by her. So I'm going to tell you a bit about what made me fall in love with her, because everyone deserves to see her the way I do."

I took another deep breath because holding back these tears was suddenly the hardest thing I had ever tried to do. "She had a way of talking to you that made you feel like you were in a different world. You were safe and you were free and you were happy. You got to see her world, and it was amazing. The way she had these plans, ideas, goals. You wanted to be a part of them. Even if they were insane. The way she spoke about them, the way she was…they weren't just dreams. It wasn't some unattainable thing. She was going to do it. There was no question." I could see her in my mind now, the fire in her eyes. The subtle determination. Things started to add up. How her brother described her. How she had refused to let anyone in for so long. How Mariah had told her she got everything she wanted. It wasn't that she got everything. It was the determination and perseverance she had that was the most beautiful thing about her.

I looked back up at the sea of black. "She amazed me. To know her past and know her determination to *live*. It may have taken a while, but she found who she was this year. And who she was…was incredible."

I chuckled to myself, thinking back on that freezing afternoon in January when she had dragged me out to the lake just to watch the snow fall. It may have been my favorite place, but I didn't exactly want to sit outside in the cold when we could have been drinking coffee in the apartment. I went anyways. Of course I went, because what she wanted, I wanted to give her. "One day, she turned to me and said, 'I know I'm not perfect. I'd just like to be for one day. Just one. Just to know what it feels like.' Now, I'm not going to lie to you, and I sure wasn't going to lie to her. So I won't give you the fantasy love story line. You know the one. Where the guy tells her, 'to me you're perfect every day.'" I bit my lip and shook my head, remembering just how she looked that afternoon as the people in the pews chuckled and batted away tears. My own were falling unchecked at this point, I had long ago lost the battle to holding them back.

"Instead, I told her she was a pain in the ass." A mixture of gasps and watery laughter followed my words. I vaguely thought of how I shouldn't be swearing in a church. "Because she was. I could never win with her. It was always a battle; a challenge. But my God, it was a challenge I wanted to accept from the day I met her. Her logic made me laugh. It made me think. It made me love her even more. She wasn't perfect. She didn't do everything right. Lord knows, I didn't, either. She made everything okay. She made me okay. She made me better than I ever was. And I loved her. So no. She wasn't perfect. She was a mess actually, I think we can all agree with that. But I was so happy to have her as my mess."

I turned my back to the audience where the sobs were becoming uncontrollable, the tears now waterfalls from almost every face. I faced the casket and thanked God that it was closed because if I hadn't completely lost it at this point, I would break if I had to look at her lying in it. I slowly knelt down before it and held out that same paper she had given to me so long ago. I ran my finger over it, over her quick, neat strokes of ink. The list of things she would never get to do. Never get to see.

"I am so sorry, Cub. You can never know how sorry I am. I made this mess and there's nothing I can do to fix it. I know you may not forgive me. I just need you to hear me one last time, okay? I love you, Carter McMillan. I love you so much I'm going to do this." I sniffled and shook the paper at the casket. "Even the stupid one that says I have to go underwater cave diving. I'm going to do it all for you. If I could have anything in the world, it would be to have you back. But this is the closest thing I've got. So I guess it's time for me to stop being afraid of living. Thank you for reminding me to live. I love you."

Made in the USA
Middletown, DE
26 November 2017